ALESSANDRO BARONCIANI

WHEN EVERYTHING TURNED BLUE™

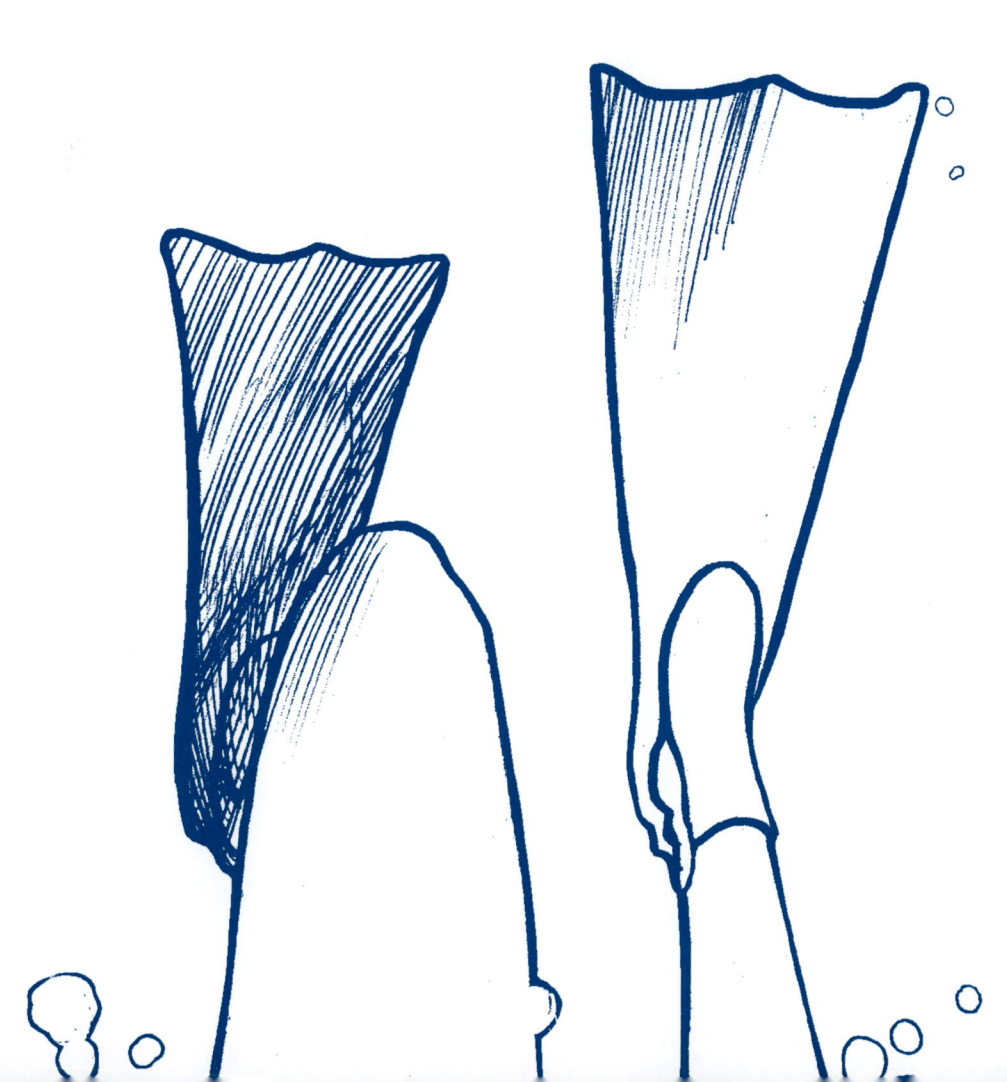

ALESSANDRO BARONCIANI

WHEN EVERYTHING TURNED BLUE™

DARK HORSE BOOKS

Lettering & Page Layout by
GIACOMO AGNELLO MODICA with OFFICINE BOLZONI

Translated by
CARLA RONCALLI DI MONTORIO

President and Publisher
MIKE RICHARDSON

Editor
BRETT ISRAEL

Assistant Editor
SANJAY DHARAWAT

Digital Art Technician
SAMANTHA HUMMER

Collection Designer
MAY HIJIKURO

Special Thanks to **KARI TORSON** at Dark Horse Comics

NEIL HANKERSON Executive Vice President TOM WEDDLE Chief Financial Officer DALE LaFOUNTAIN Chief Information Officer TIM WIESCH Vice President of Licensing MATT PARKINSON Vice President of Marketing VANESSA TODD-HOLMES Vice President of Production and Scheduling MARK BERNARDI Vice President of Book Trade and Digital Sales RANDY LAHRMAN Vice President of Product Development KEN LIZZI General Counsel DAVE MARSHALL Editor in Chief DAVEY ESTRADA Editorial Director CHRIS WARNER Senior Books Editor CARY GRAZZINI Director of Specialty Projects LIA RIBACCHI Art Director MATT DRYER Director of Digital Art and Prepress MICHAEL GOMBOS Senior Director of Licensed Publications KARI YADRO Director of Custom Programs KARI TORSON Director of International Licensing

Published by Dark Horse Books
A division of Dark Horse Comics LLC
10956 SE Main Street, Milwaukie, OR 97222

First edition: October 2022
Ebook ISBN 978-1-50672-676-2 | Hardcover ISBN 978-1-50672-673-1

10 9 8 7 6 5 4 3 2 1
Printed in China

WHEN EVERYTHING TURNED BLUE
Original title: Quando tutto diventò blu
When Everything Turned Blue ™ and © 2020, 2022 Alessandro Baronciani. All names, characters and related indicia contained in this book are exclusively licensed to BAO Publishing srl in their original version. Their translated and/or adapted versions are property of BAO Publishing srl. All rights reserved. International Rights © BAO Publishing, via Leopardi 8 - 20123 Milano — Italia— foreignrights@baopublishing.it. No part of this book may be stored, reproduced or transmitted in any form or by any means, electronic or mechanical, including photocopying, recording, or by any information storage and retrieval system without written permission from the copyright holder. For information address BAO Publishing.
Dark Horse Books® and the Dark Horse logo are registered trademarks of Dark Horse Comics LLC. All rights reserved. Names, characters, places, and incidents featured in this publication either are the product of the author's imagination or are used fictitiously. Any resemblance to actual persons (living or dead), events, institutions, or locales, without satiric intent, is coincidental.

Library of Congress Cataloging-in-Publication Data

Names: Baronciani, Alessandro, author, artist.
Title: When everything turned blue / Alessandro Baronciani.
Other titles: Quando tutto diventò blu. English
Description: First edition. | Milwaukie, OR : Dark Horse Books, 2022. |
   Summary: "Chiara lives her life afraid of many things, but most of all
   the fear of an undiagnosed illness. As she delves further and further
   down a rabbit hole of denial and disassociation, she will be forced to
   make a decision that will alter her life forever"-- Provided by
   publisher.
Identifiers: LCCN 2022020310 | ISBN 9781506726731 (hardcover) | ISBN
   9781506726762 (ebook)
Subjects: LCGFT: Graphic novels.
Classification: LCC PN6767.B38 Q3613 2022 | DDC
   741.5/945--dc23/eng/20220506
LC record available at https://lccn.loc.gov/2022020310

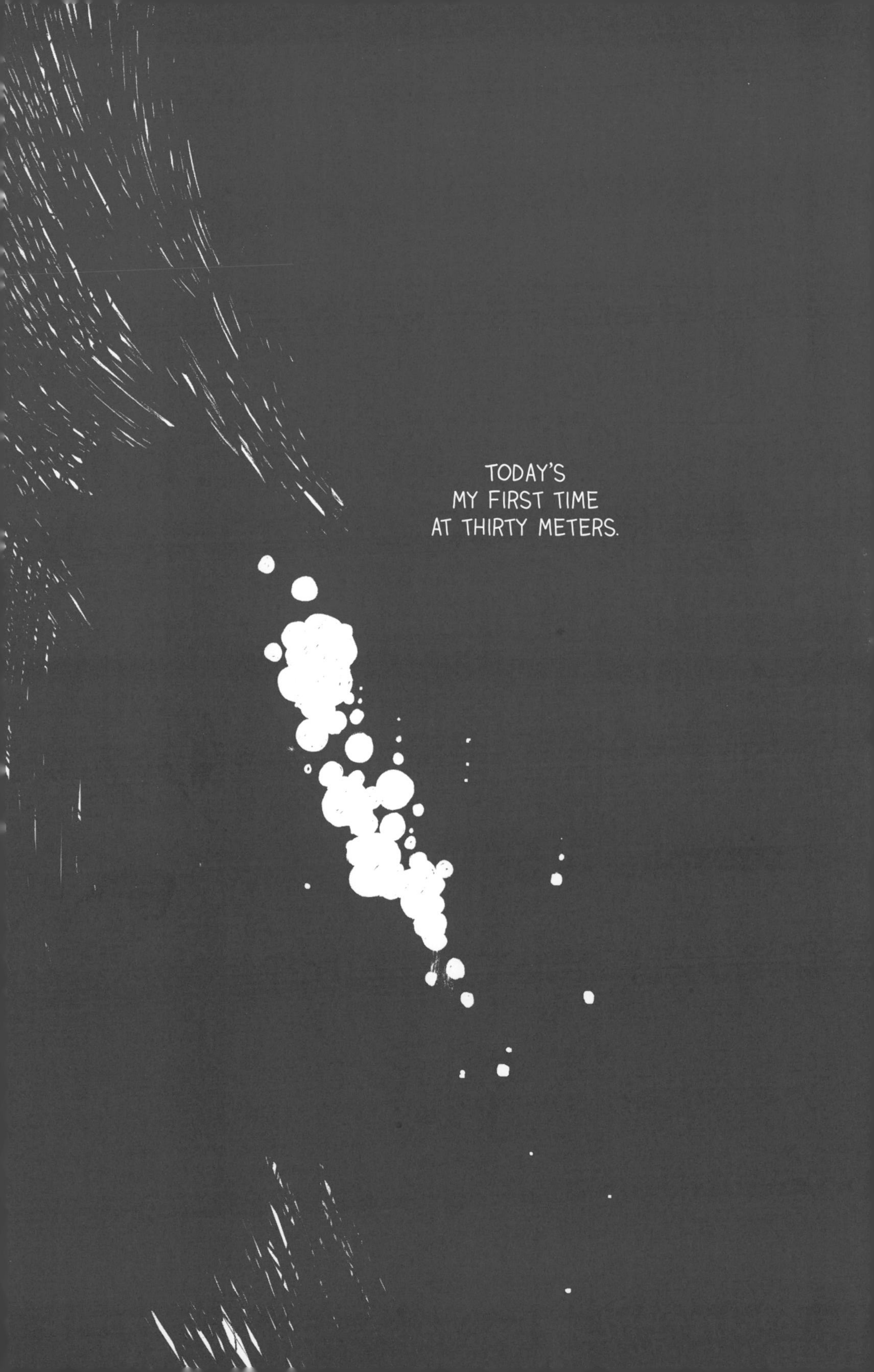
TODAY'S MY FIRST TIME AT THIRTY METERS.

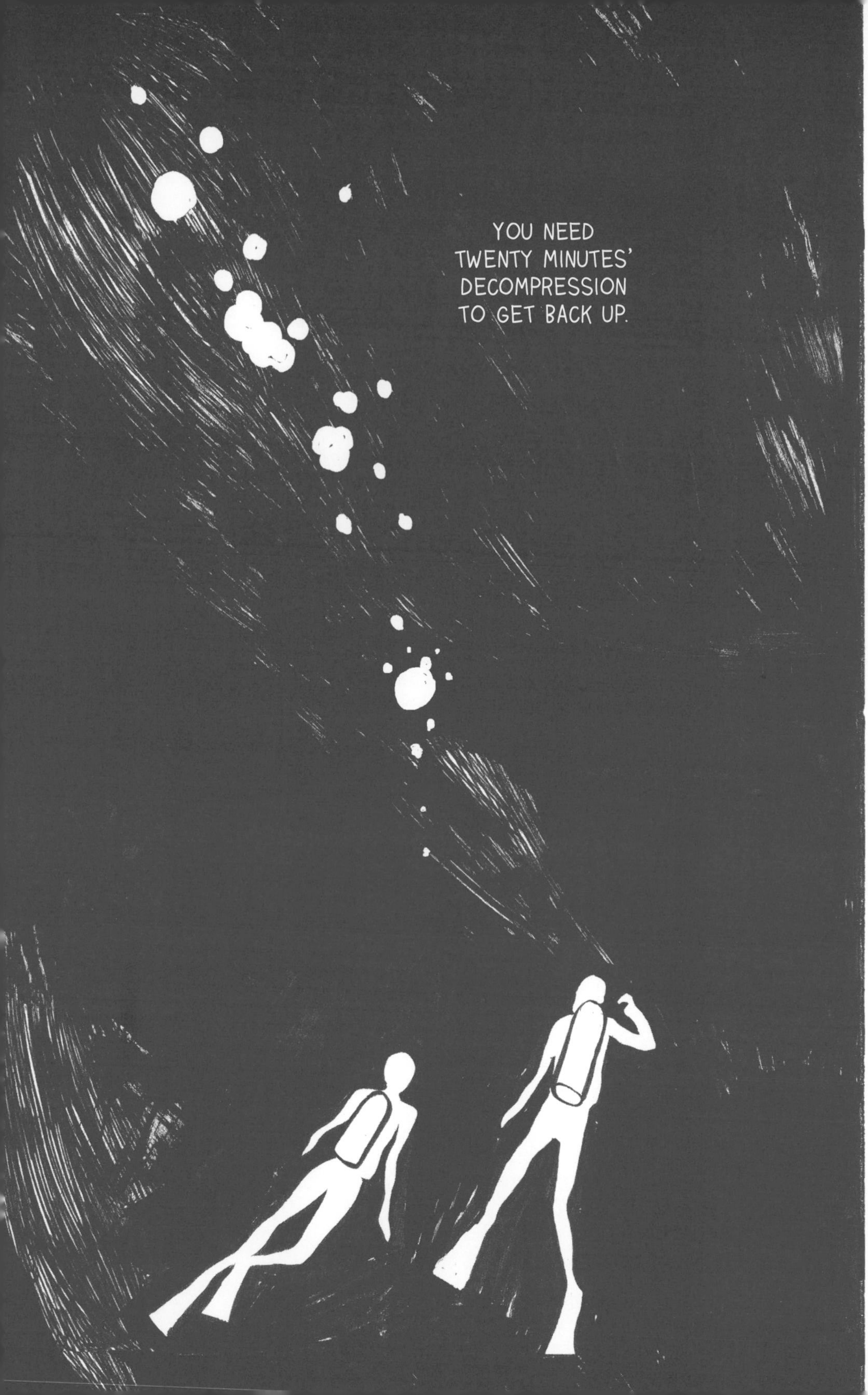
YOU NEED
TWENTY MINUTES'
DECOMPRESSION
TO GET BACK UP.

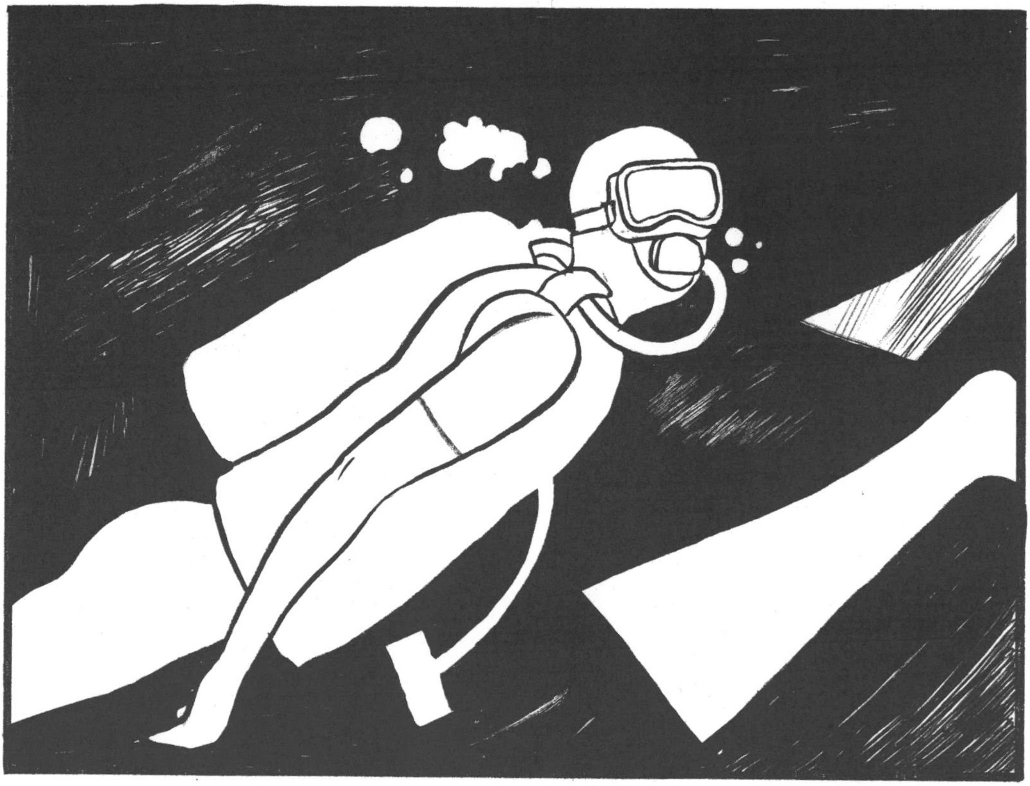

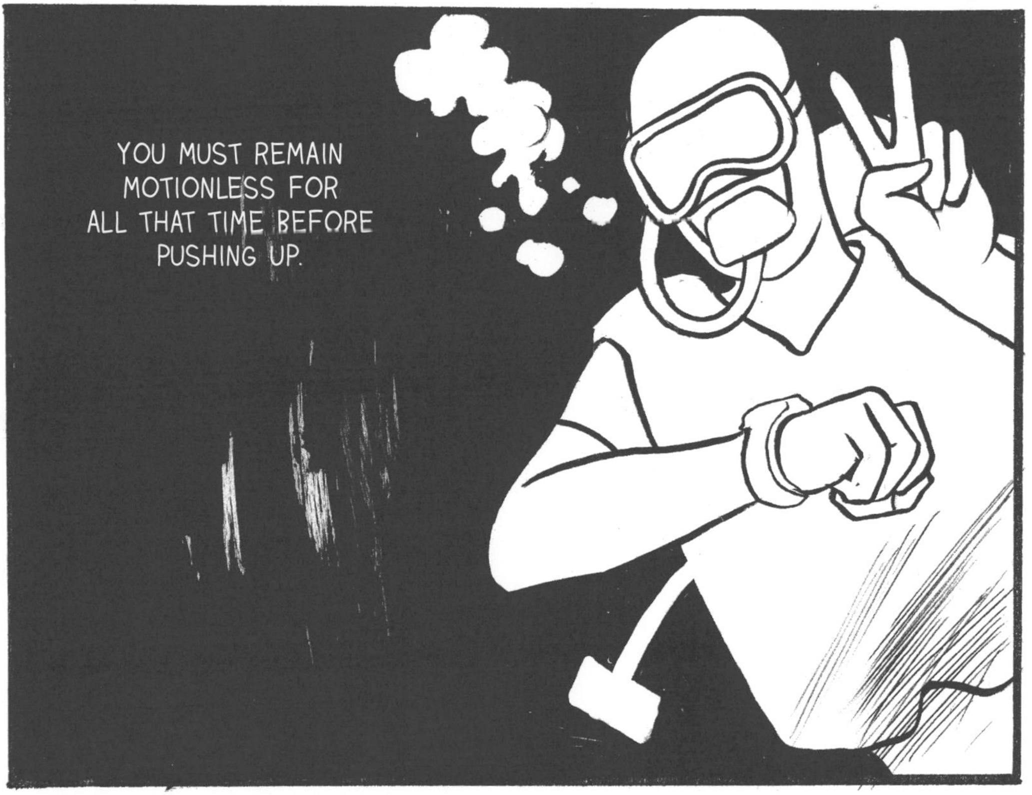
YOU MUST REMAIN MOTIONLESS FOR ALL THAT TIME BEFORE PUSHING UP.

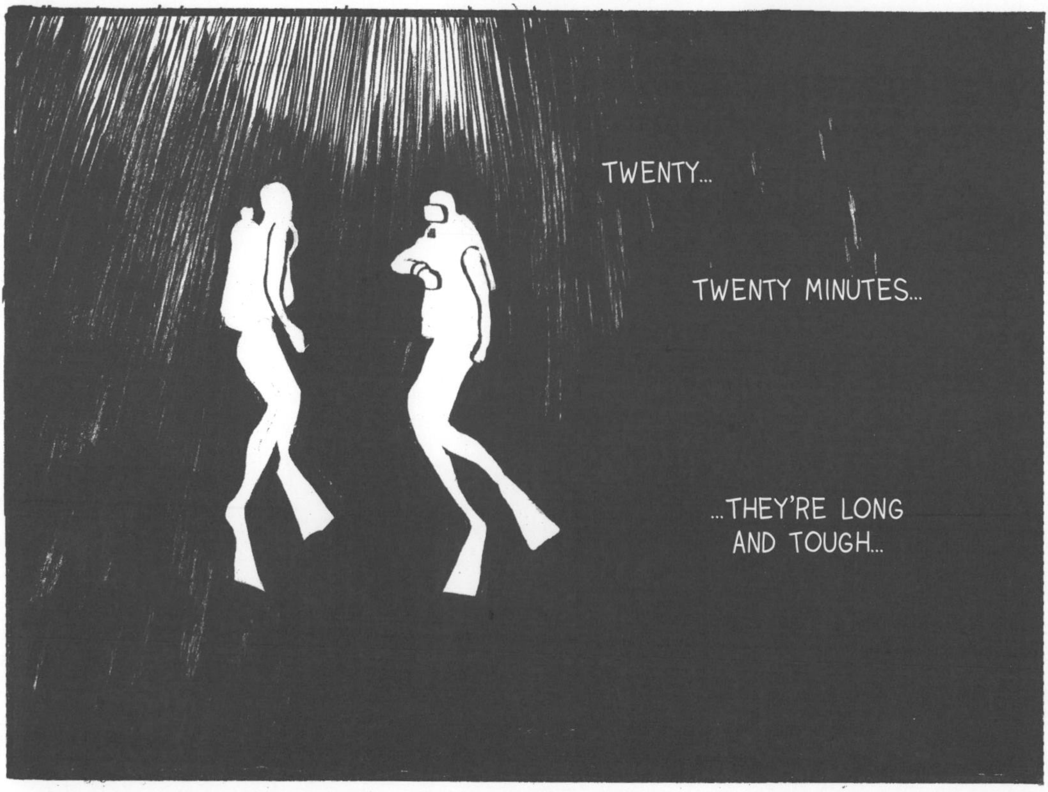
TWENTY...
TWENTY MINUTES...
...THEY'RE LONG
AND TOUGH...

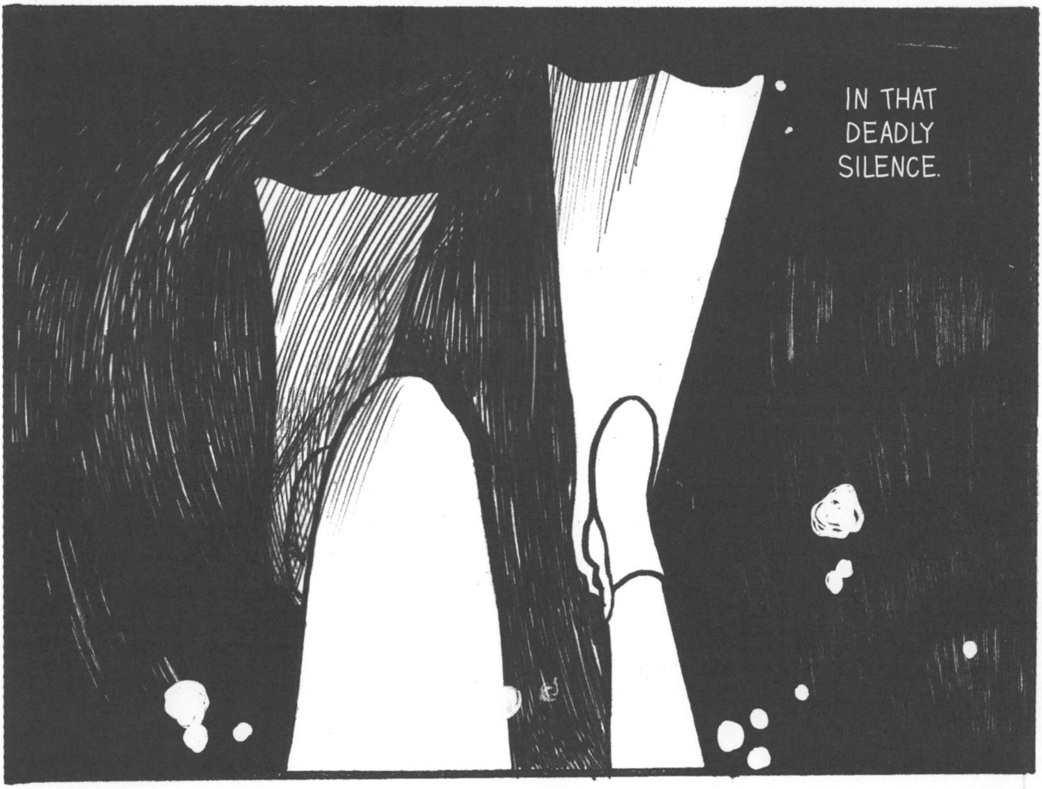
IN THAT
DEADLY
SILENCE.

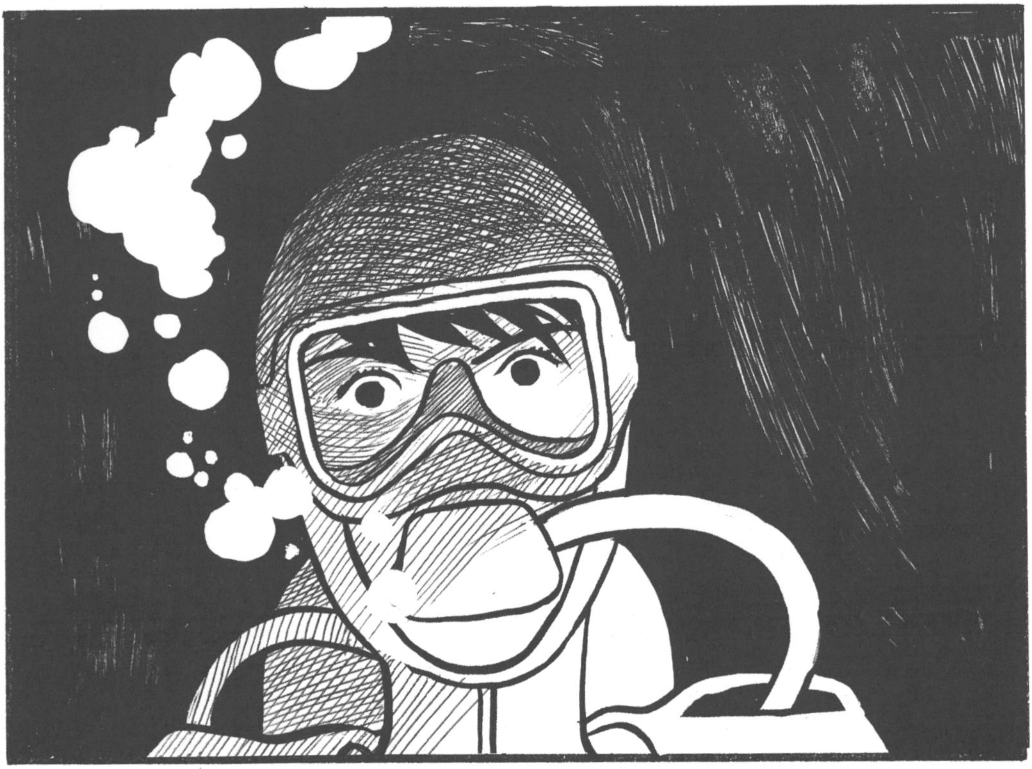

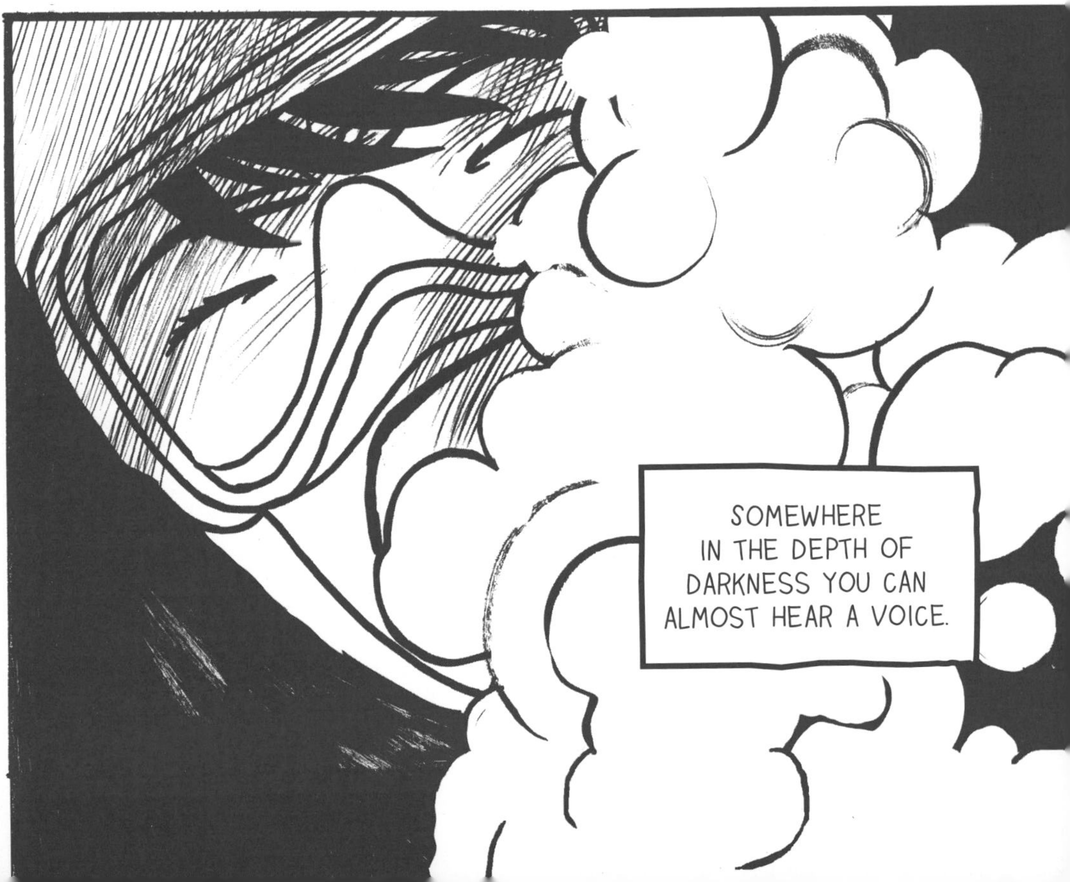
SOMEWHERE IN THE DEPTH OF DARKNESS YOU CAN ALMOST HEAR A VOICE.

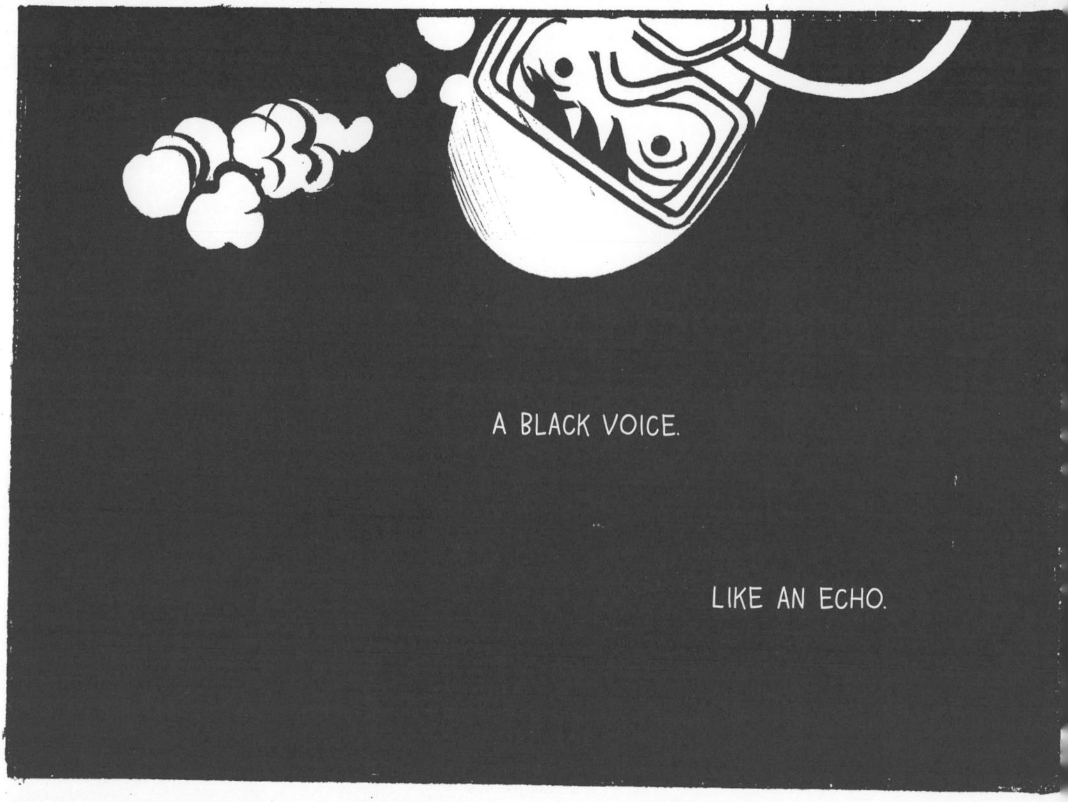
A BLACK VOICE.
LIKE AN ECHO.
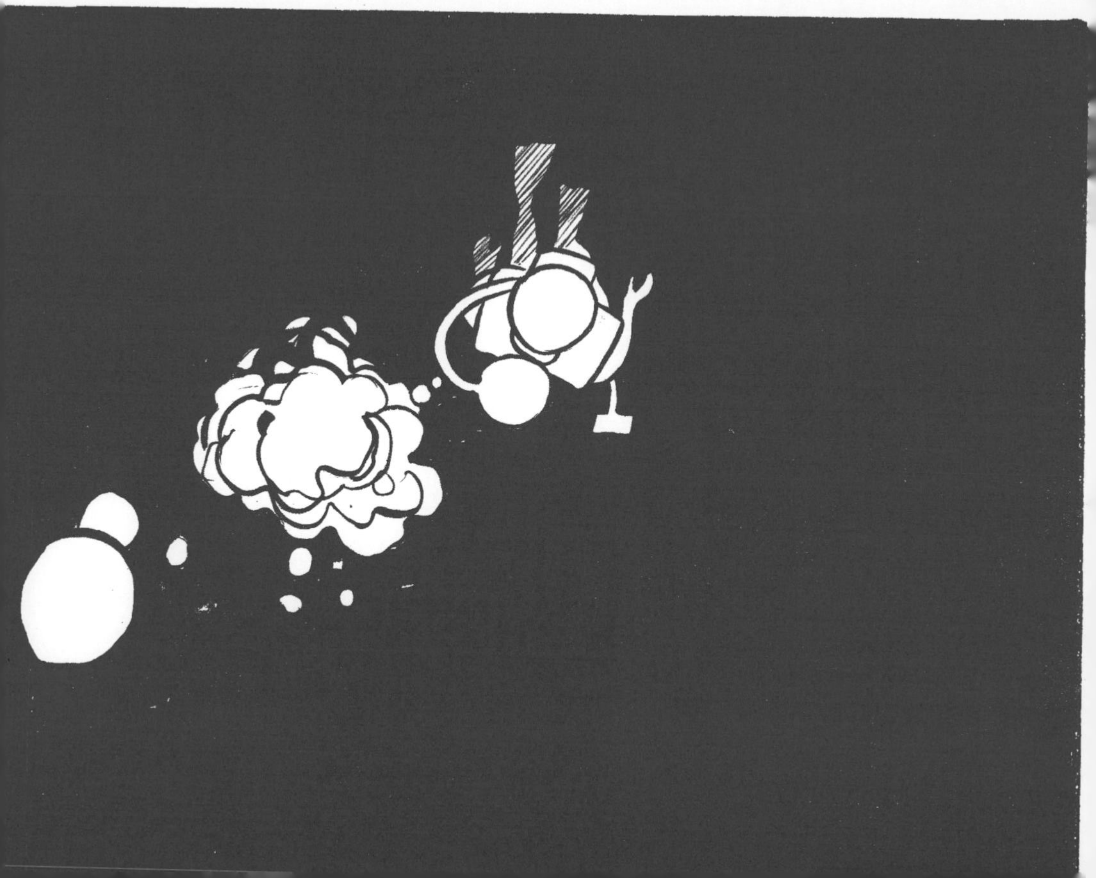

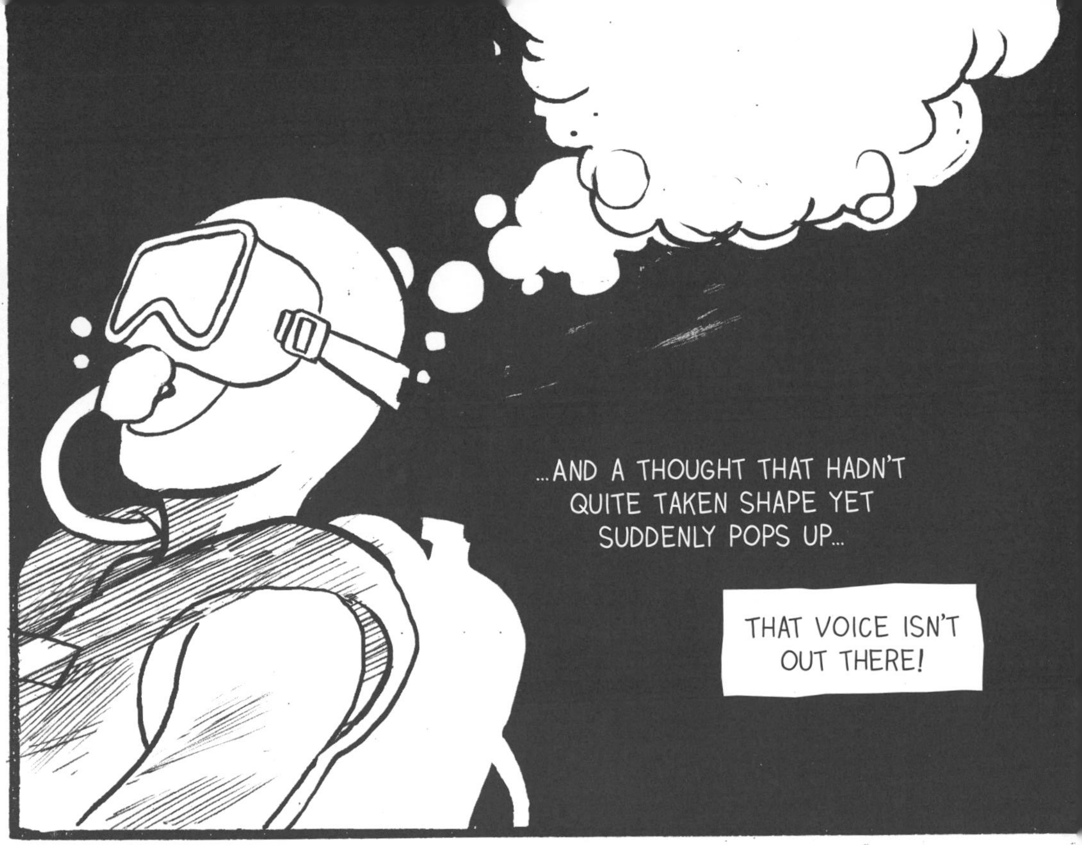
...AND A THOUGHT THAT HADN'T QUITE TAKEN SHAPE YET SUDDENLY POPS UP...
THAT VOICE ISN'T OUT THERE!

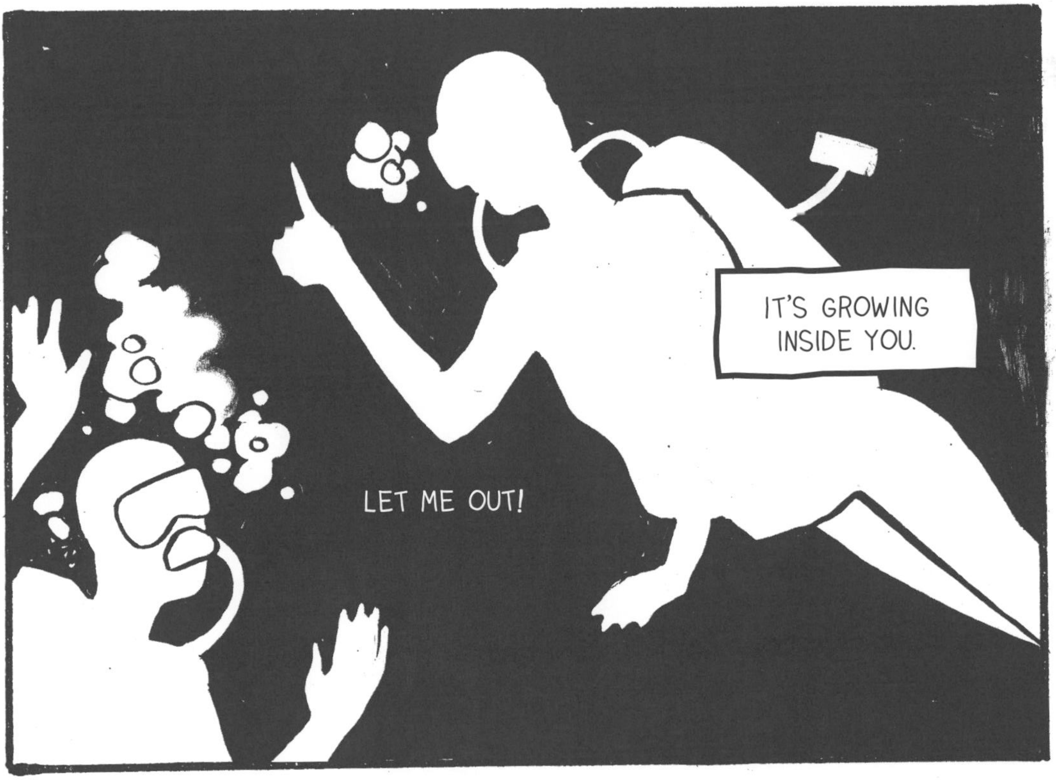
IT'S GROWING INSIDE YOU.
LET ME OUT!

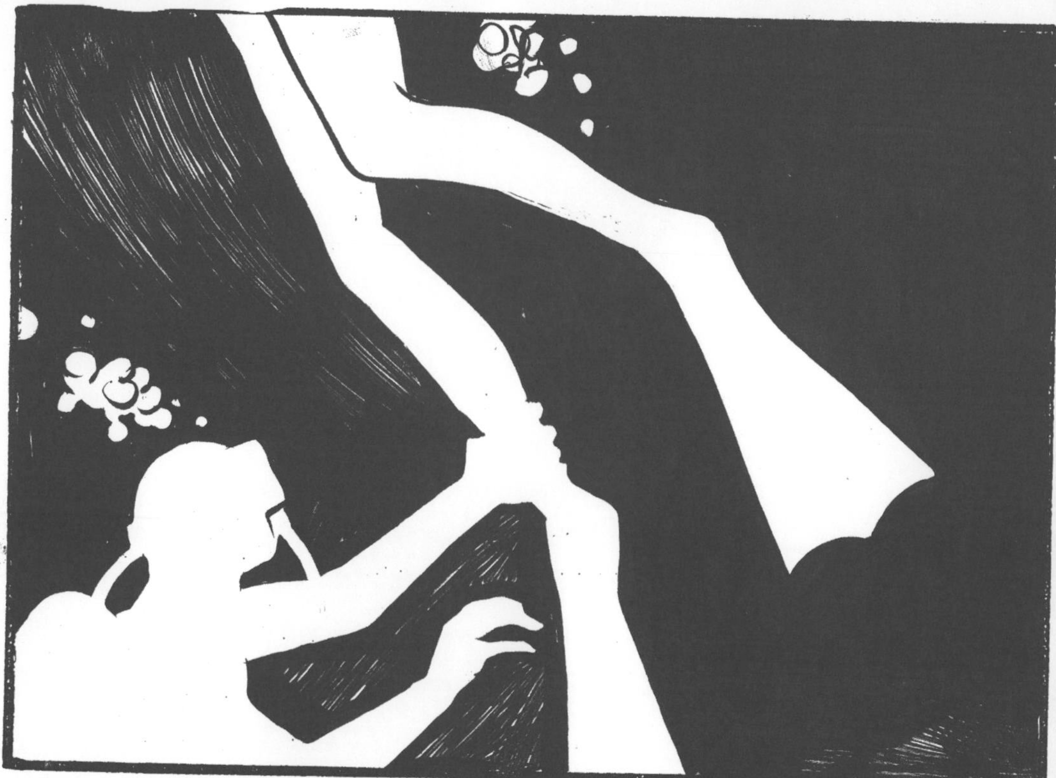

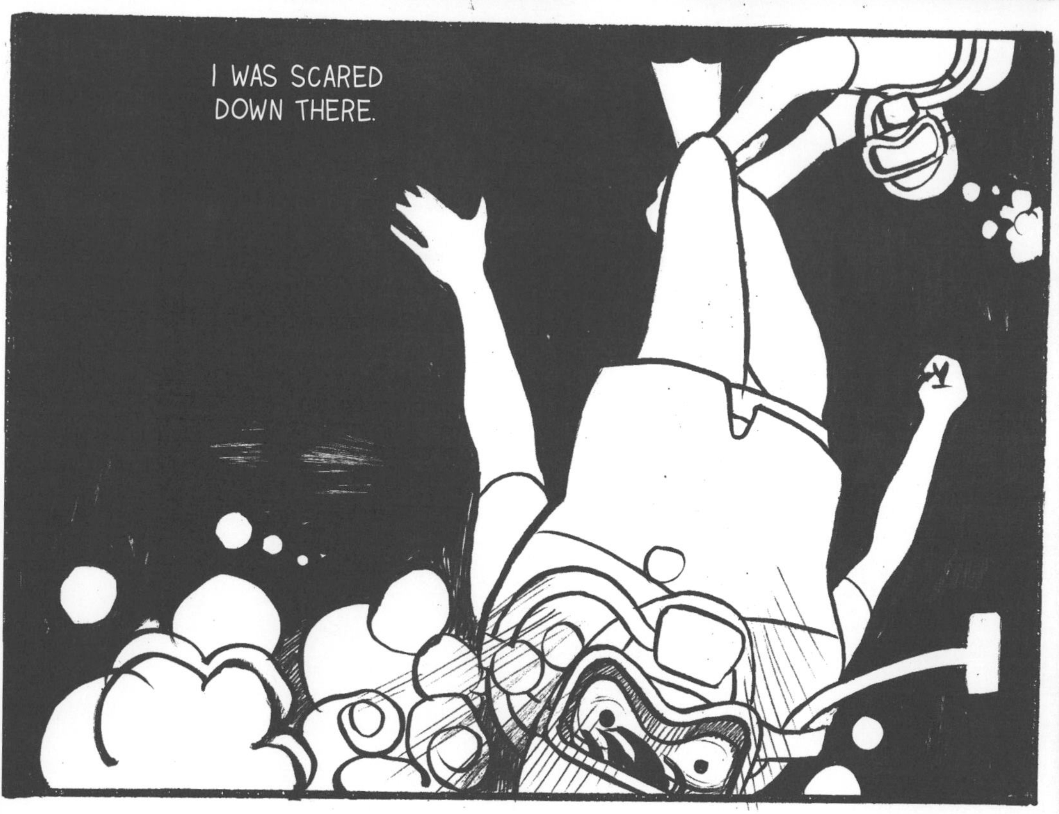
I WAS SCARED DOWN THERE.

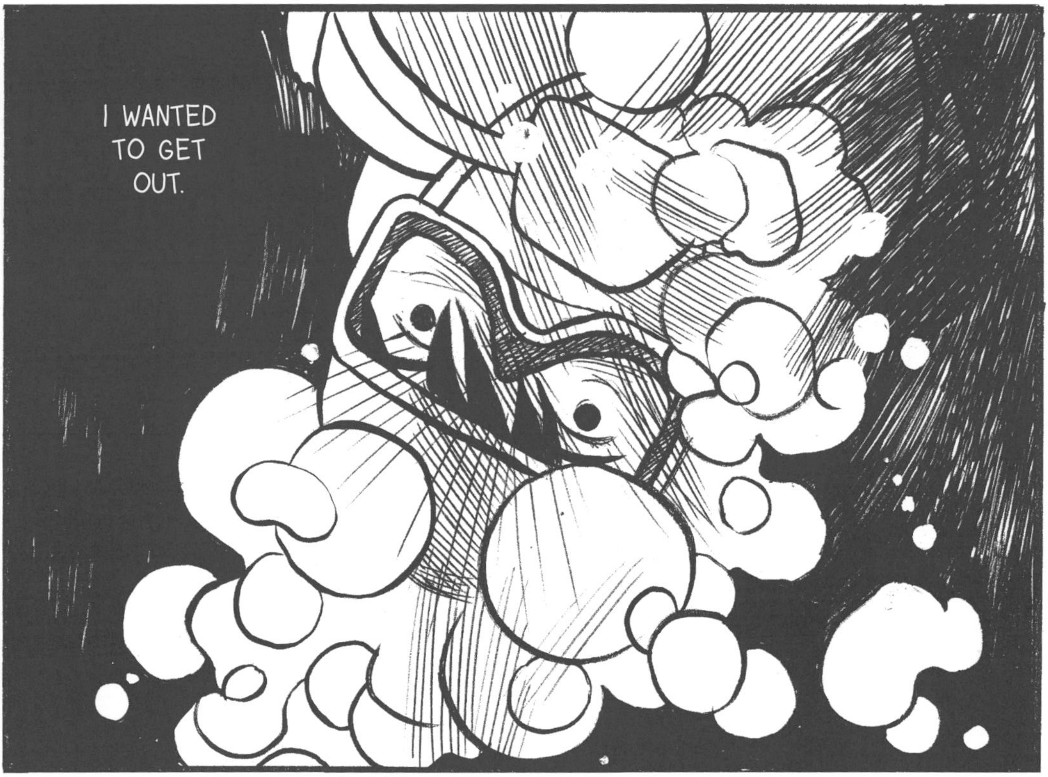
I WANTED
TO GET
OUT.

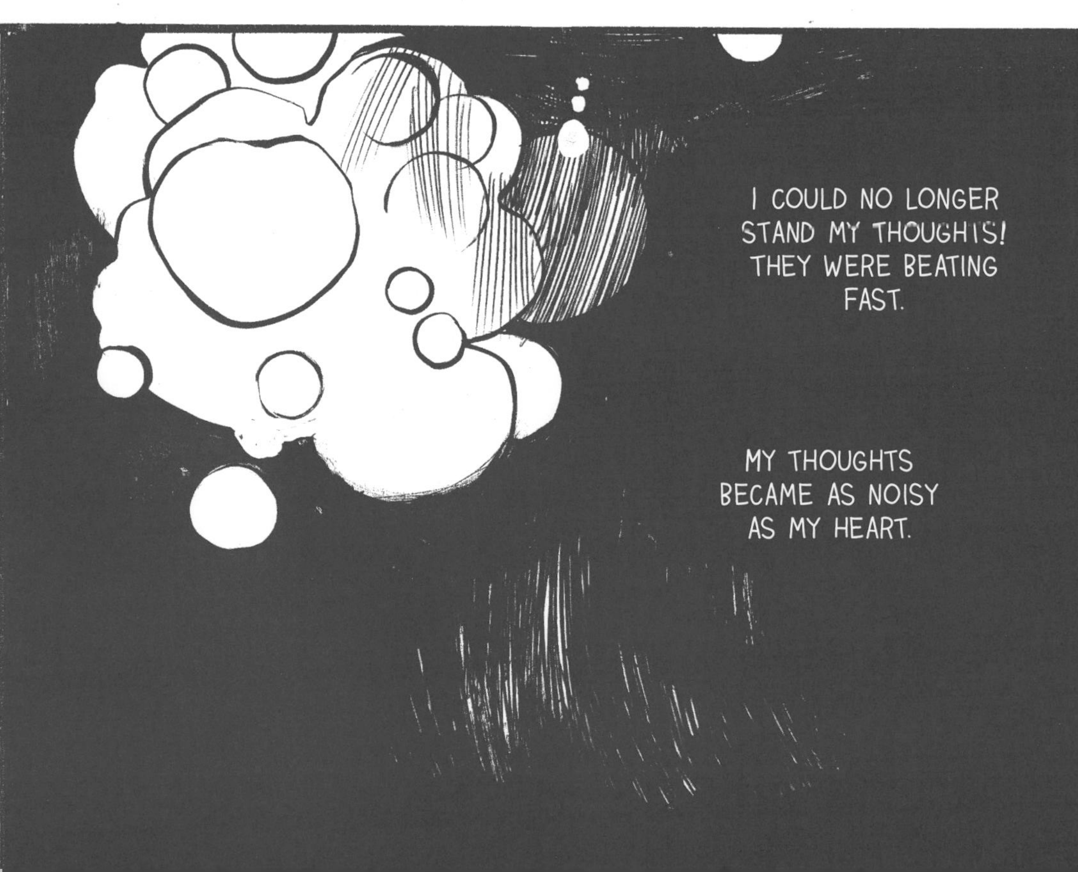
I COULD NO LONGER
STAND MY THOUGHTS!
THEY WERE BEATING
FAST.
MY THOUGHTS
BECAME AS NOISY
AS MY HEART.

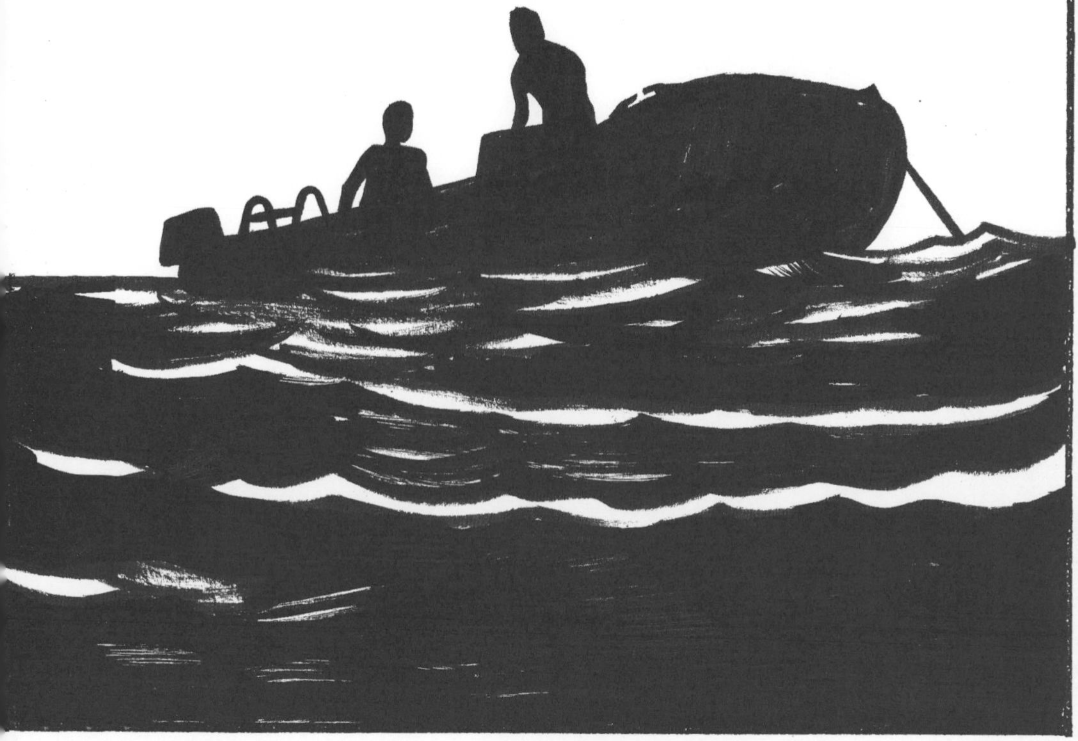

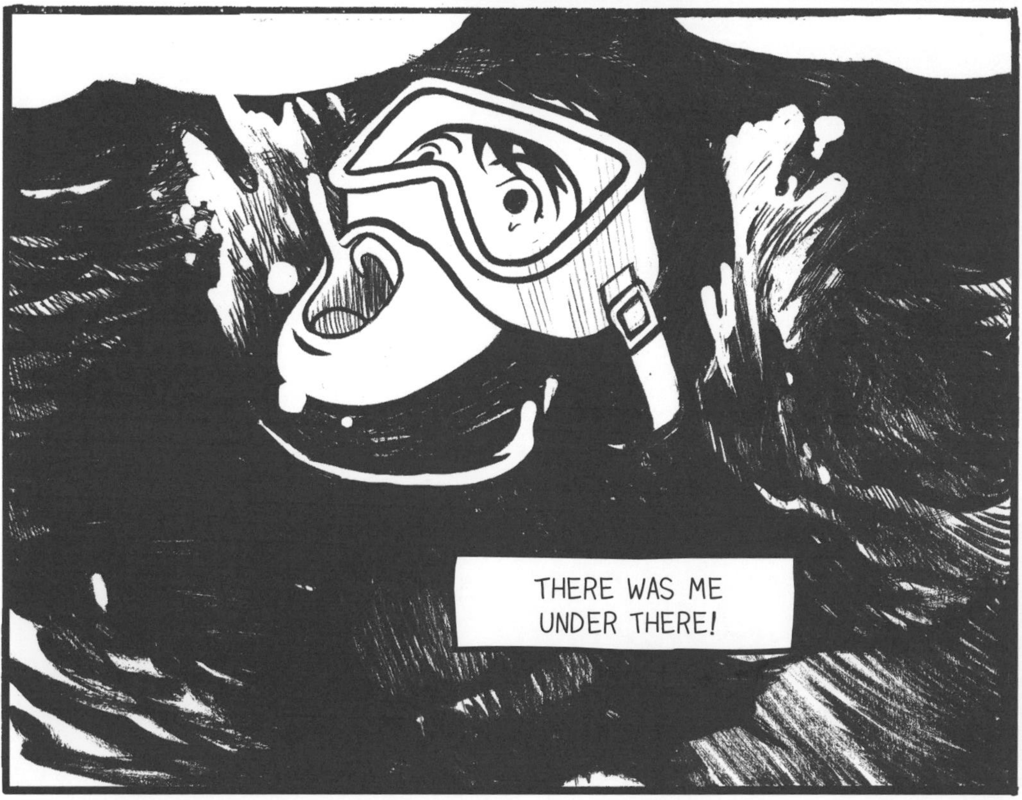
THERE WAS ME
UNDER THERE!

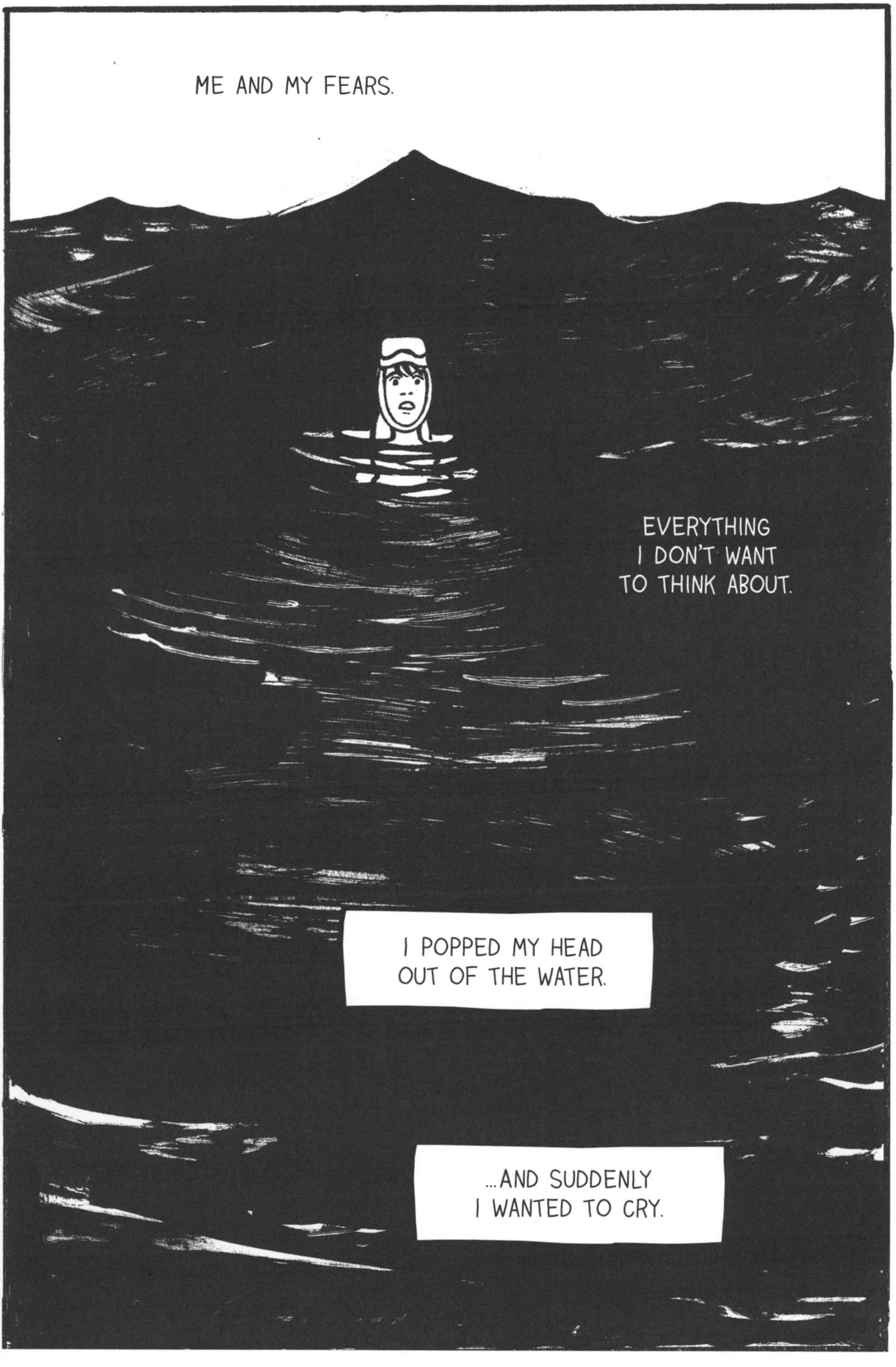
ME AND MY FEARS.
EVERYTHING I DON'T WANT TO THINK ABOUT.
I POPPED MY HEAD OUT OF THE WATER.
...AND SUDDENLY I WANTED TO CRY.

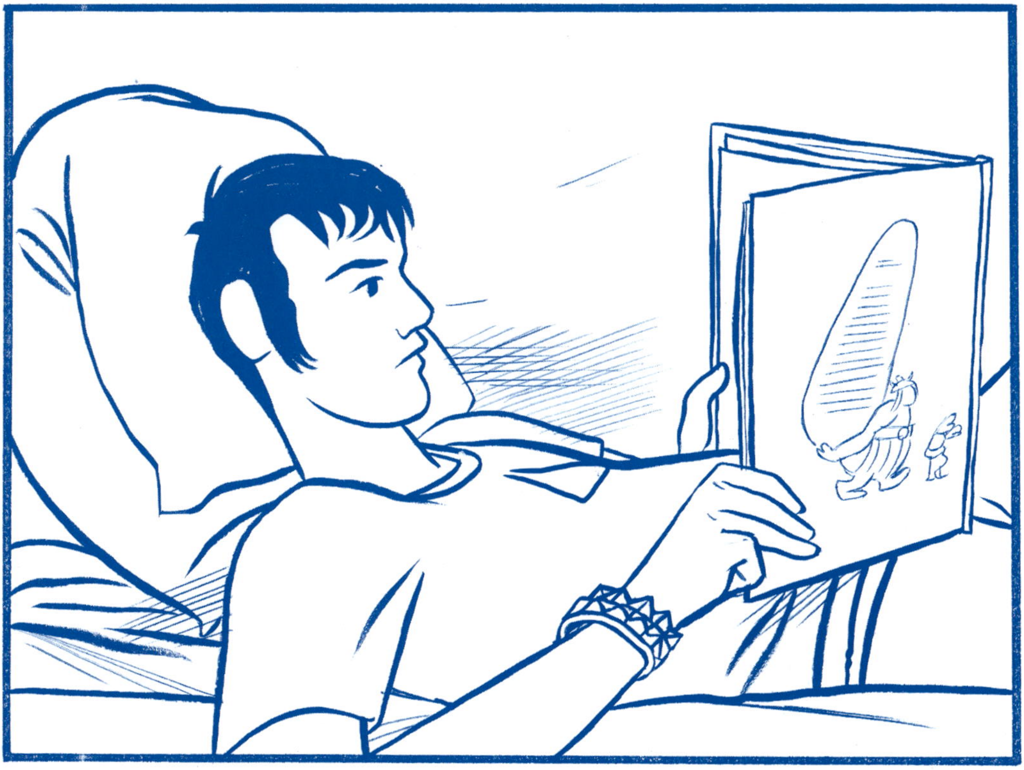

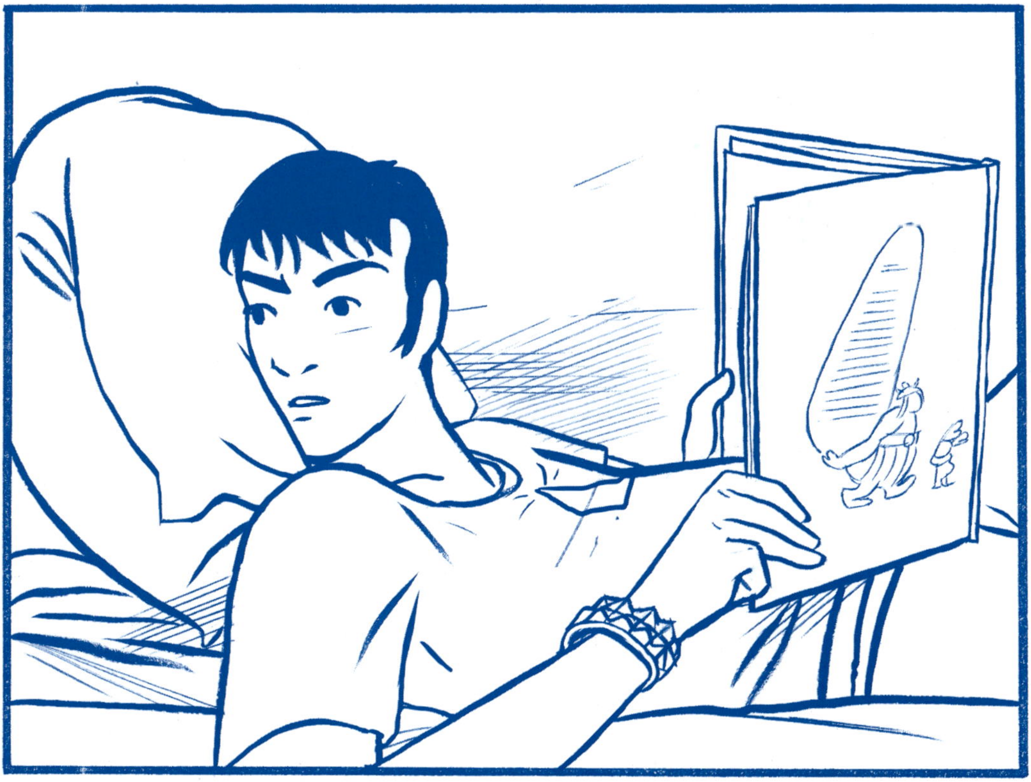

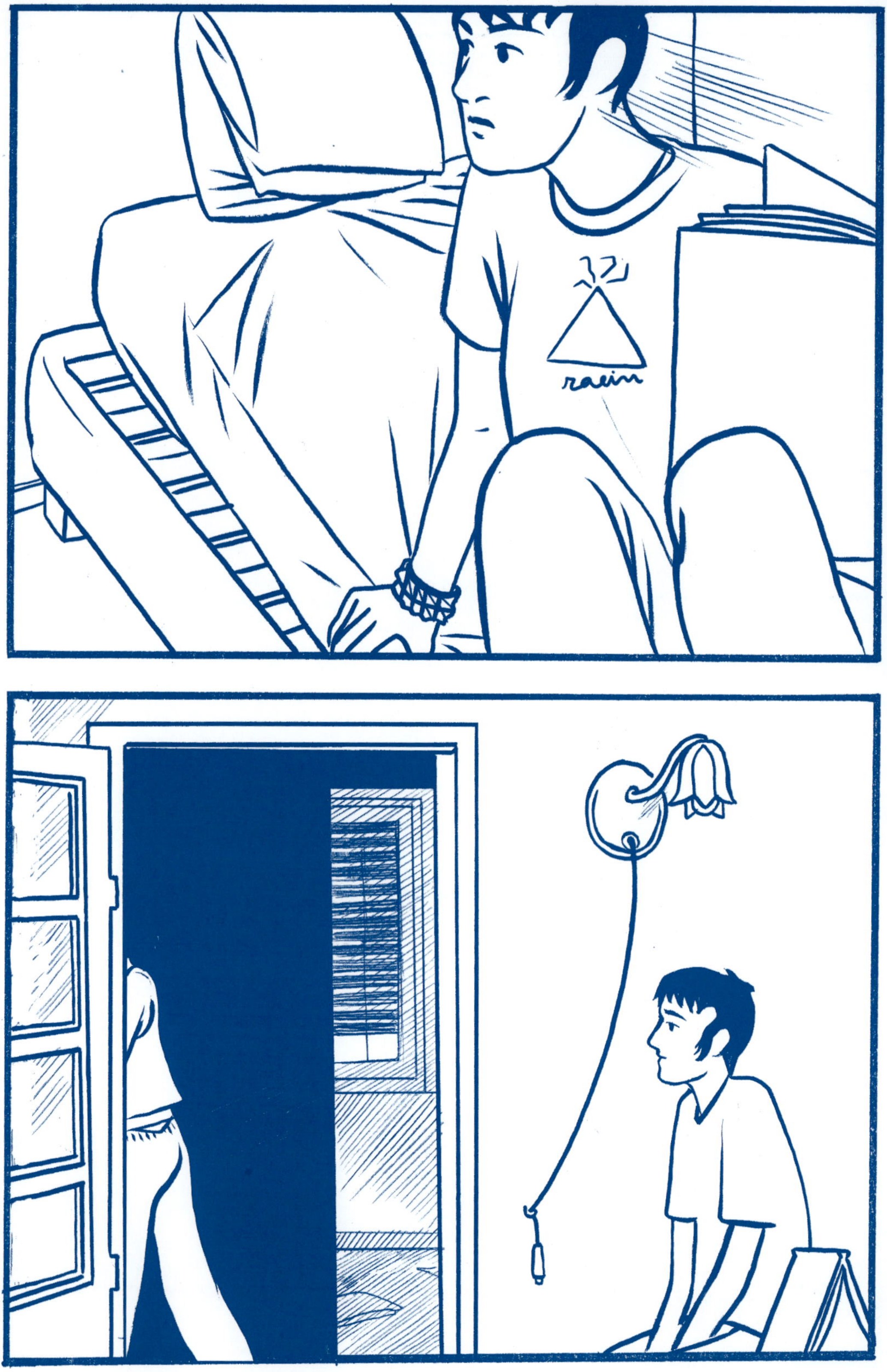
raein

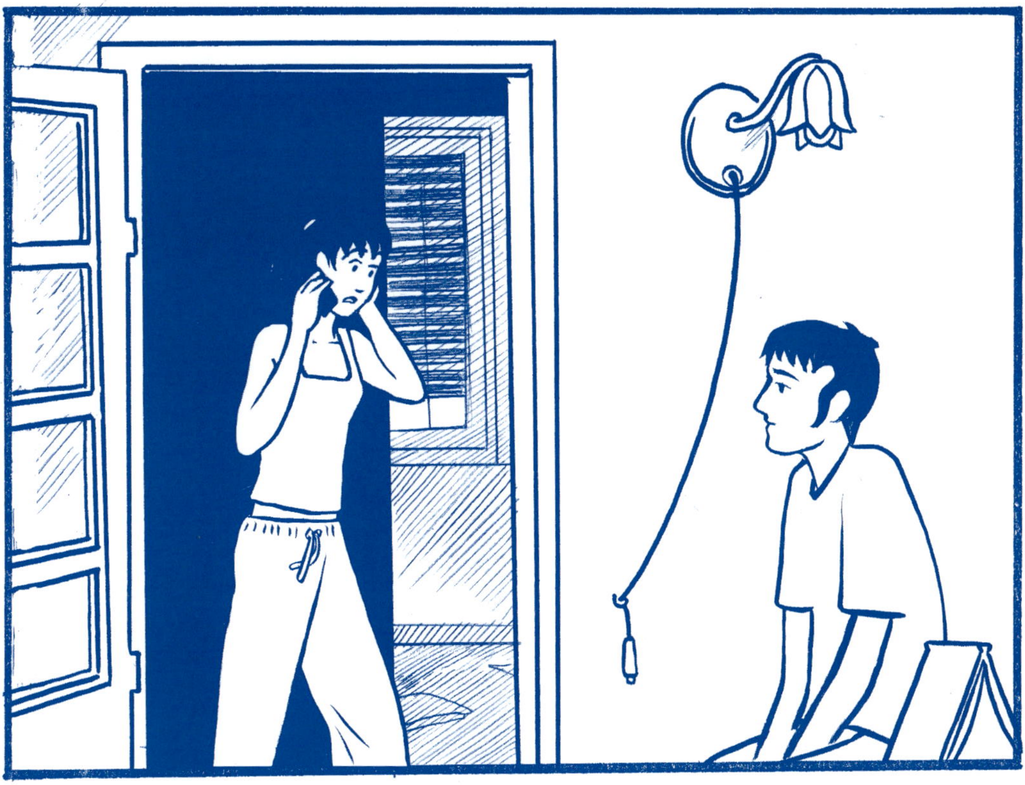

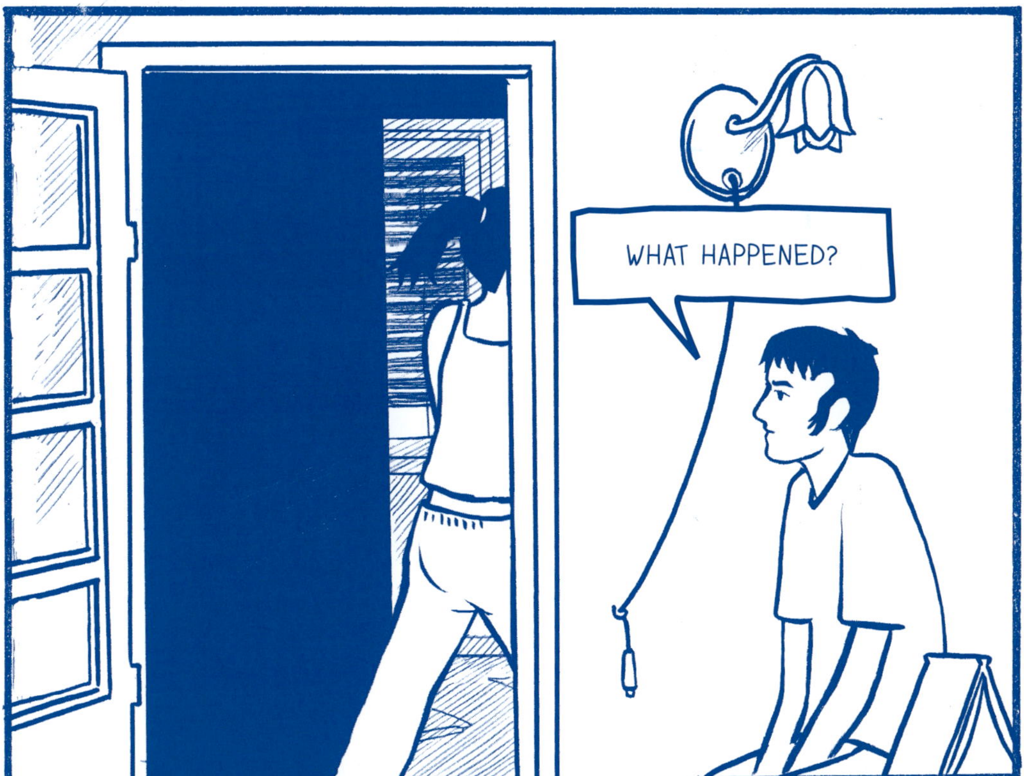
WHAT HAPPENED?

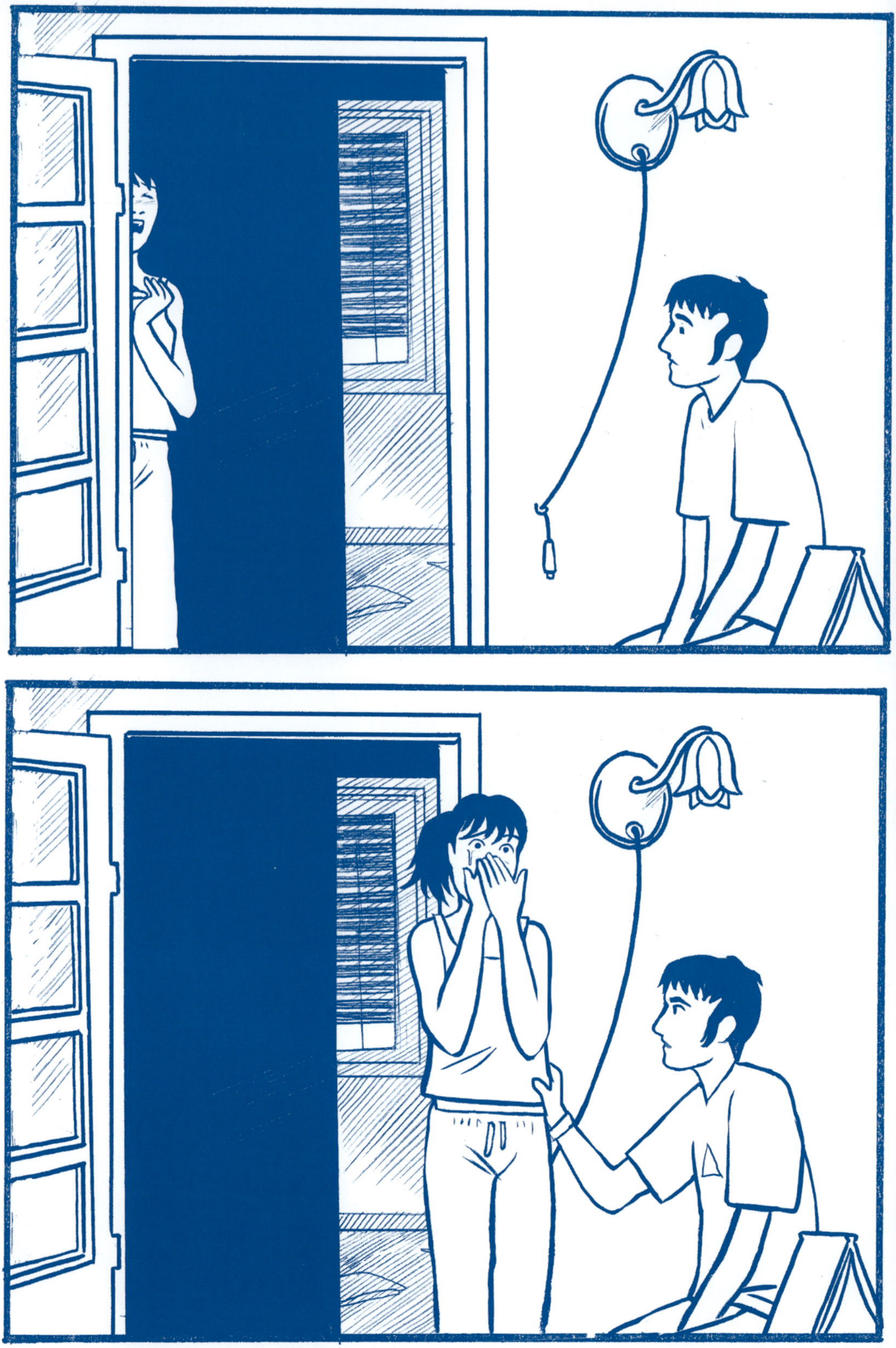

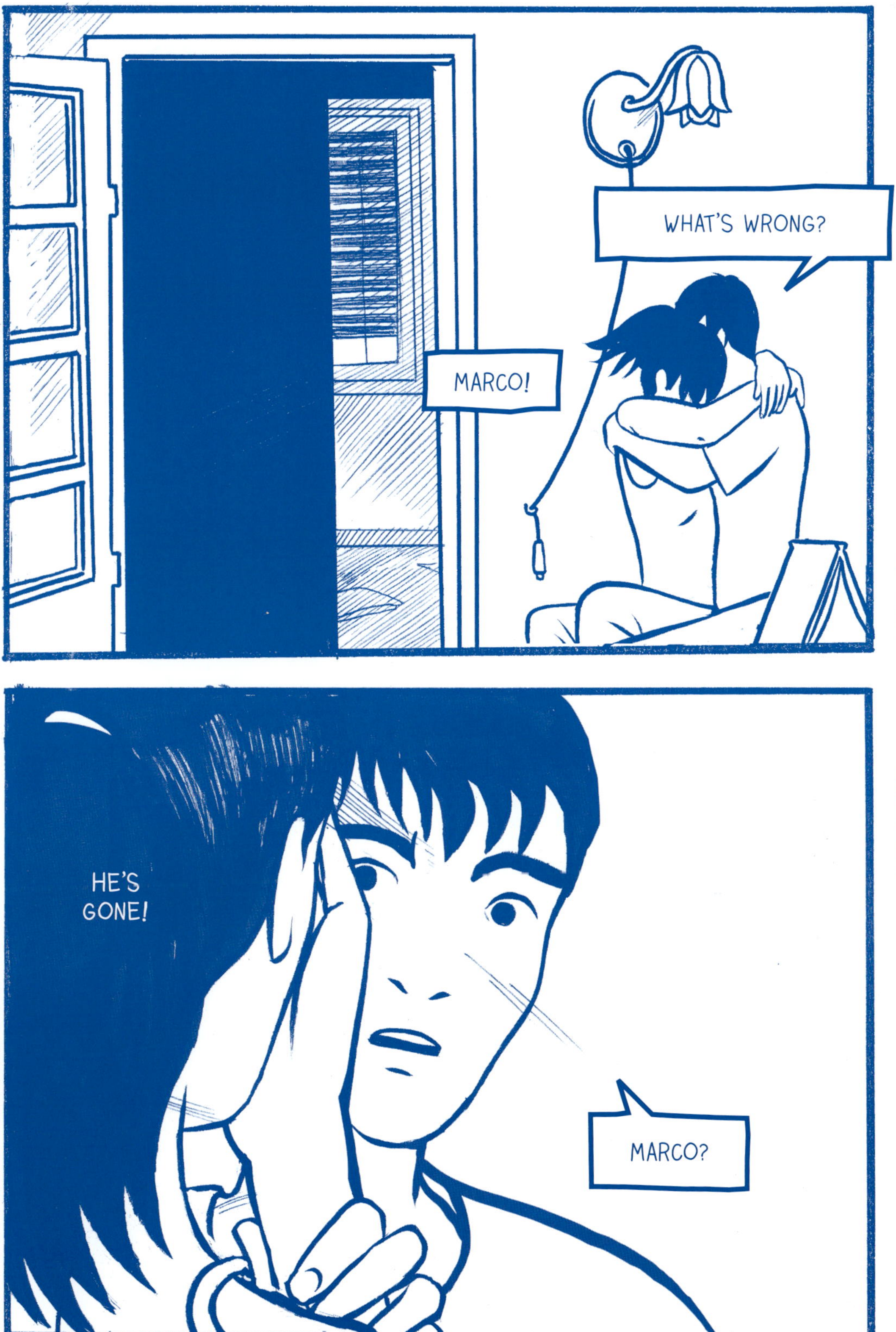
MARCO!
WHAT'S WRONG?
HE'S GONE!
MARCO?

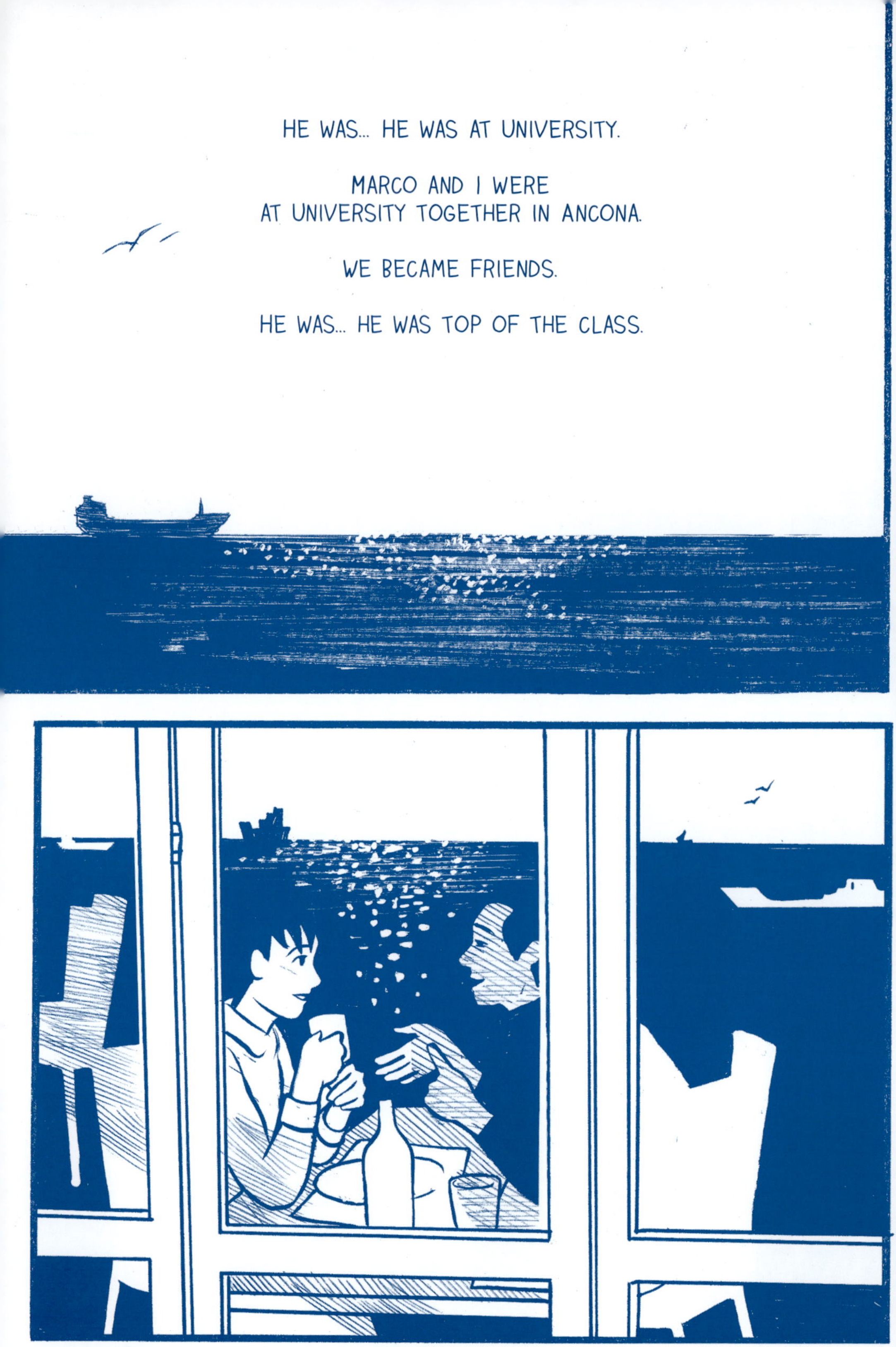
HE WAS... HE WAS AT UNIVERSITY.
MARCO AND I WERE AT UNIVERSITY TOGETHER IN ANCONA.
WE BECAME FRIENDS.
HE WAS... HE WAS TOP OF THE CLASS.

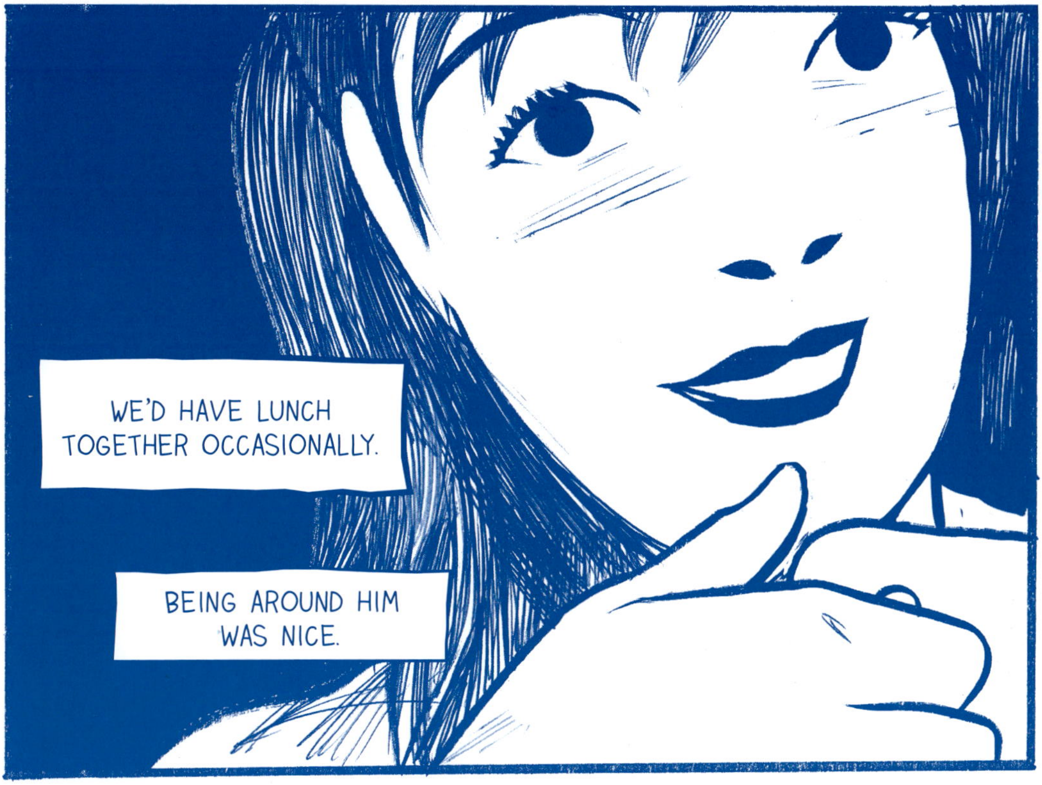
WE'D HAVE LUNCH TOGETHER OCCASIONALLY.
BEING AROUND HIM WAS NICE.

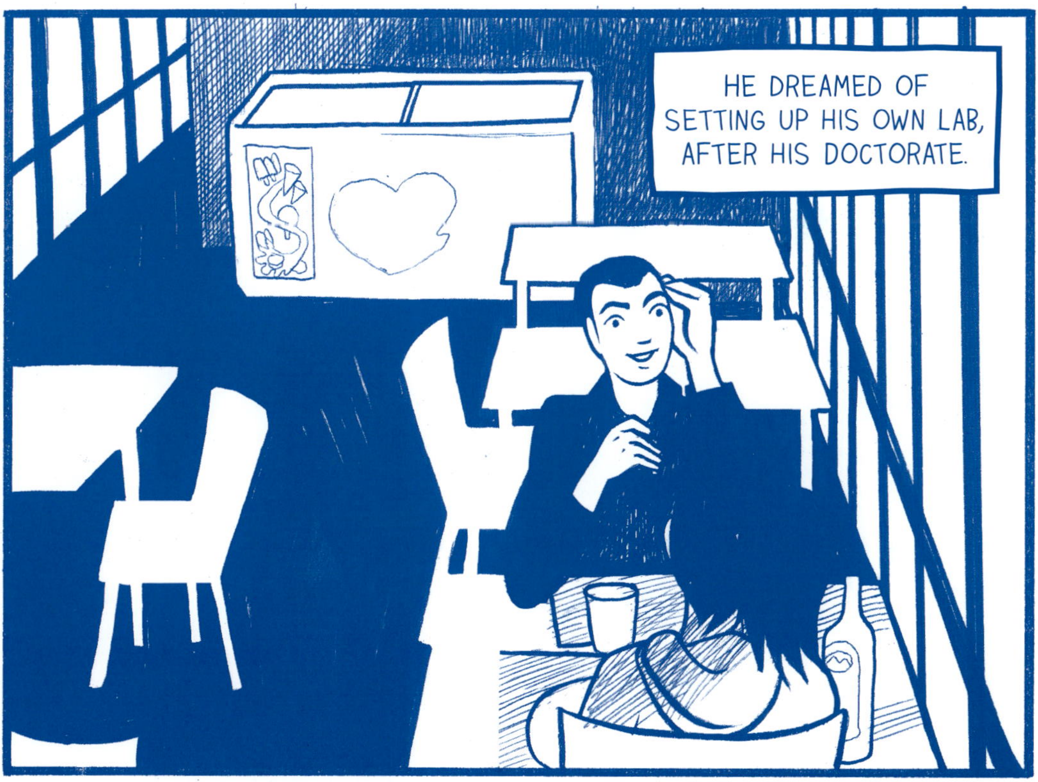
HE DREAMED OF SETTING UP HIS OWN LAB, AFTER HIS DOCTORATE.

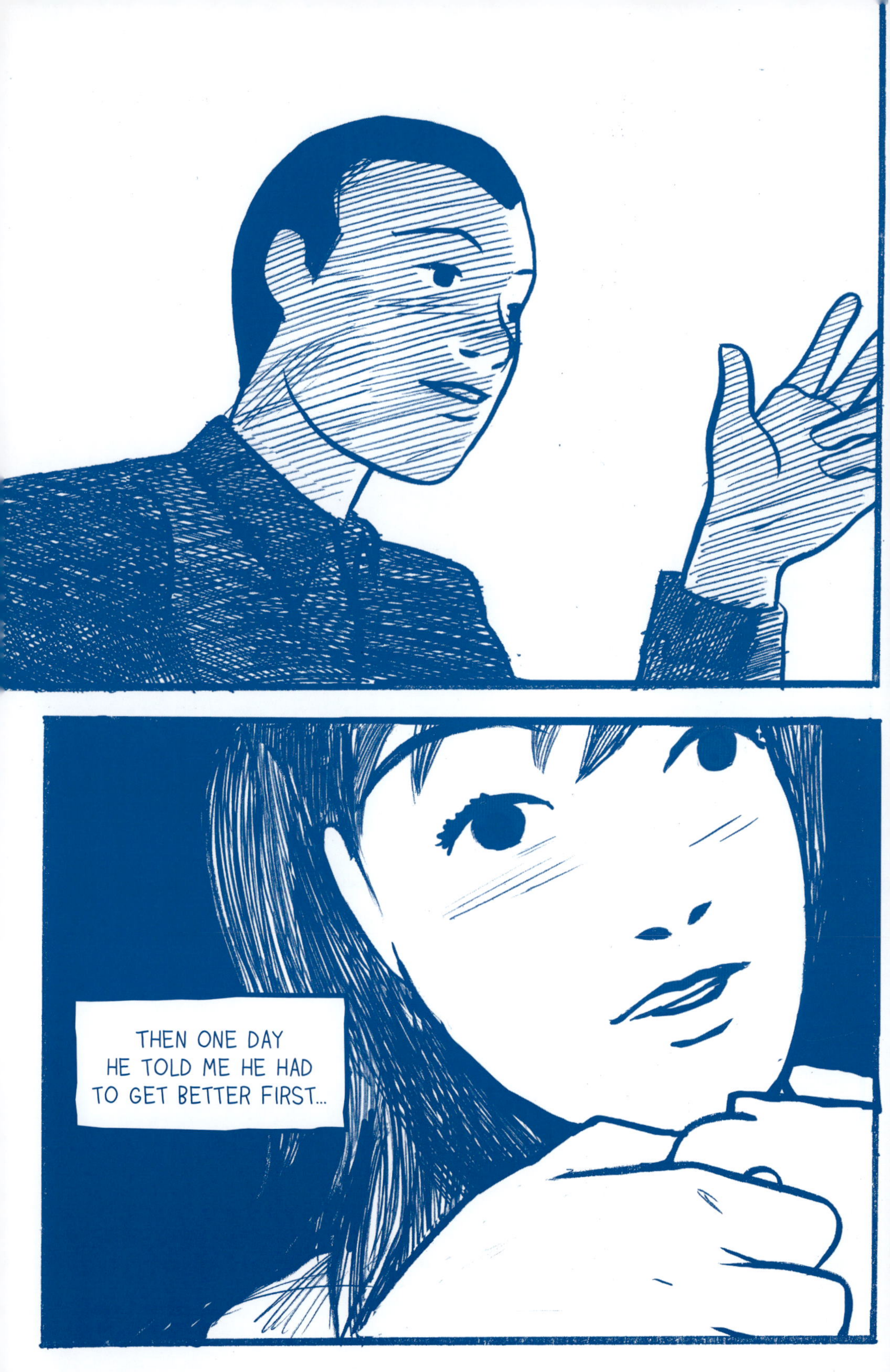
THEN ONE DAY
HE TOLD ME HE HAD
TO GET BETTER FIRST...

I SMILED.
MUST HAVE BEEN A CLUMSY SMILE.

WHEN HE TOLD ME HE WAS SICK...
...I DIDN'T THINK IT WAS SERIOUS.

HE WAS SO CONFIDENT WHEN HE SPOKE ABOUT HIMSELF AND THE FUTURE.
HIS PLANS.

SAME EVERY TIME WE SPOKE ON THE PHONE.

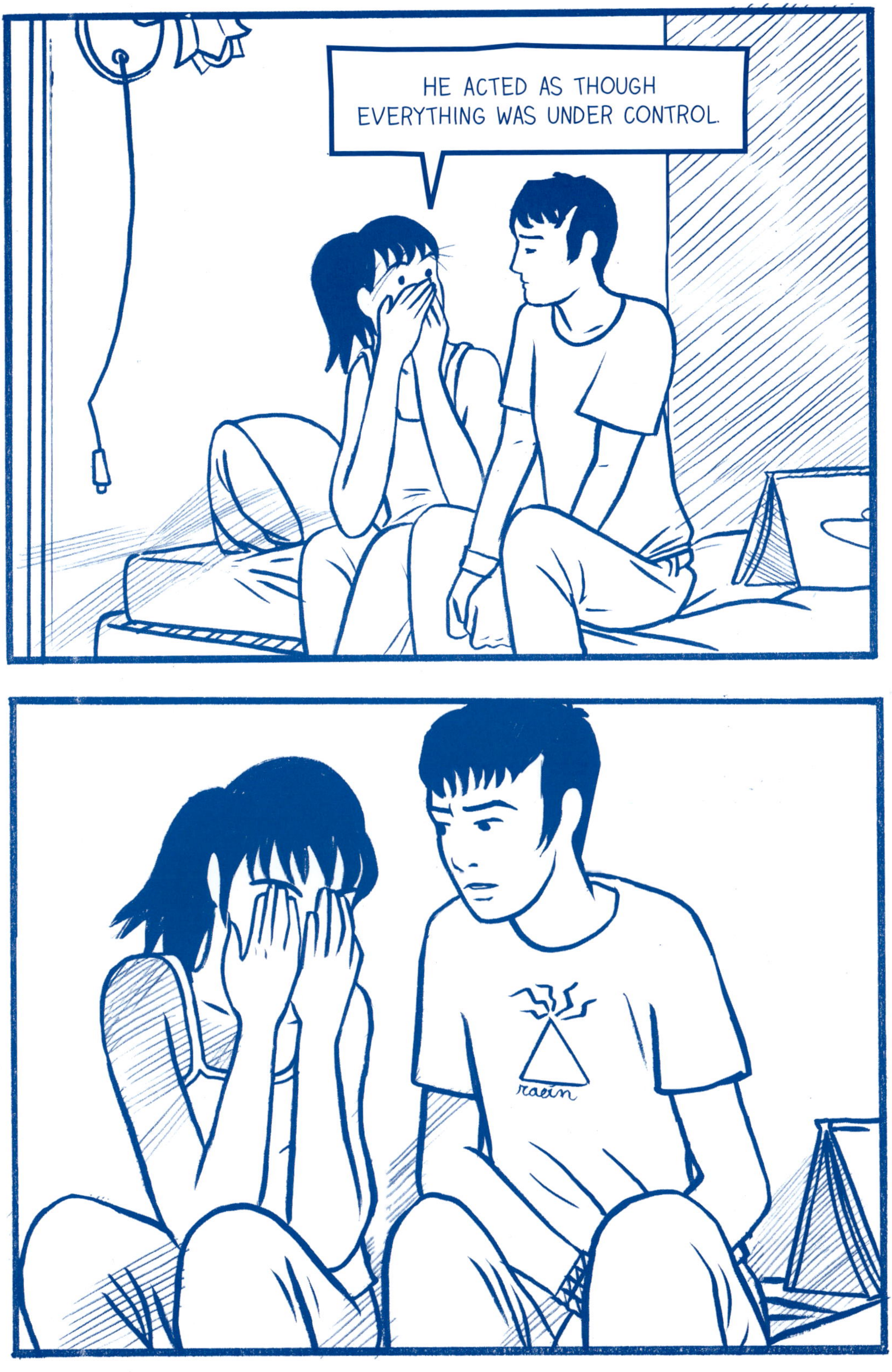
HE ACTED AS THOUGH EVERYTHING WAS UNDER CONTROL.
raein

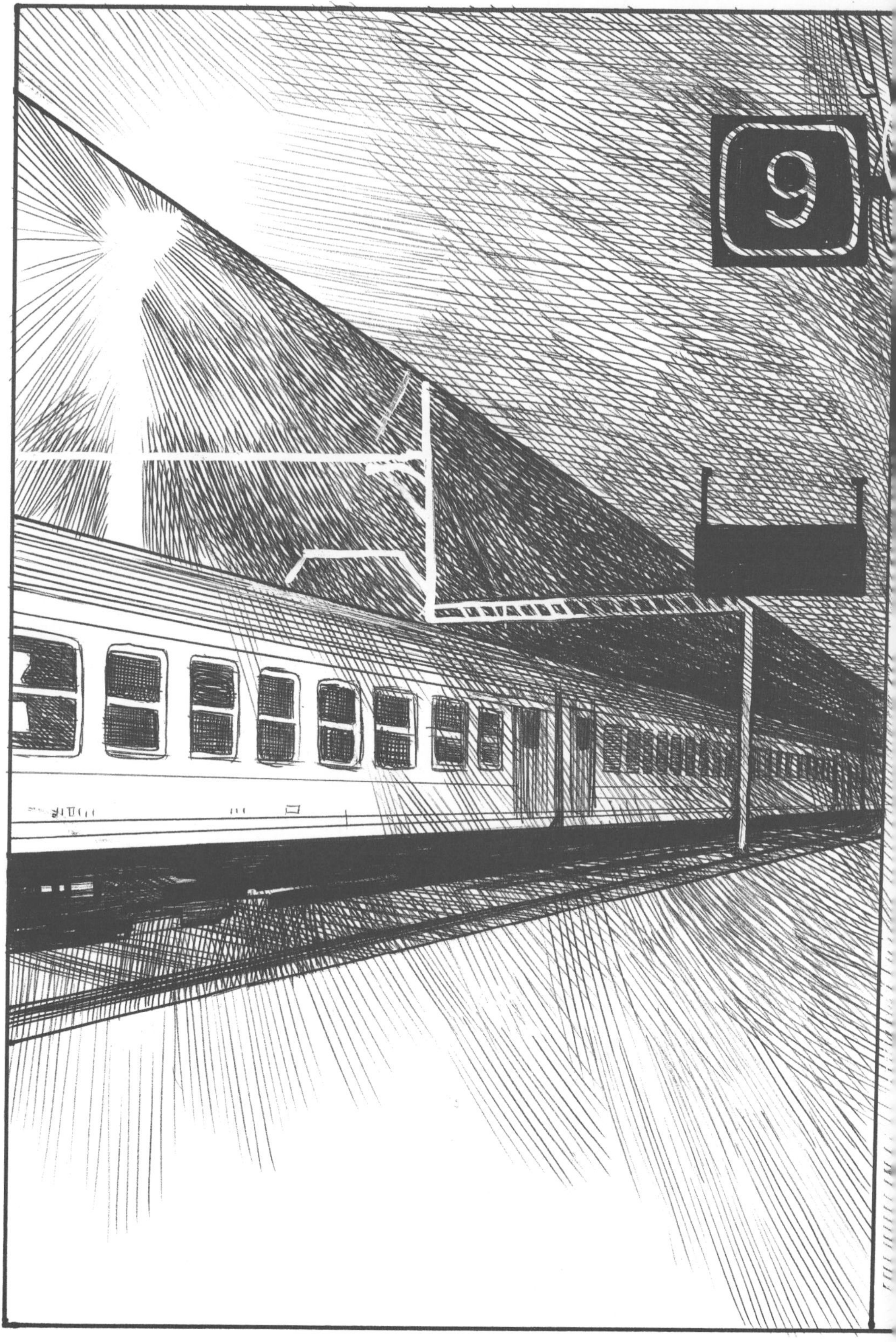
9

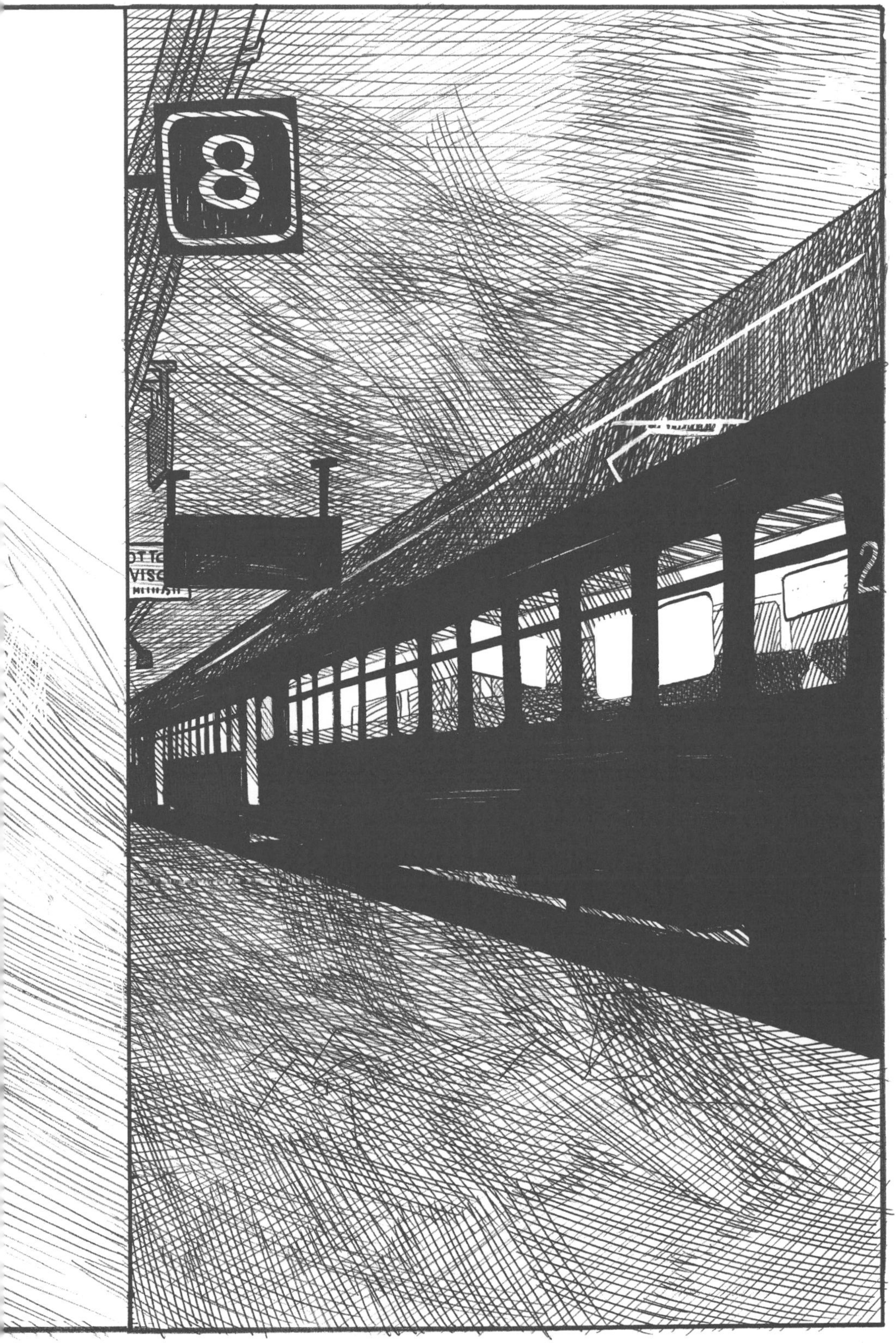
8
2

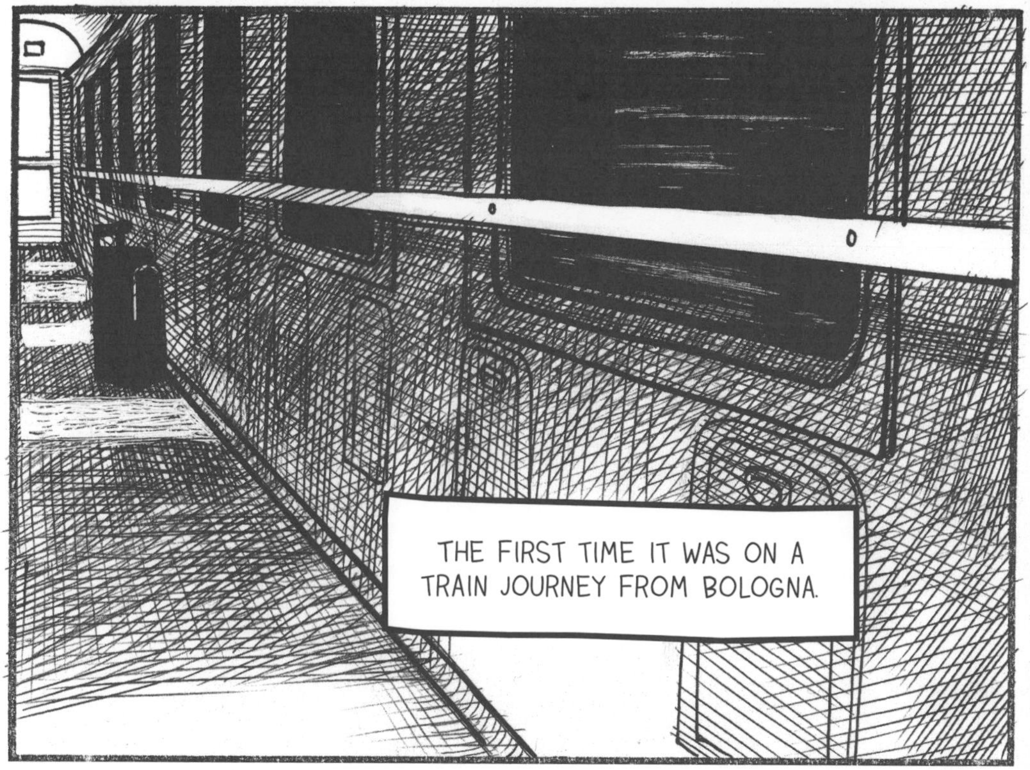
THE FIRST TIME IT WAS ON A TRAIN JOURNEY FROM BOLOGNA.

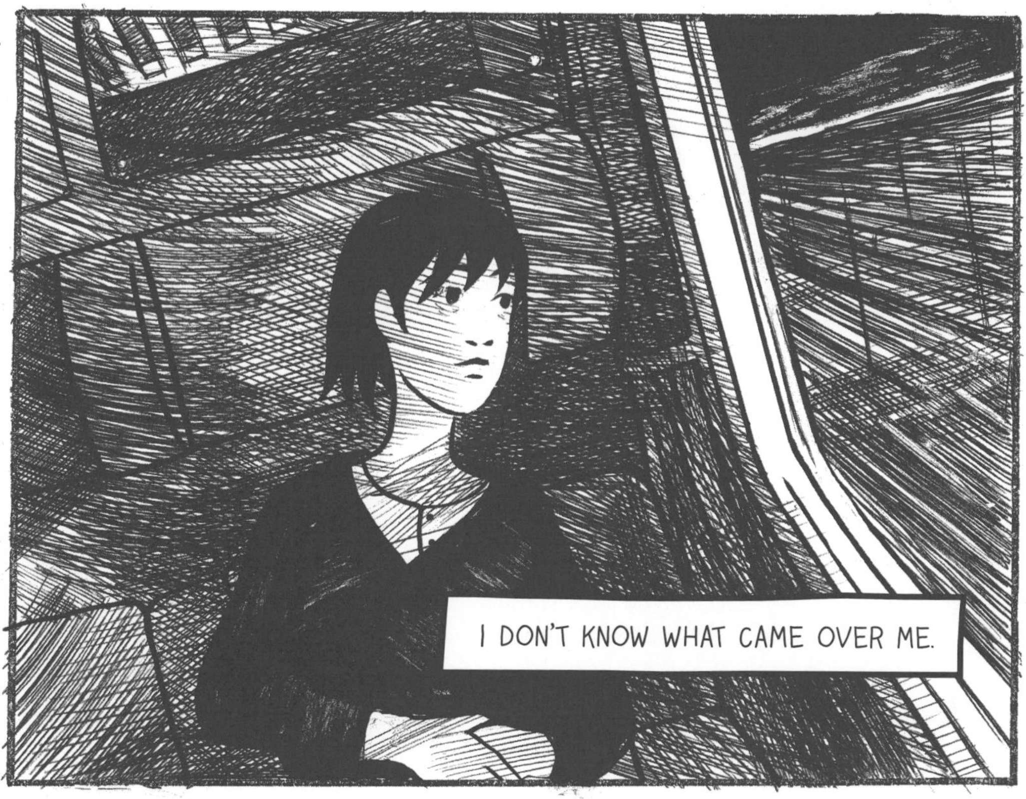
I DON'T KNOW WHAT CAME OVER ME.

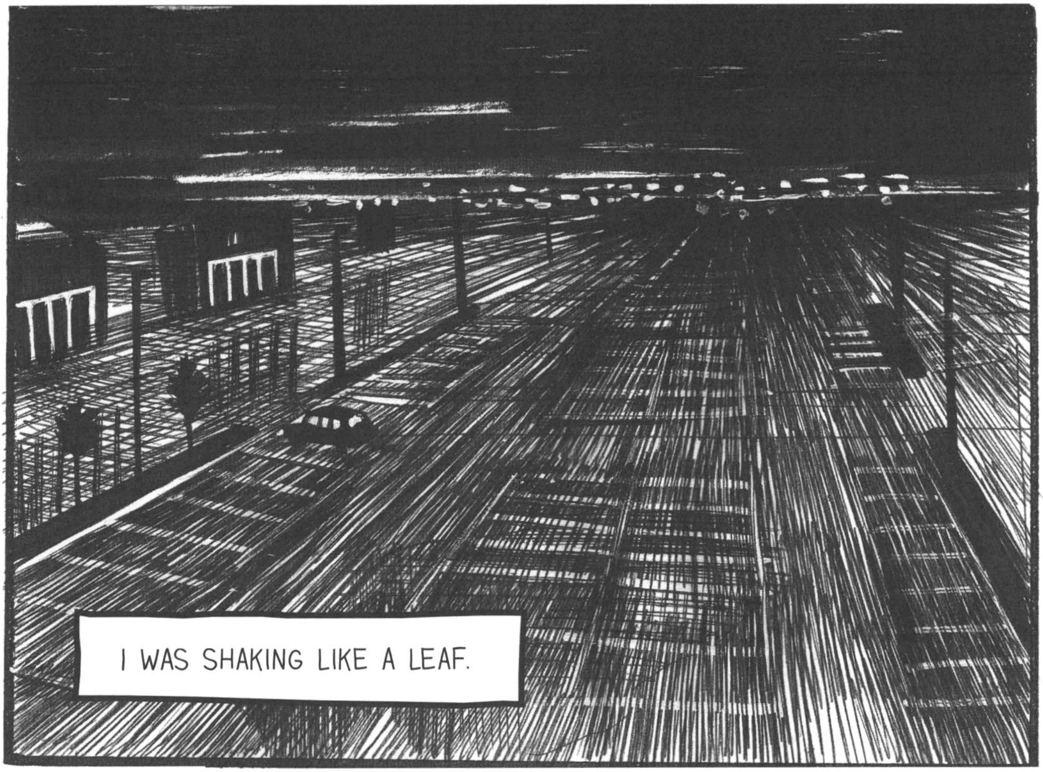
I WAS SHAKING LIKE A LEAF.

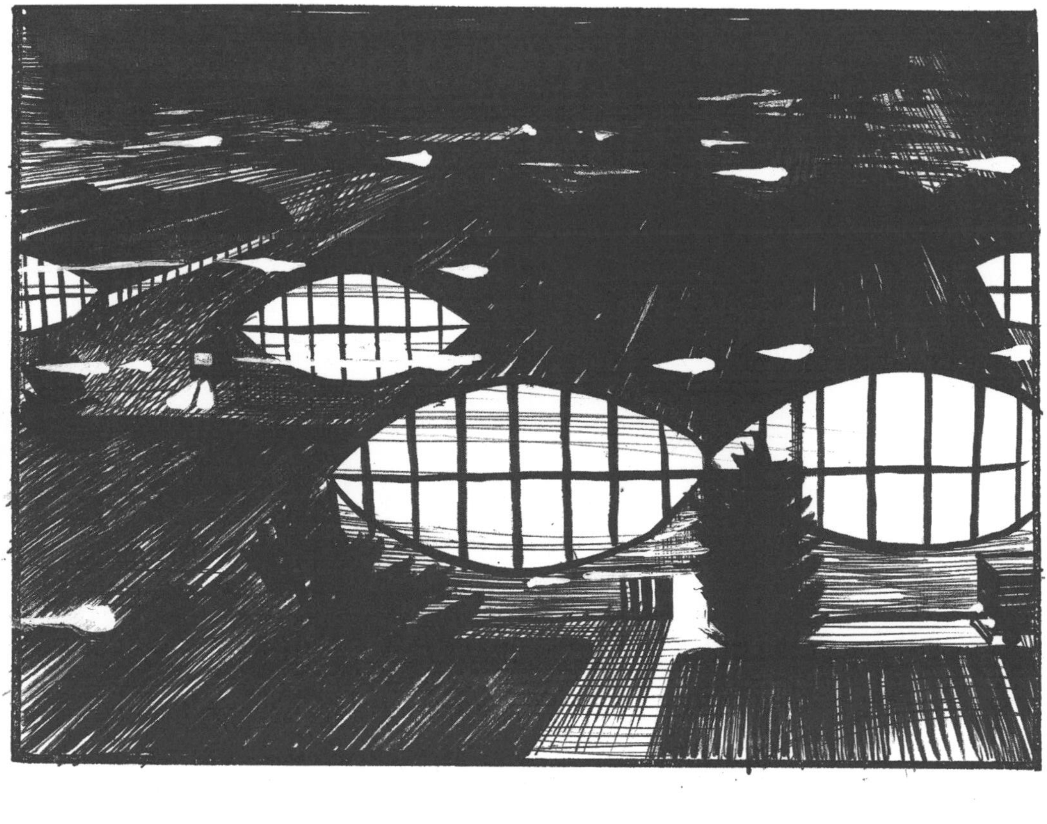

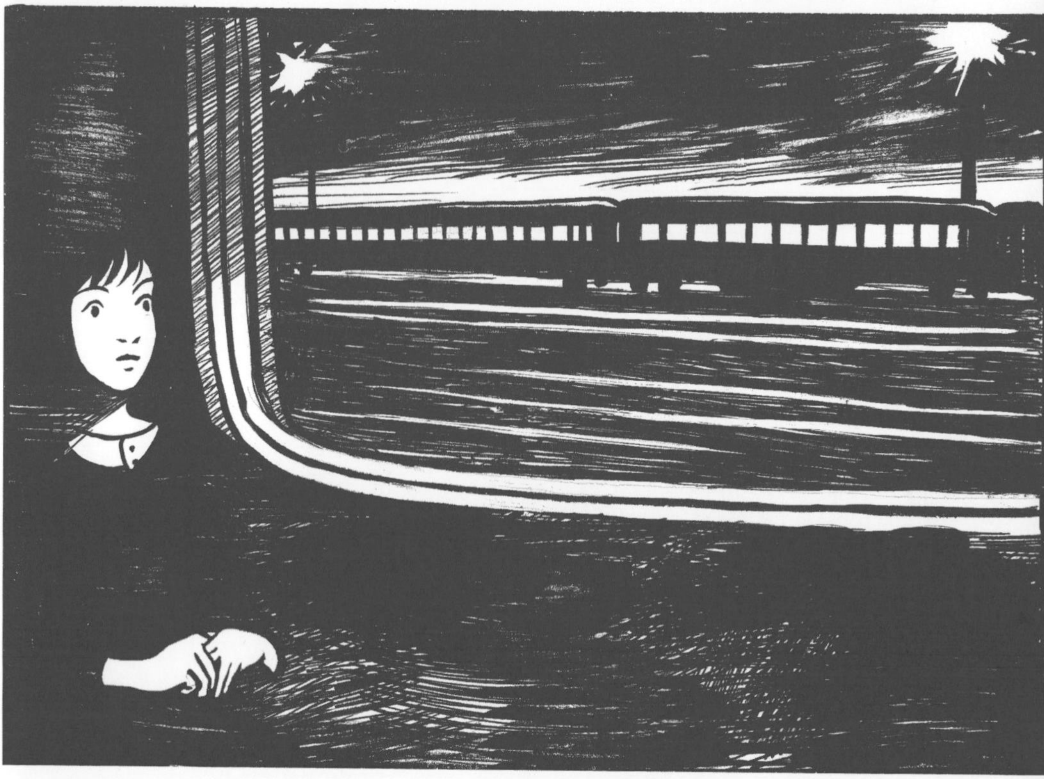

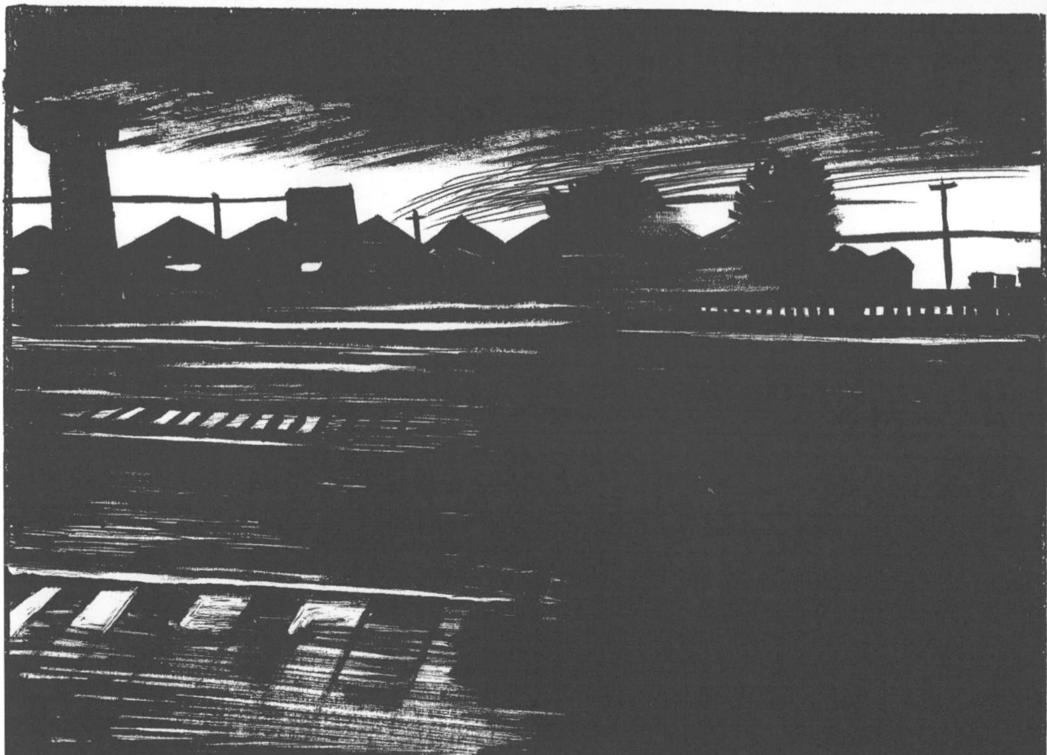

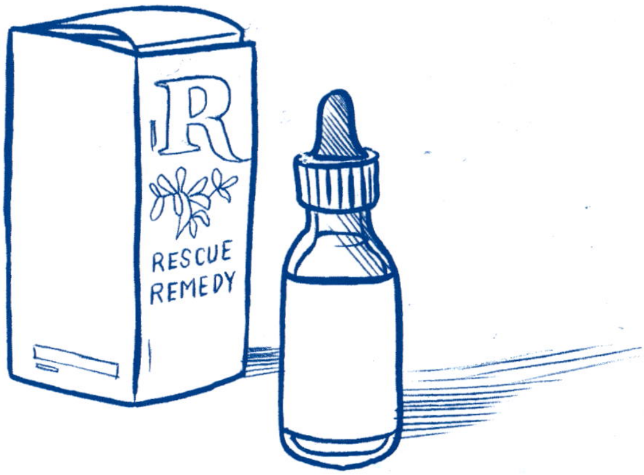
R
RESCUE REMEDY

THE FACT THAT MARCO
WAS NOT AFRAID
OF HIS FUTURE...

OF BEING ILL...
WELL, IT MADE ME EVEN
MORE FRIGHTENED.

BECAUSE
HE WAS SO POSITIVE
HE COULD MAKE IT.

I'M GOING TO CRASH!

I FEEL HOT.
EVERYONE'S LOOKING. AM I GOING TO PASS OUT?
...TOO MANY LAYERS ON.

THE BUS IS NOT LEAVING,
I'LL MISS MY TRAIN,
IT'S ONLY A FEW STOPS.
EXCUSE ME, MISS
MISS!

I'M ABOUT TO CRASH.
SUDDENLY, MY HEART BEATS FASTER.
MISS!

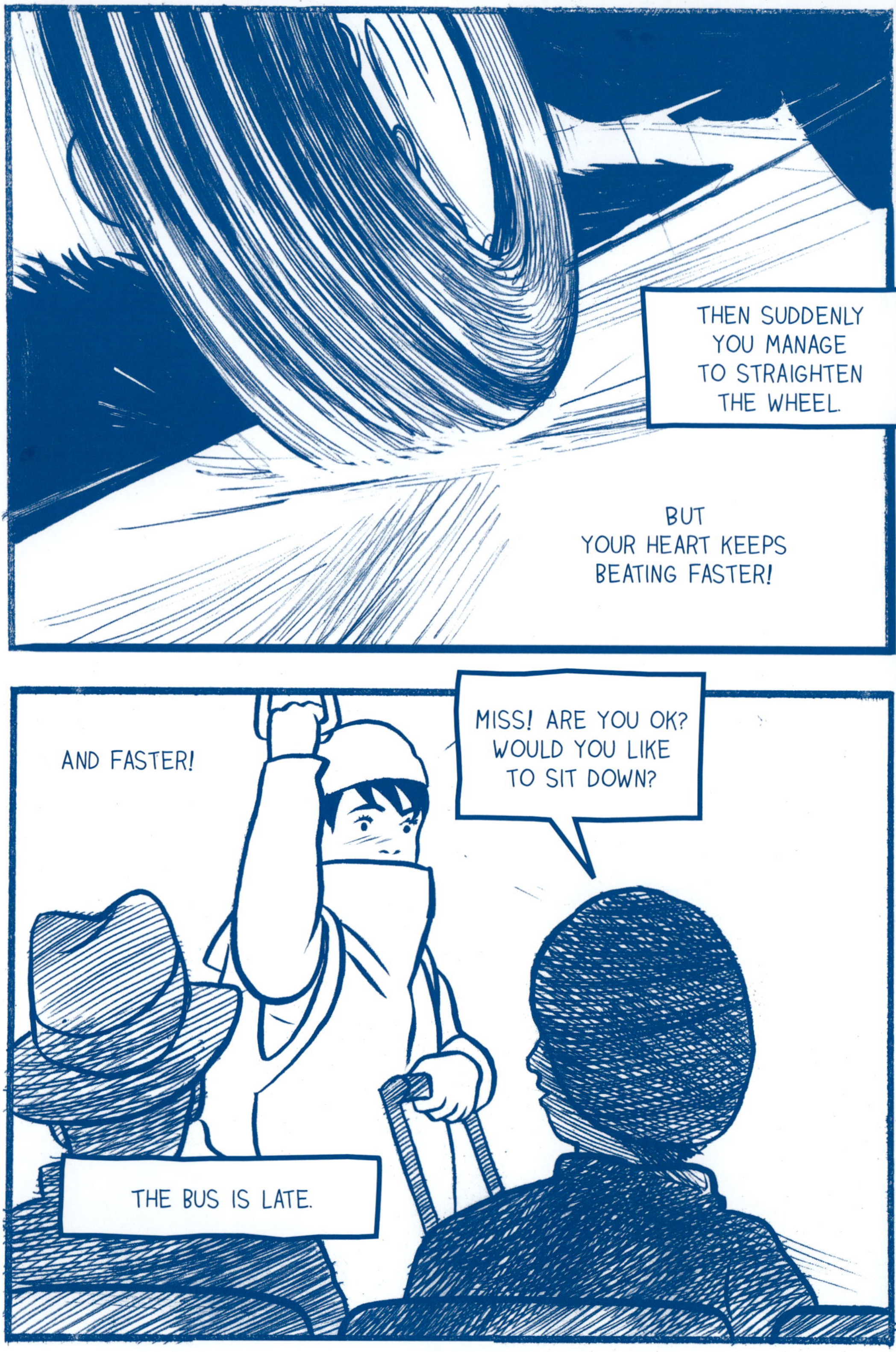
THEN SUDDENLY YOU MANAGE TO STRAIGHTEN THE WHEEL.
BUT YOUR HEART KEEPS BEATING FASTER!
AND FASTER!
MISS! ARE YOU OK? WOULD YOU LIKE TO SIT DOWN?
THE BUS IS LATE.

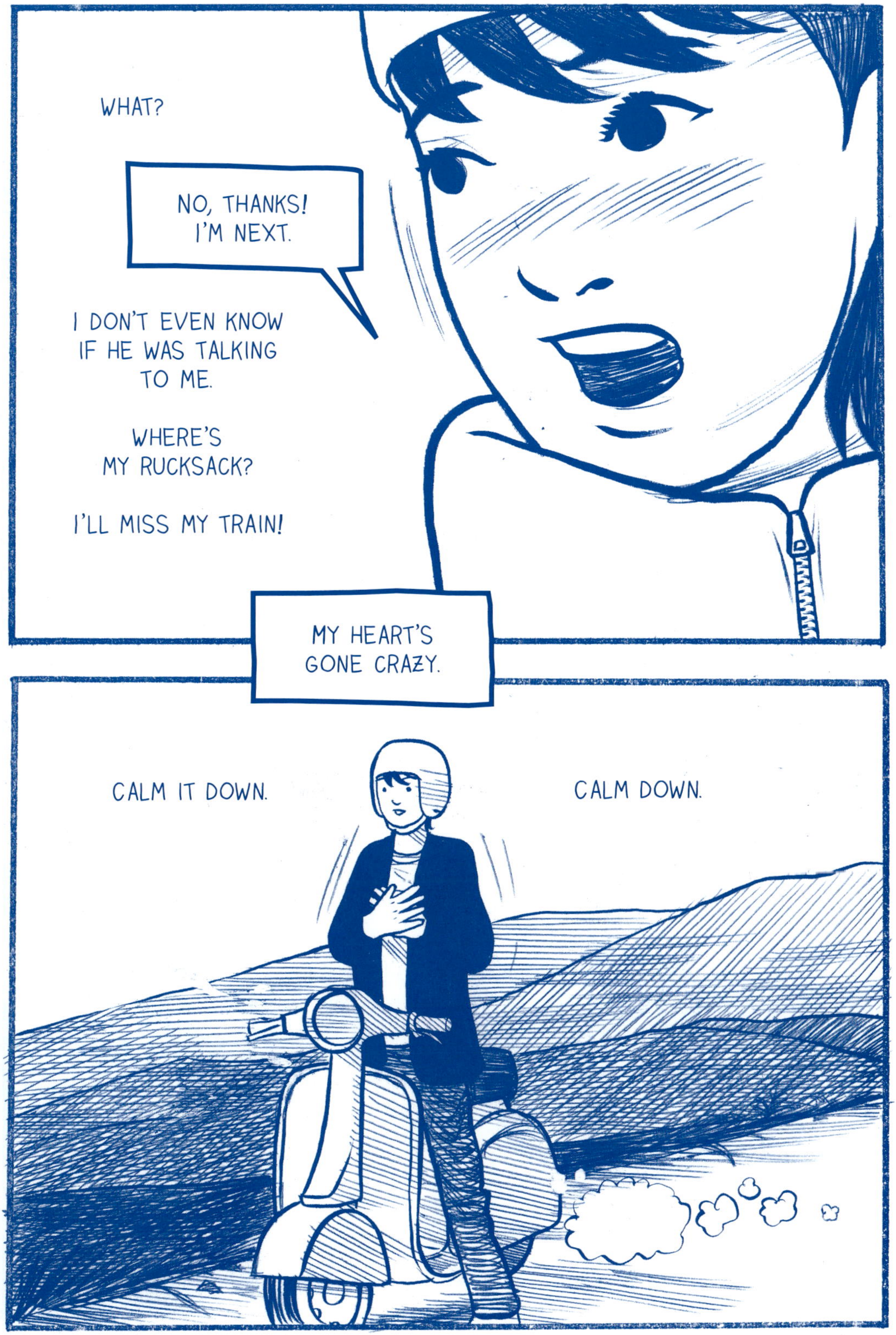
WHAT?
NO, THANKS! I'M NEXT.
I DON'T EVEN KNOW IF HE WAS TALKING TO ME.
WHERE'S MY RUCKSACK?
I'LL MISS MY TRAIN!
MY HEART'S GONE CRAZY.
CALM IT DOWN.
CALM DOWN.

MY HEART'S GONE CRAZY.
I'LL CALM DOWN NOW.
...BUT I'LL MISS MY TRAIN.
CORSO COMPUTER
ATLANTIDE
SUMO

IT'S LIKE IT WAS
BURSTING OUT
OF MY CHEST...

IT'S LIKE IT KEPT
BEATING FASTER
AND FASTER.

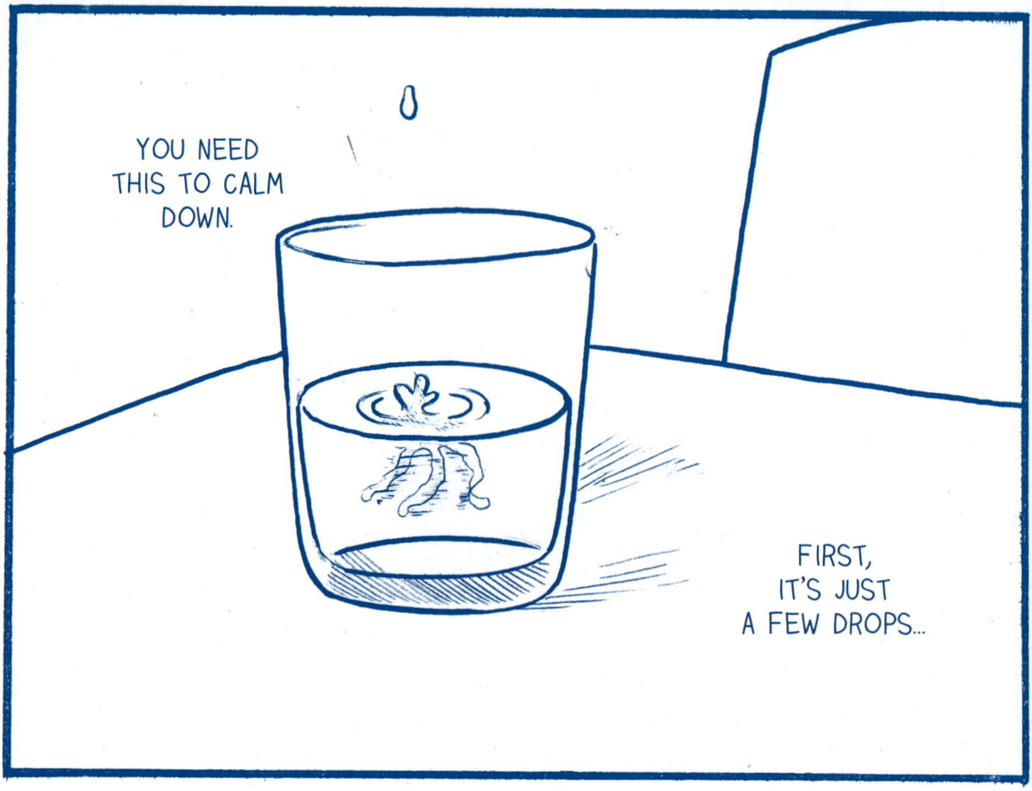
YOU NEED THIS TO CALM DOWN.
FIRST, IT'S JUST A FEW DROPS...

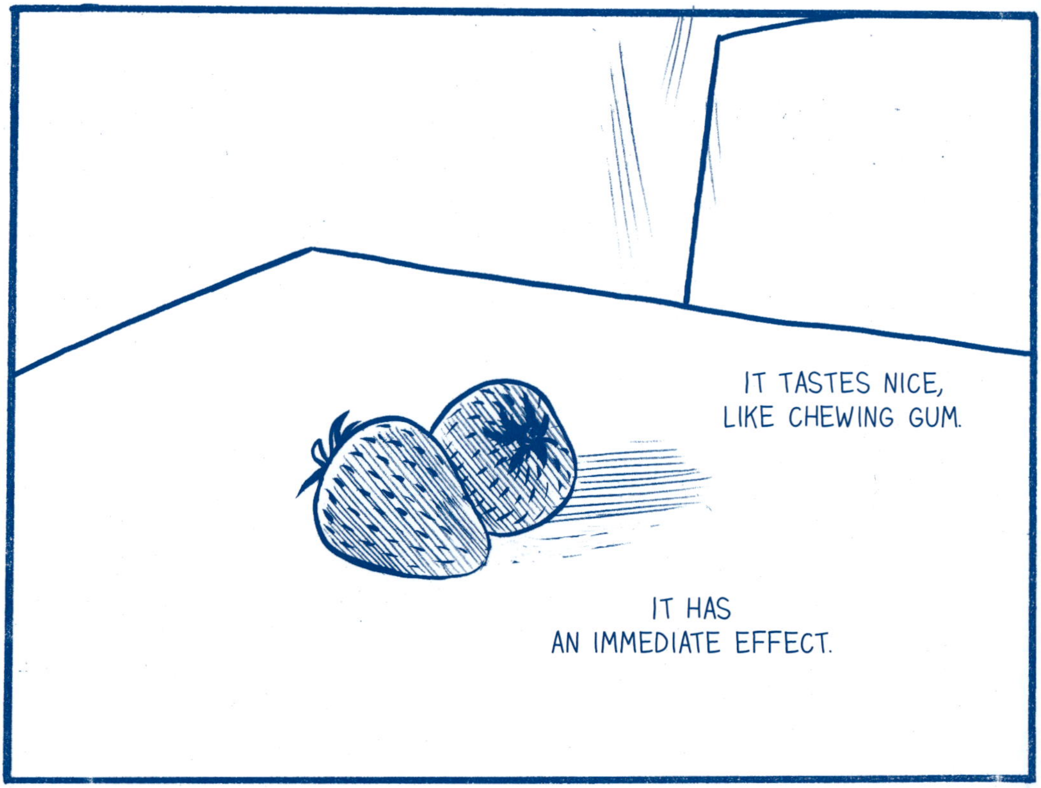
IT TASTES NICE, LIKE CHEWING GUM.
IT HAS AN IMMEDIATE EFFECT.

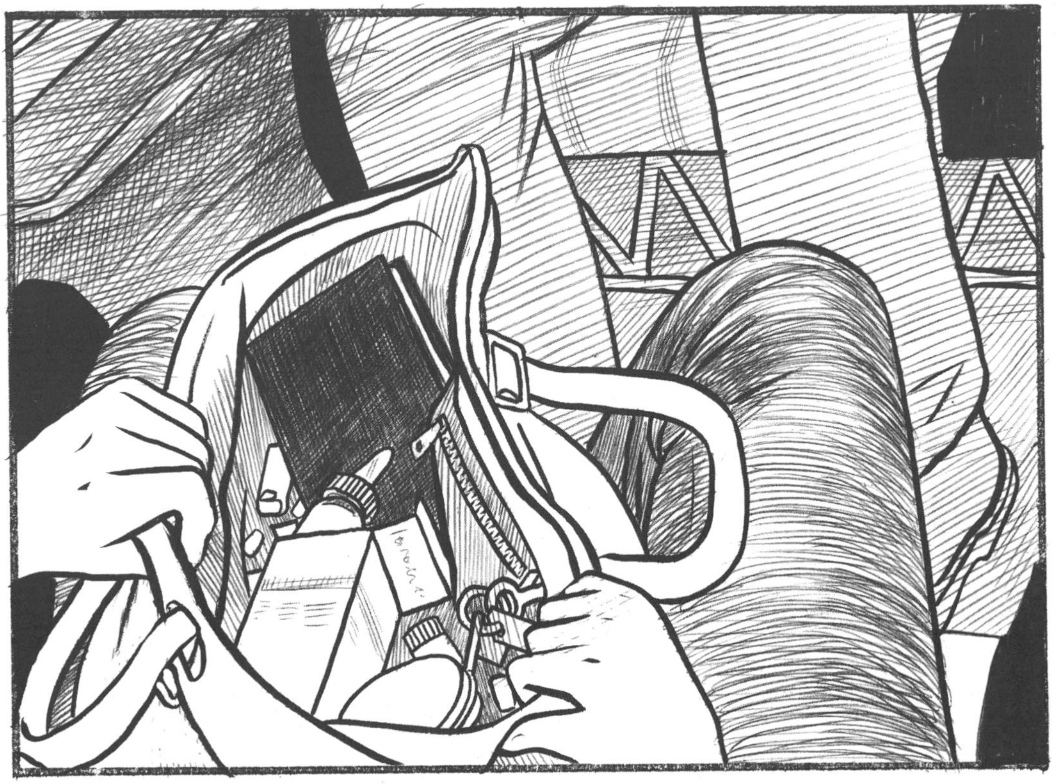

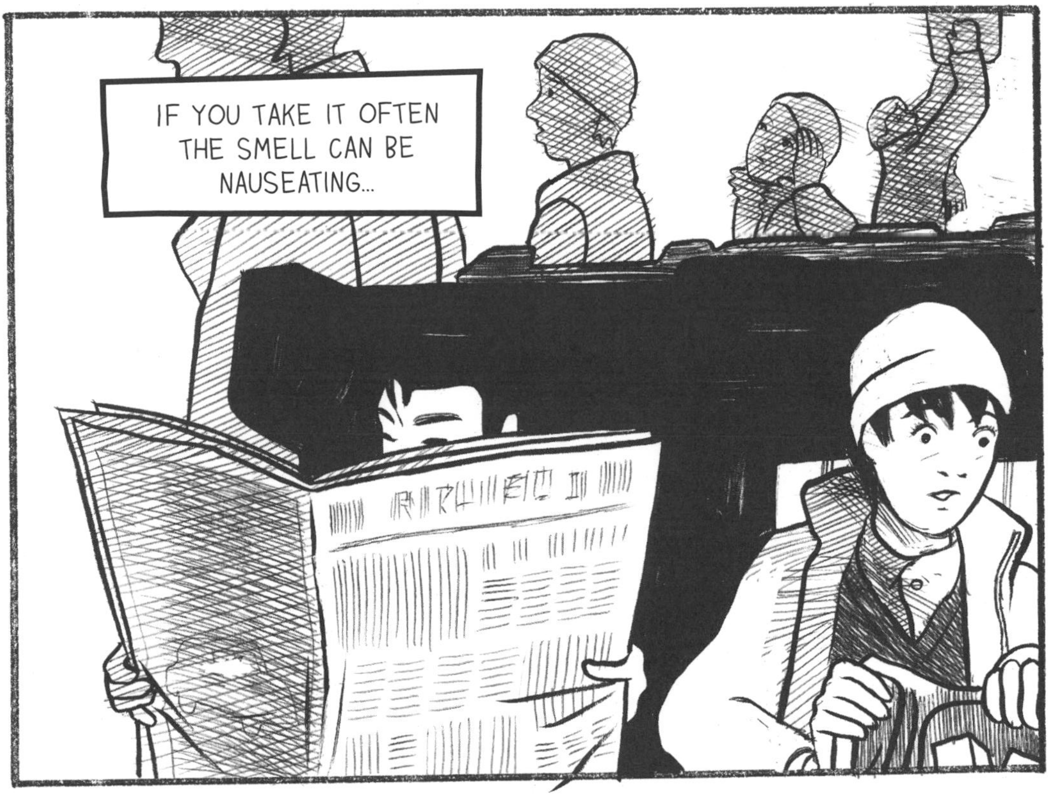
IF YOU TAKE IT OFTEN THE SMELL CAN BE NAUSEATING...

I WAS ON THE TRAIN HOME ONE DAY AND IT OPENED INSIDE MY HANDBAG...

...I HAD TO GIVE EVERYTHING TO THE DRY CLEANER.

I SECURE IT IN A BAG, NOW.

YOU CAN'T DO WITHOUT...

YOU MUST TAKE IT WITH YOU AT ALL TIMES.

YOU CAN'T EVEN IMAGINE TRAVELING WITHOUT IT.

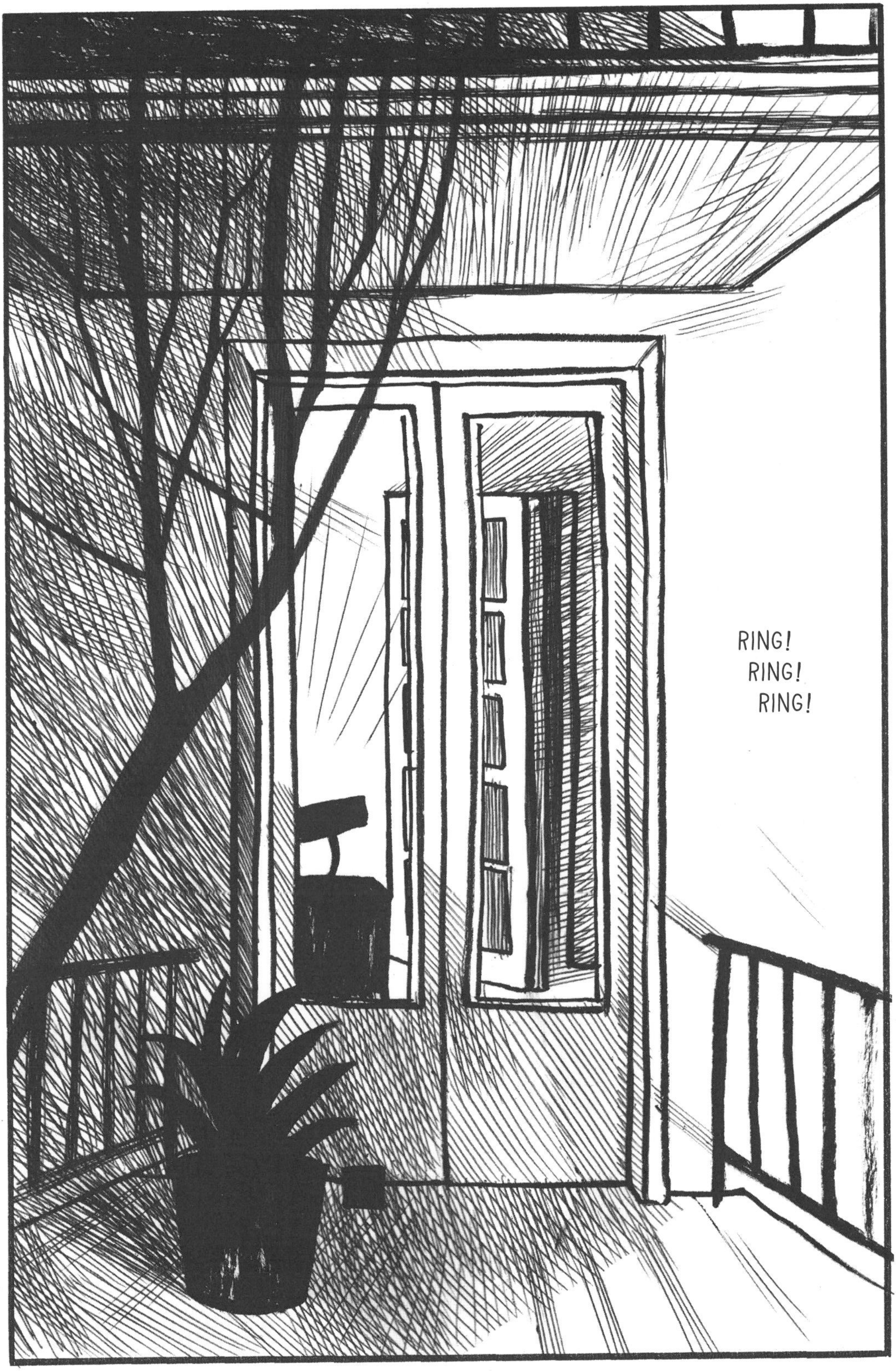
RING!
RING!
RING!

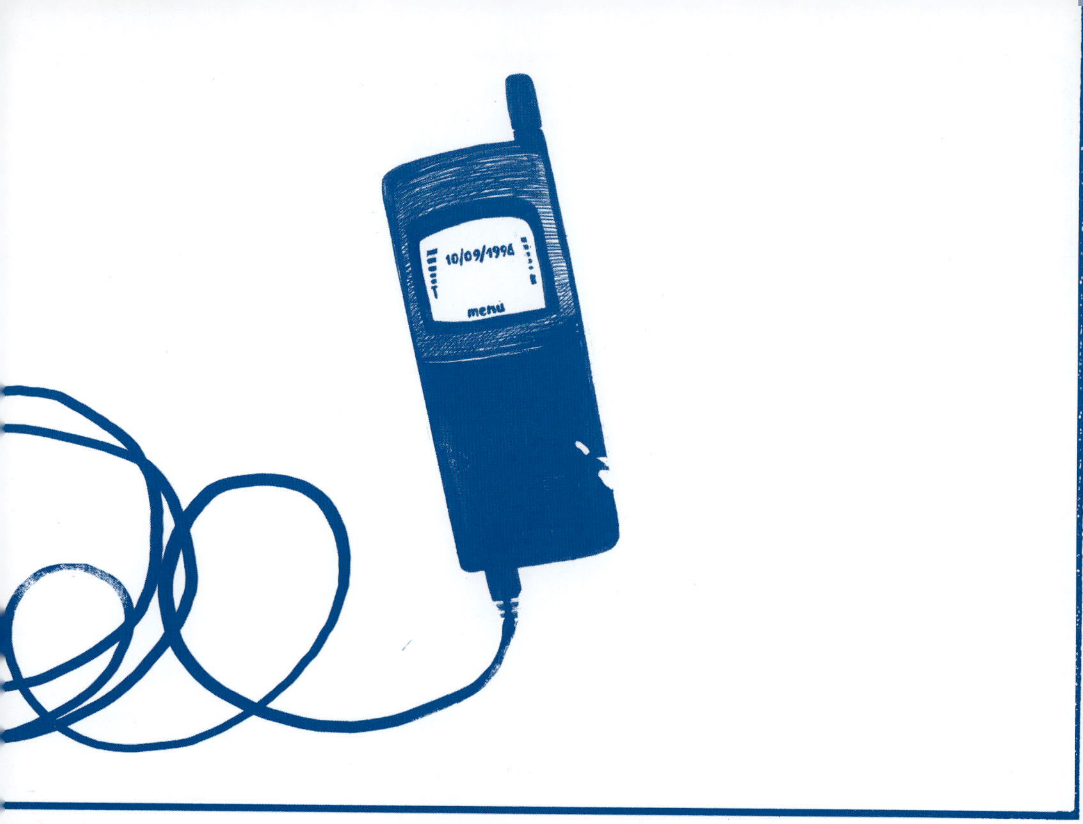
10/09/1996
menu

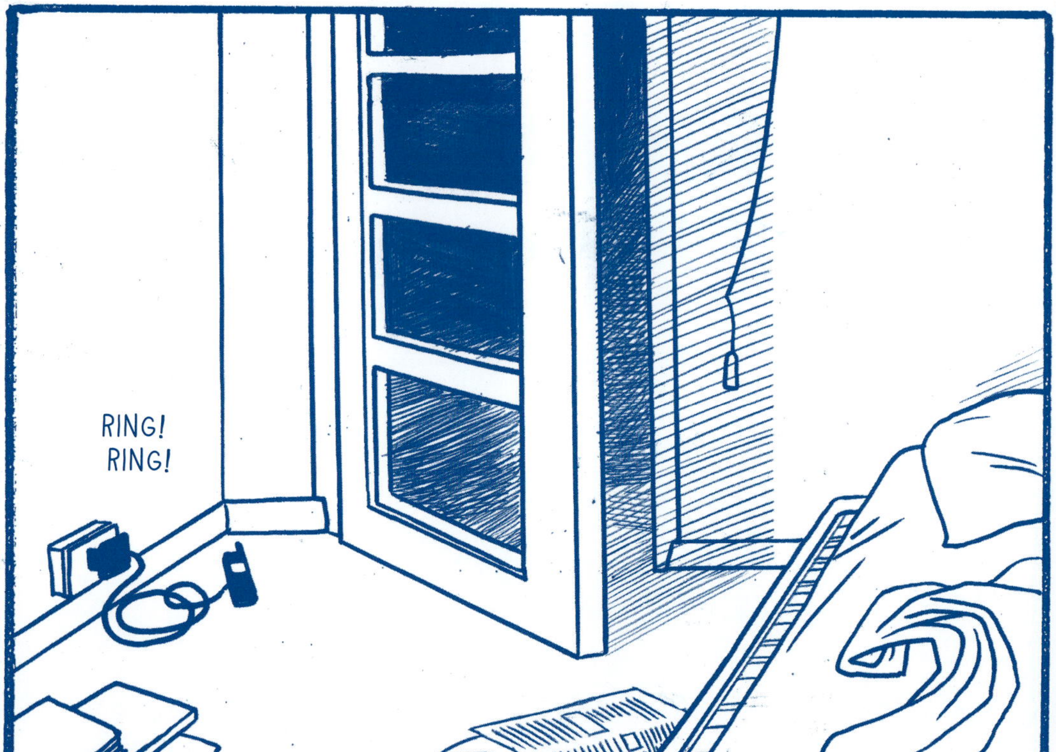
RING!
RING!

RING!
RING!
RING!
RING!

HELLO.
HELLO?
WHERE ARE YOU? HOME?
I...I'M SCARED!

WERE YOU ASLEEP?
NO, DID YOU TAKE THE DROPS?
YES, BUT I'M SCARED!
THEY'RE DOING NOTHING THIS TIME...
DON'T SAY THAT!
MY HEAD'S THUMPING!
...TRY TO CALM DOWN!
I HATE IT WHEN YOU TELL ME TO CALM DOWN!
ARE YOU LYING DOWN?
NO!
LIE DOWN!
OK!

WHEN'S IT GOING TO BE OVER?
SOON!
NO!
YES!
IT'S NOT TRUE!
I CAN'T BREATHE!

I'M SCARED!
WHY CAN'T I BREATHE?
WHAT USE ARE YOU, IF I CAN'T BREATHE?

THE FIRST THING
YOU THINK IS
IT'S YOUR HEART.

...MAYBE
THEY'RE NOT
PANIC ATTACKS.

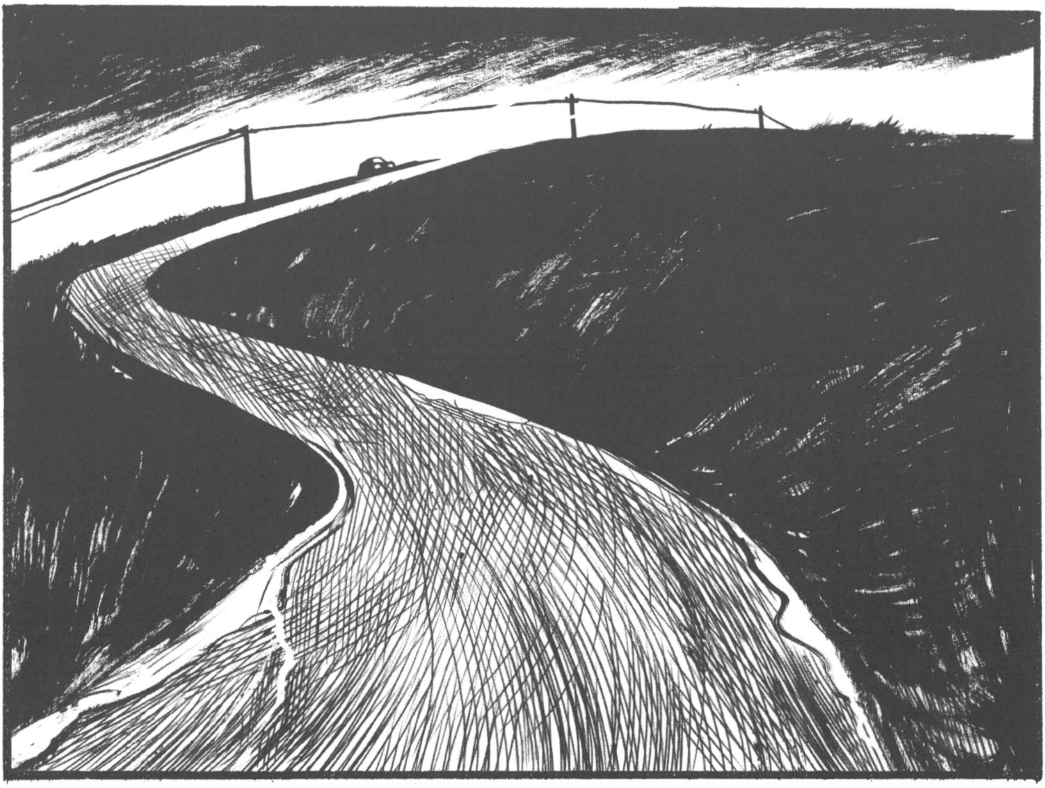

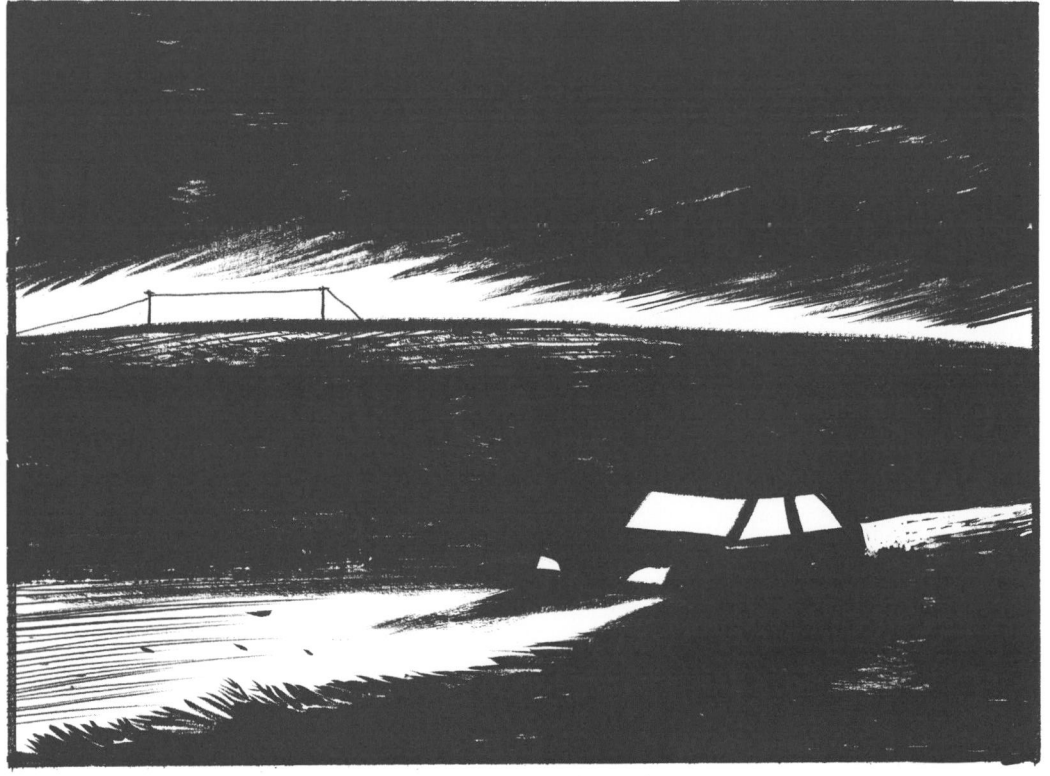

THIS IS
A CARDIAC HOLTER.
IT'S USED IN MEDICAL TESTS.

INSIDE IT IS
A TAPE RECORDING
YOUR HEARTBEAT
FOR TWENTY-FOUR HOURS.

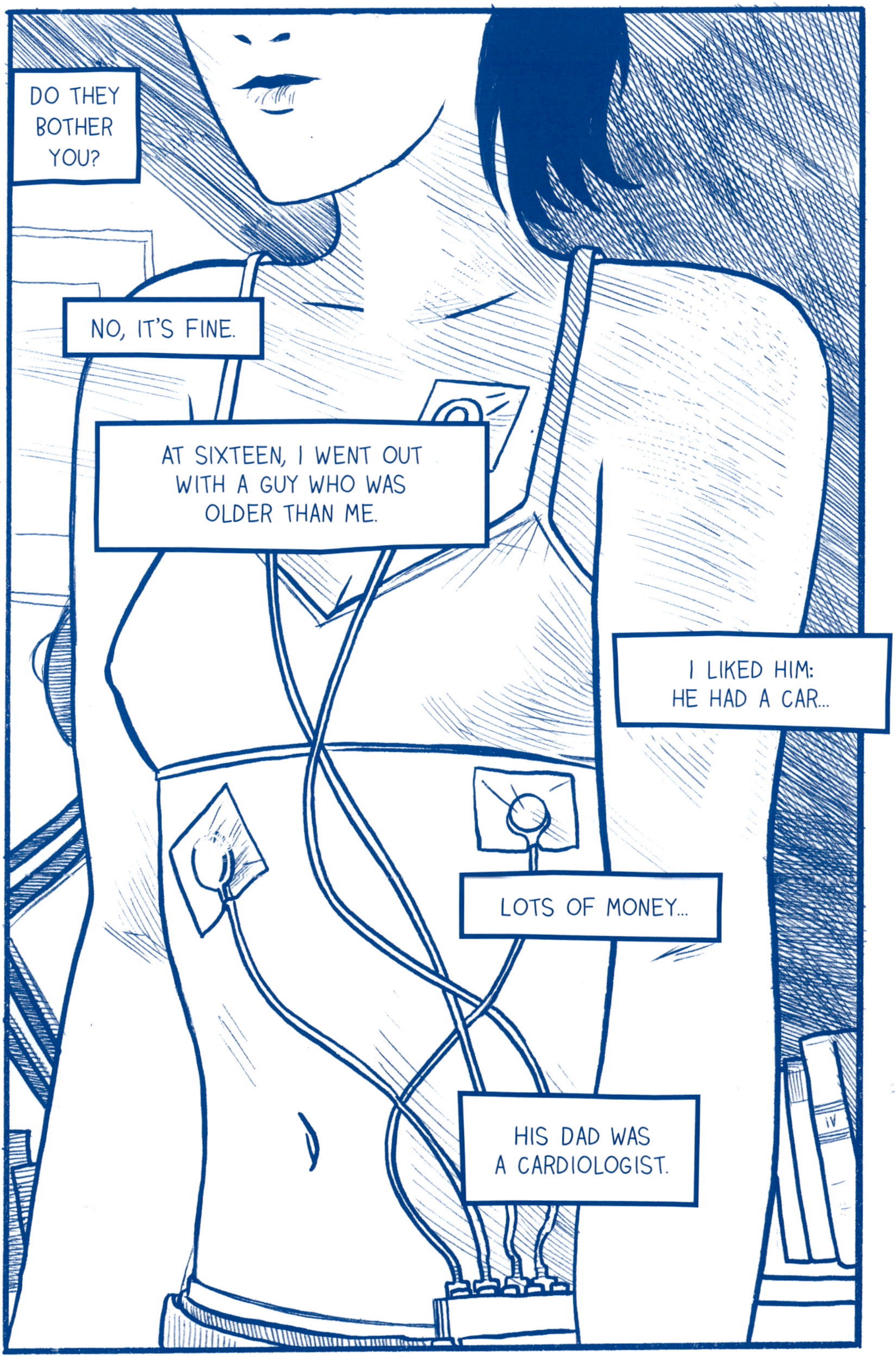
DO THEY BOTHER YOU?
NO, IT'S FINE.
AT SIXTEEN, I WENT OUT WITH A GUY WHO WAS OLDER THAN ME.
I LIKED HIM: HE HAD A CAR...
LOTS OF MONEY...
HIS DAD WAS A CARDIOLOGIST.
IV

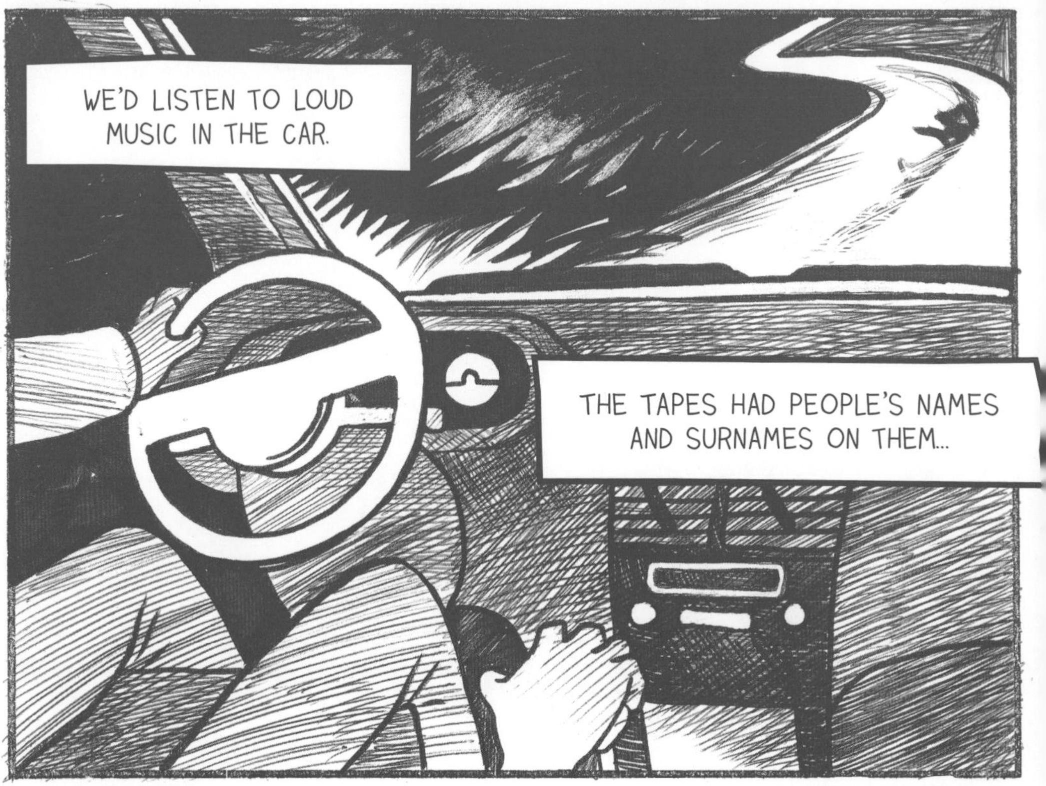
WE'D LISTEN TO LOUD MUSIC IN THE CAR.
THE TAPES HAD PEOPLE'S NAMES AND SURNAMES ON THEM...

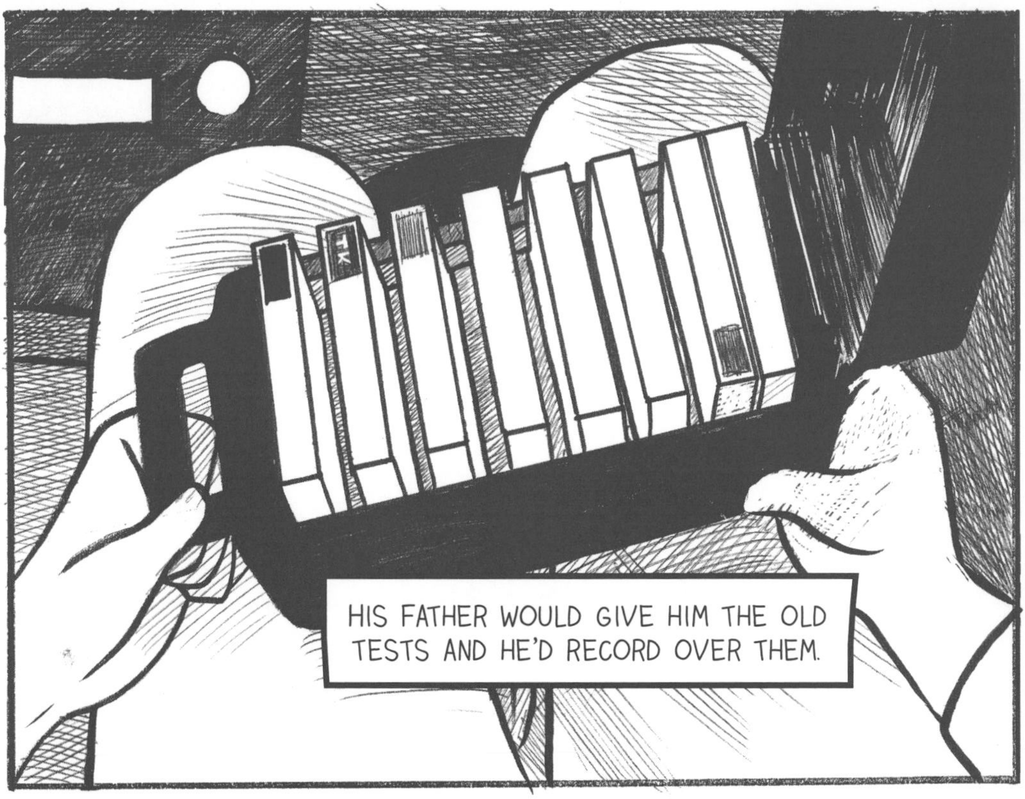
TK
HIS FATHER WOULD GIVE HIM THE OLD TESTS AND HE'D RECORD OVER THEM.

WE ONCE GOT LOST AT A CROSSROADS.
THE MUSIC ENDED AT THAT PRECISE MOMENT.
TUM!
TUM!

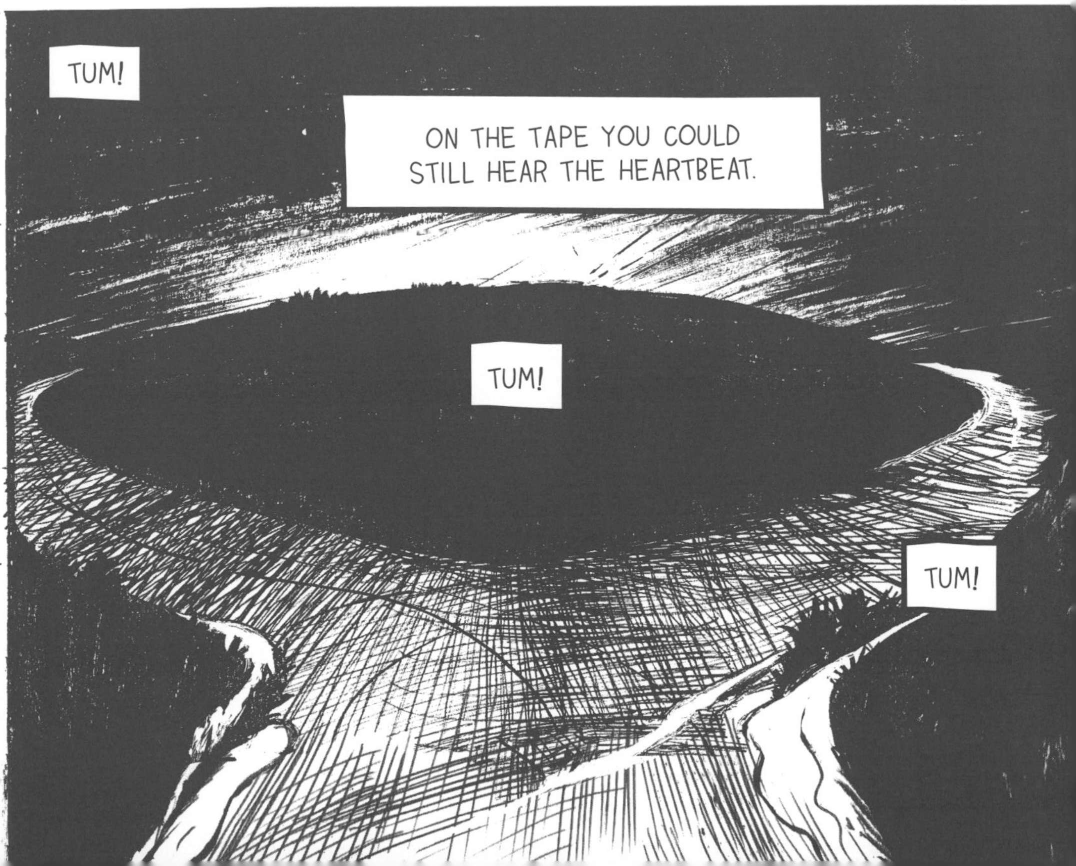
TUM!
ON THE TAPE YOU COULD STILL HEAR THE HEARTBEAT.
TUM!
TUM!

TUM!
TUM!
THAT LITTLE BOX PREVENTS YOU FROM SLEEPING AT NIGHT.
IT'S REALLY ANNOYING.
TUM!
YOU TURN TO ONE SIDE.
THEN THE OTHER.
SURELY THE TEST WILL FIND SOMETHING.
...YOU HOPE!

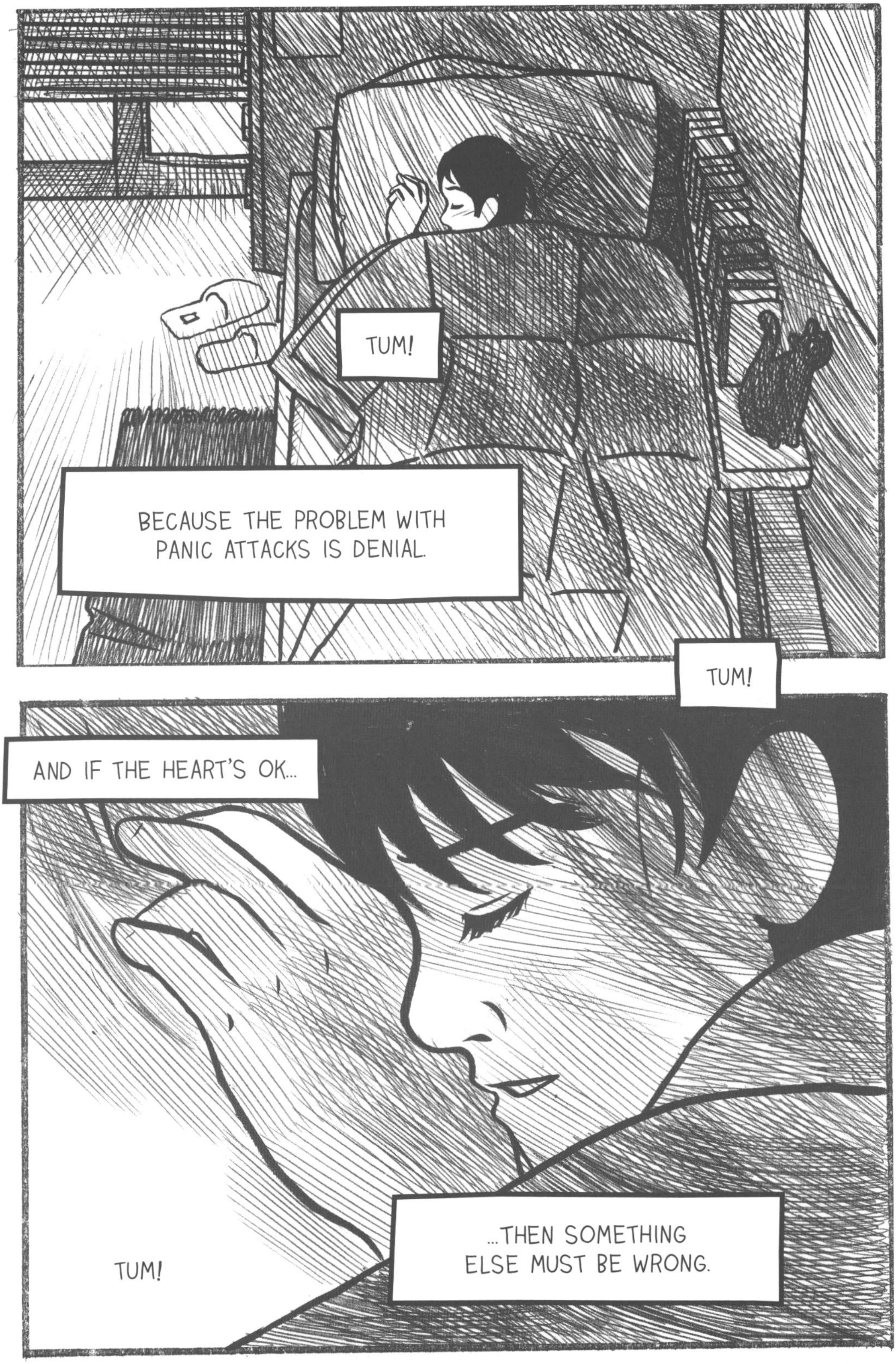
TUM!
BECAUSE THE PROBLEM WITH PANIC ATTACKS IS DENIAL.
TUM!
AND IF THE HEART'S OK...
...THEN SOMETHING ELSE MUST BE WRONG.
TUM!

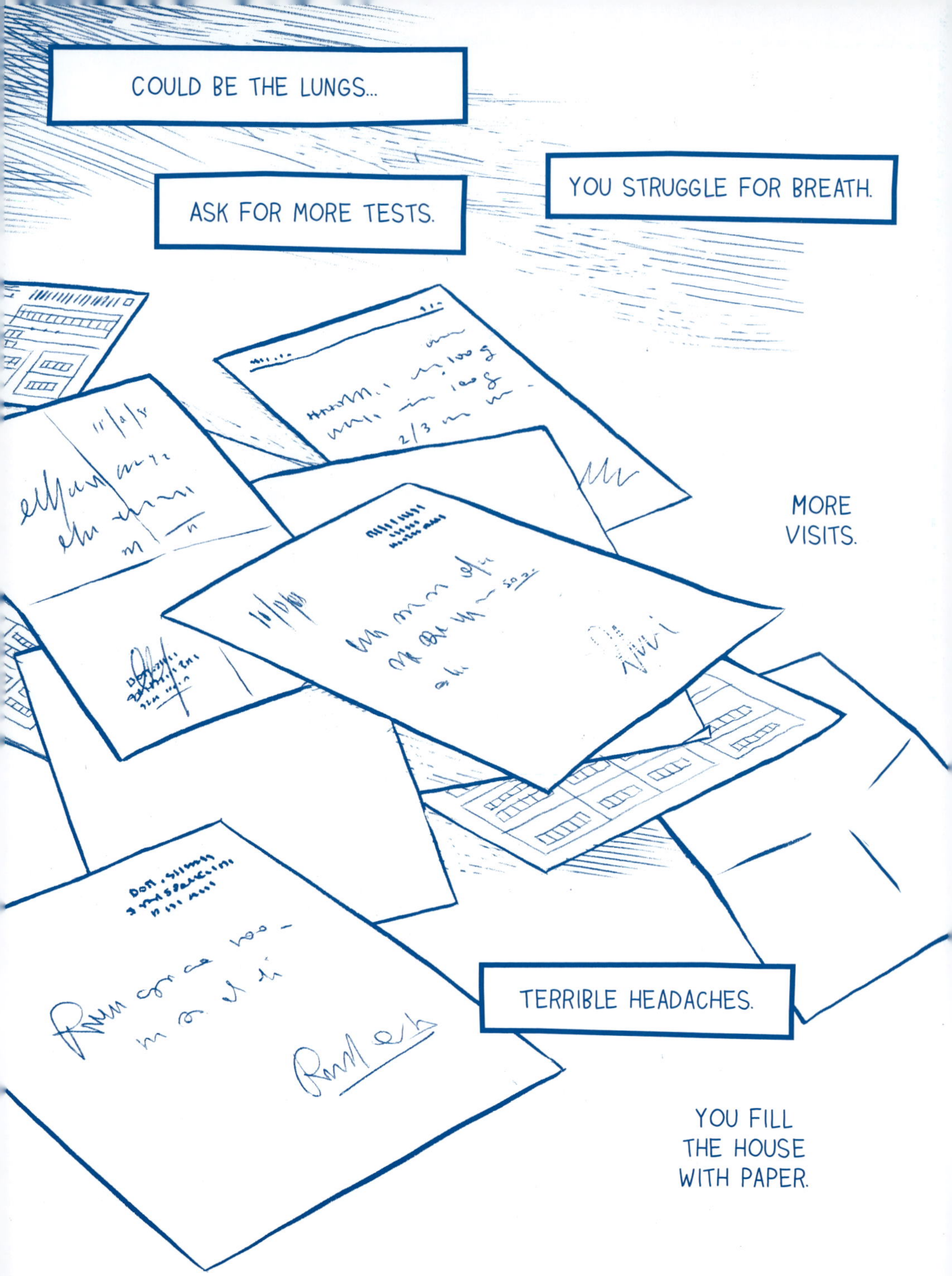
COULD BE THE LUNGS...
ASK FOR MORE TESTS.
YOU STRUGGLE FOR BREATH.
MORE VISITS.
TERRIBLE HEADACHES.
YOU FILL THE HOUSE WITH PAPER.

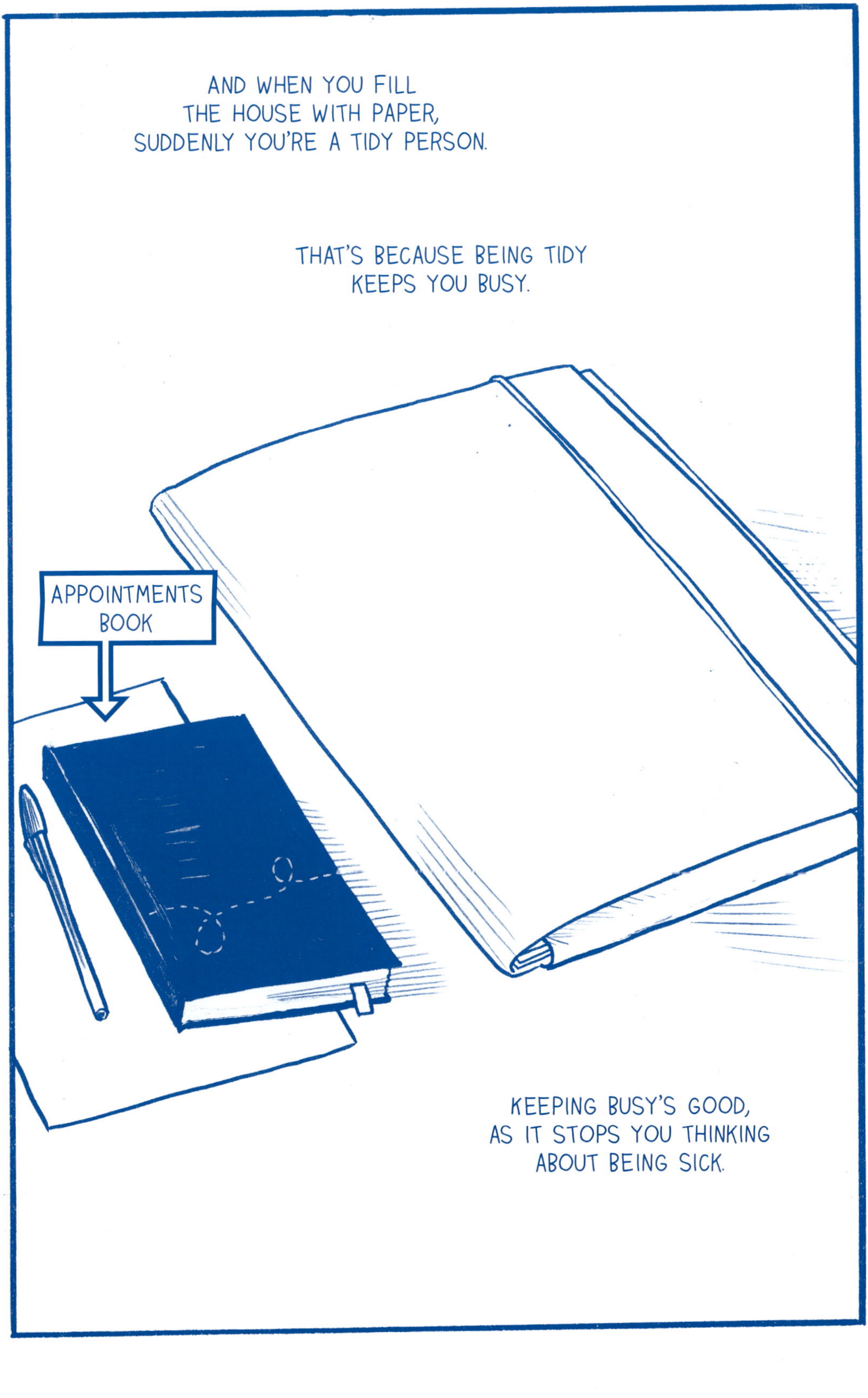
AND WHEN YOU FILL THE HOUSE WITH PAPER, SUDDENLY YOU'RE A TIDY PERSON.
THAT'S BECAUSE BEING TIDY KEEPS YOU BUSY.
APPOINTMENTS BOOK
KEEPING BUSY'S GOOD, AS IT STOPS YOU THINKING ABOUT BEING SICK.

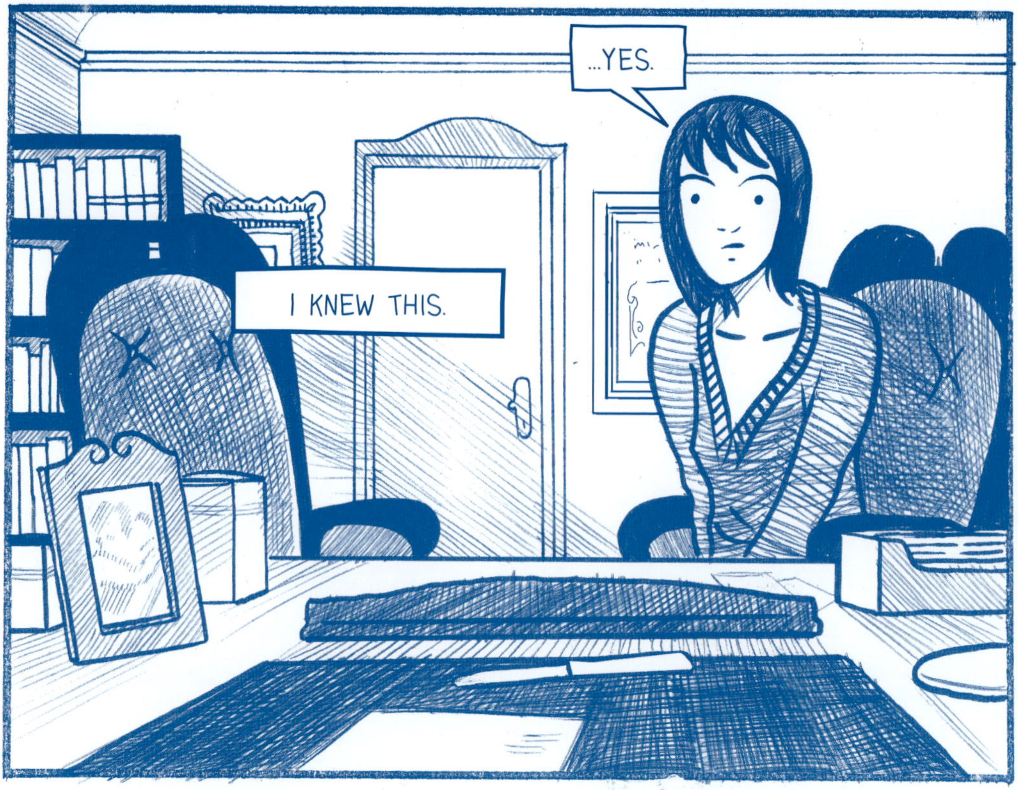
...YES.
I KNEW THIS.

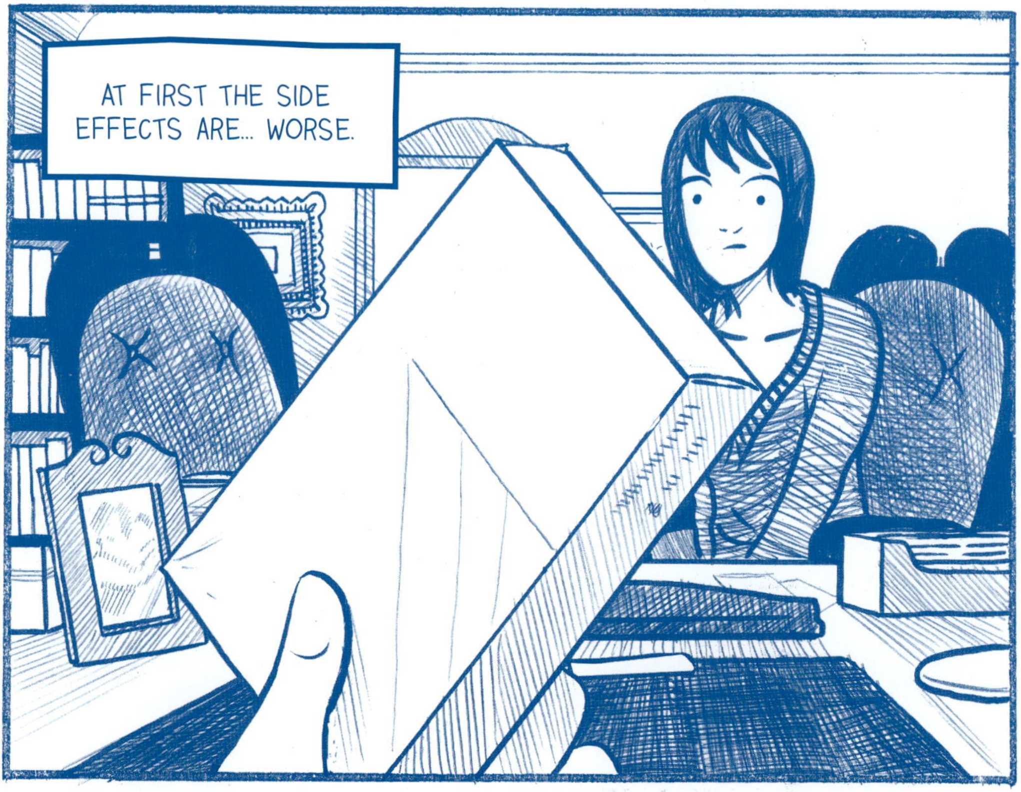
AT FIRST THE SIDE EFFECTS ARE... WORSE.

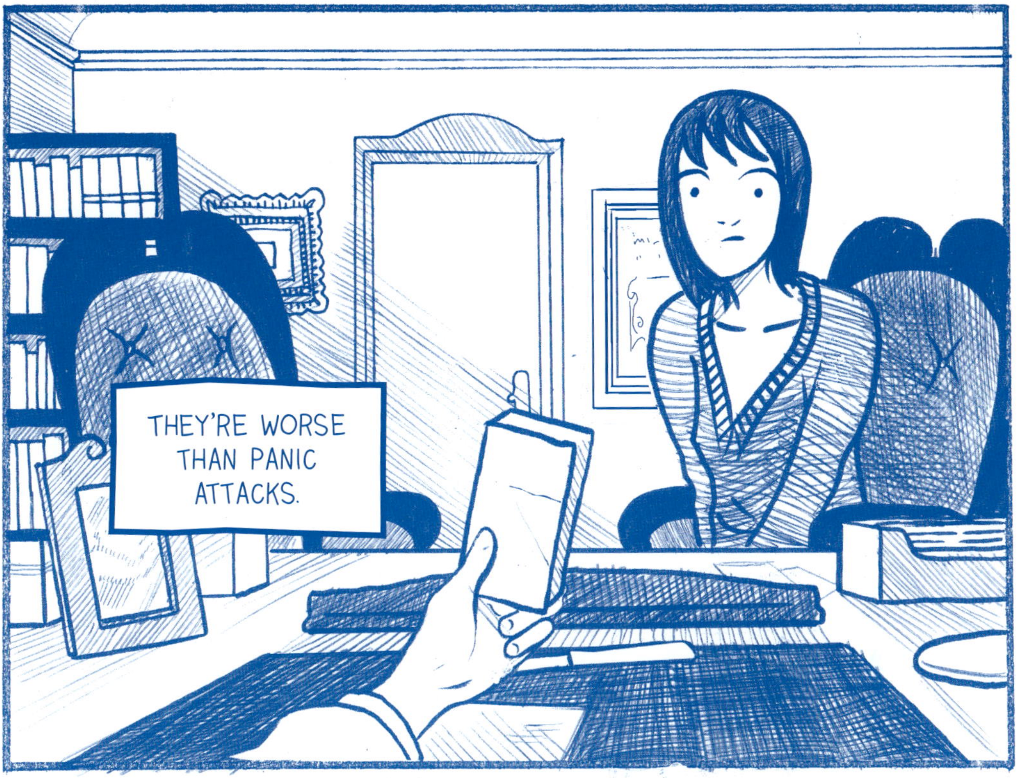
THEY'RE WORSE THAN PANIC ATTACKS.
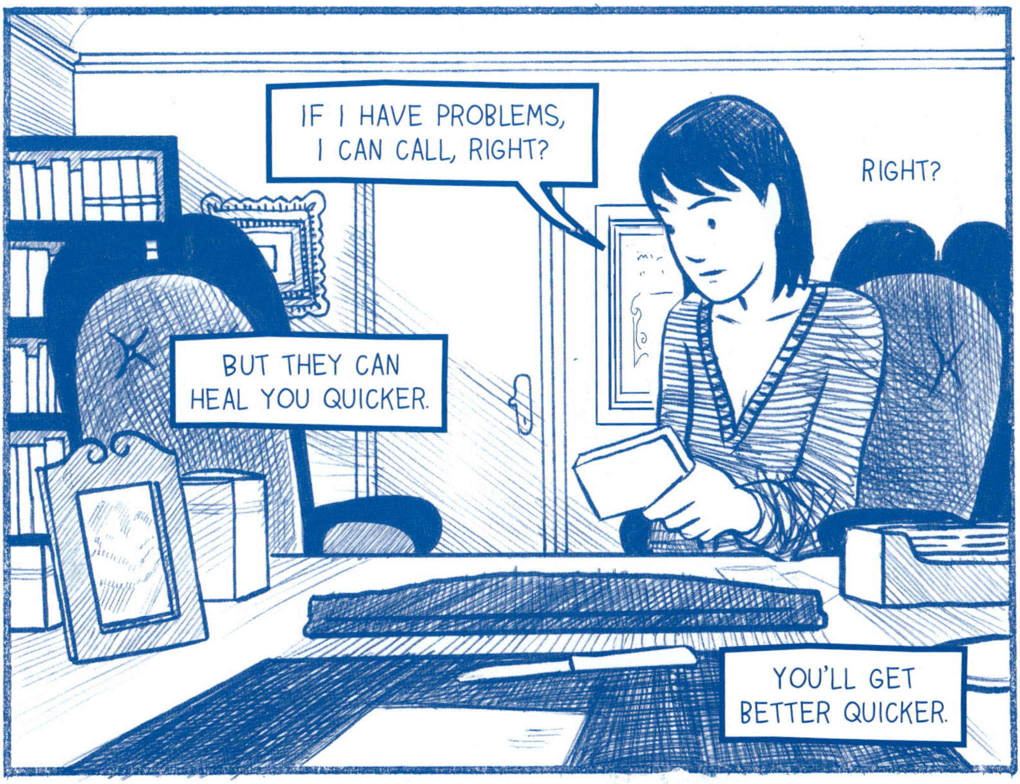
BUT THEY CAN HEAL YOU QUICKER.
IF I HAVE PROBLEMS, I CAN CALL, RIGHT?
RIGHT?
YOU'LL GET BETTER QUICKER.

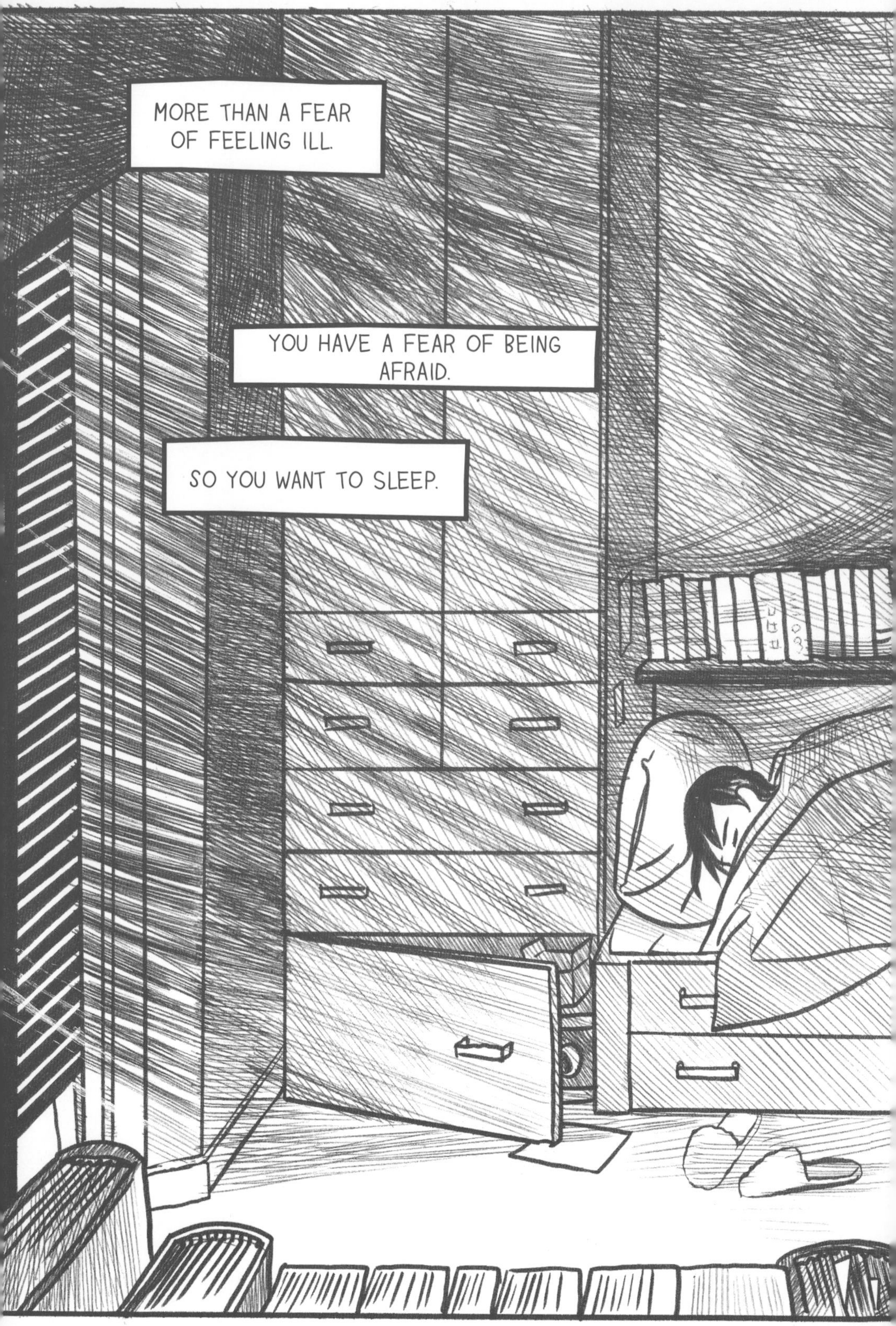
MORE THAN A FEAR OF FEELING ILL.
YOU HAVE A FEAR OF BEING AFRAID.
SO YOU WANT TO SLEEP.

SLEEP.
THAT'S THE SIDE EFFECT.
SLEEP...
I SLEEP, BECAUSE IF I DON'T, I GET A HEADACHE.
I SLEEP, BECAUSE WHEN I SLEEP, I'M SAFE.

WHEN I'M NOT SLEEPING,
I WORK...

THAT'S HOW I SPEND MY TIME...

MY DAYS.

CONTROLLING MYSELF.

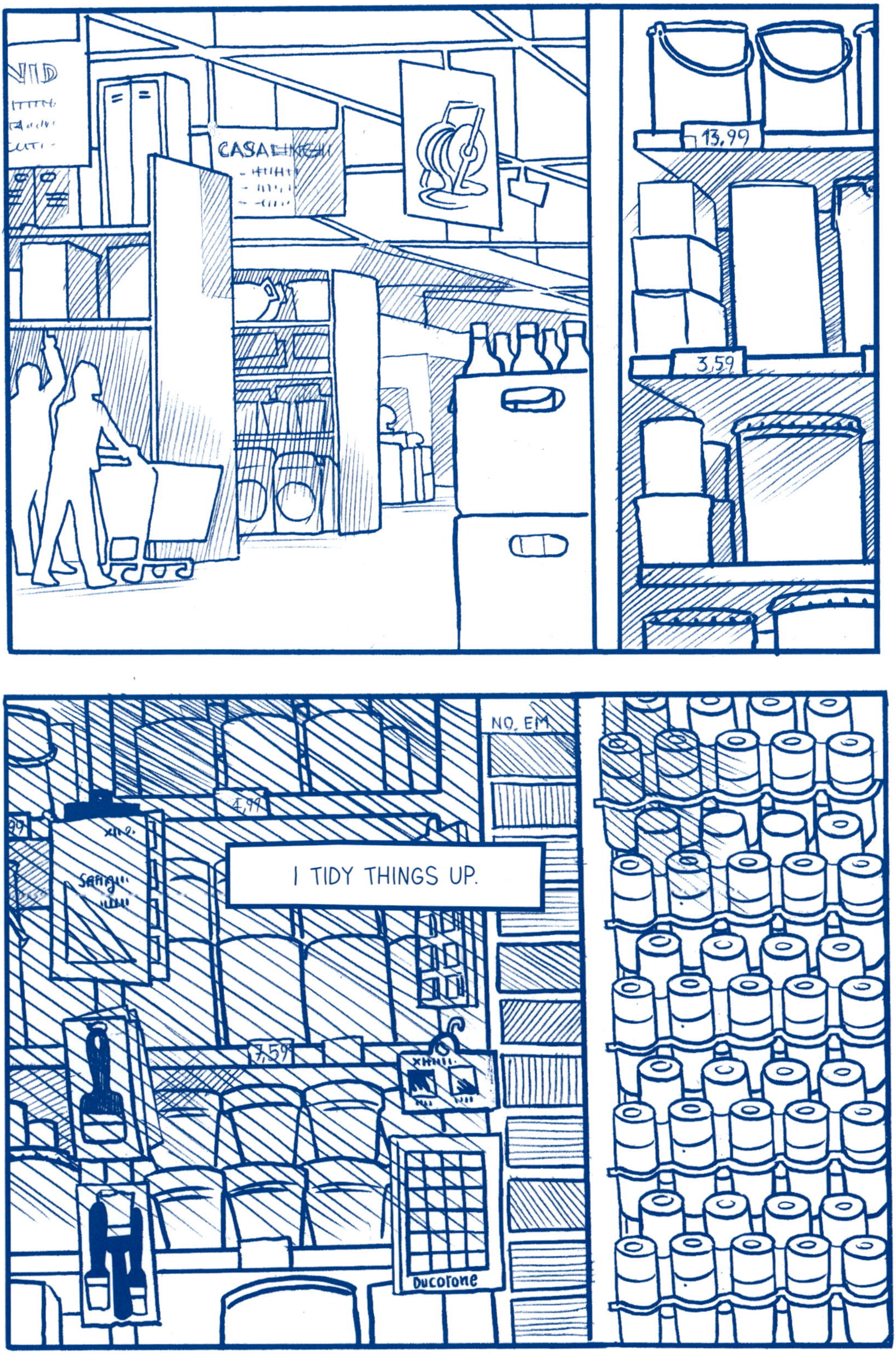
13,99
3,59
4,99
I TIDY THINGS UP.
7,59

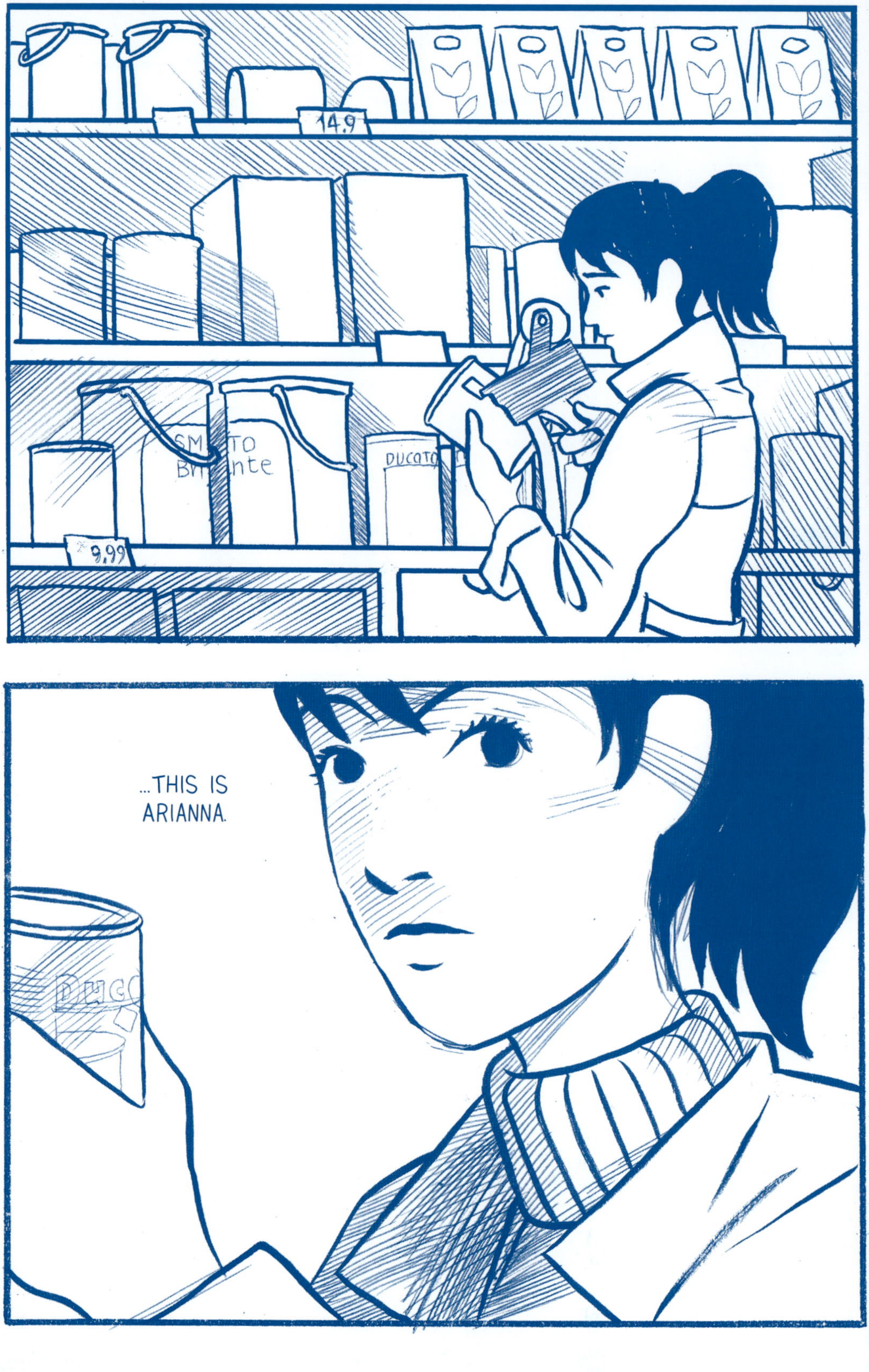
14.9
DUCATO
9,99
...THIS IS ARIANNA.

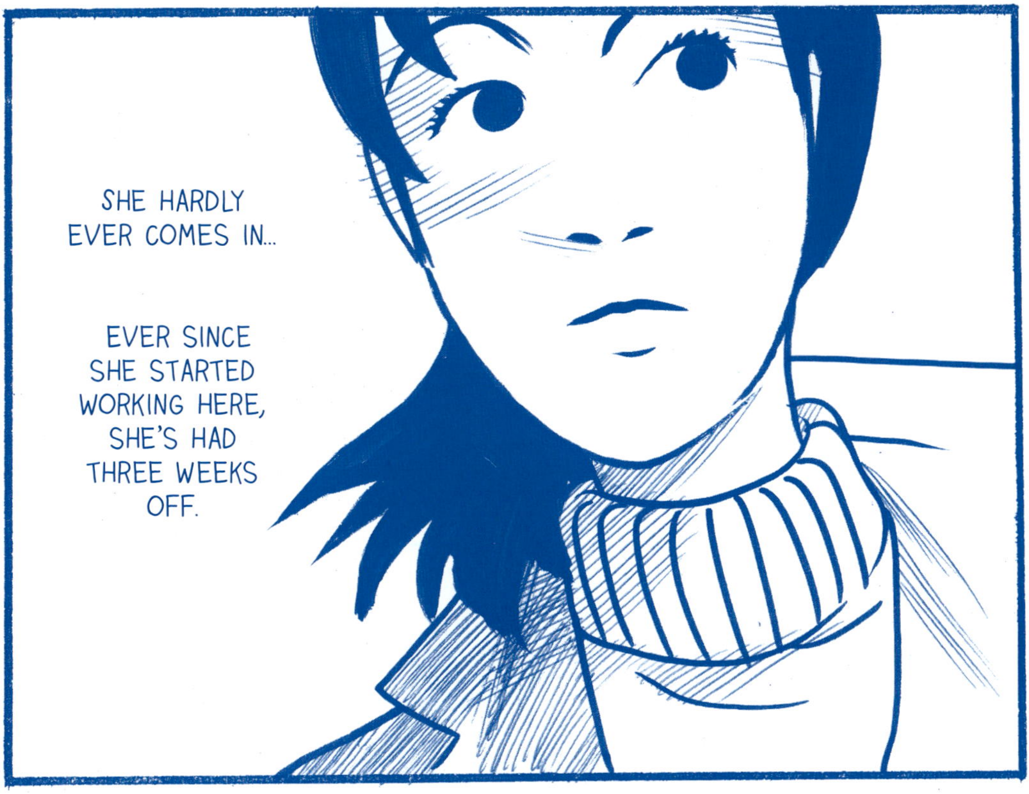
SHE HARDLY EVER COMES IN...
EVER SINCE SHE STARTED WORKING HERE, SHE'S HAD THREE WEEKS OFF.

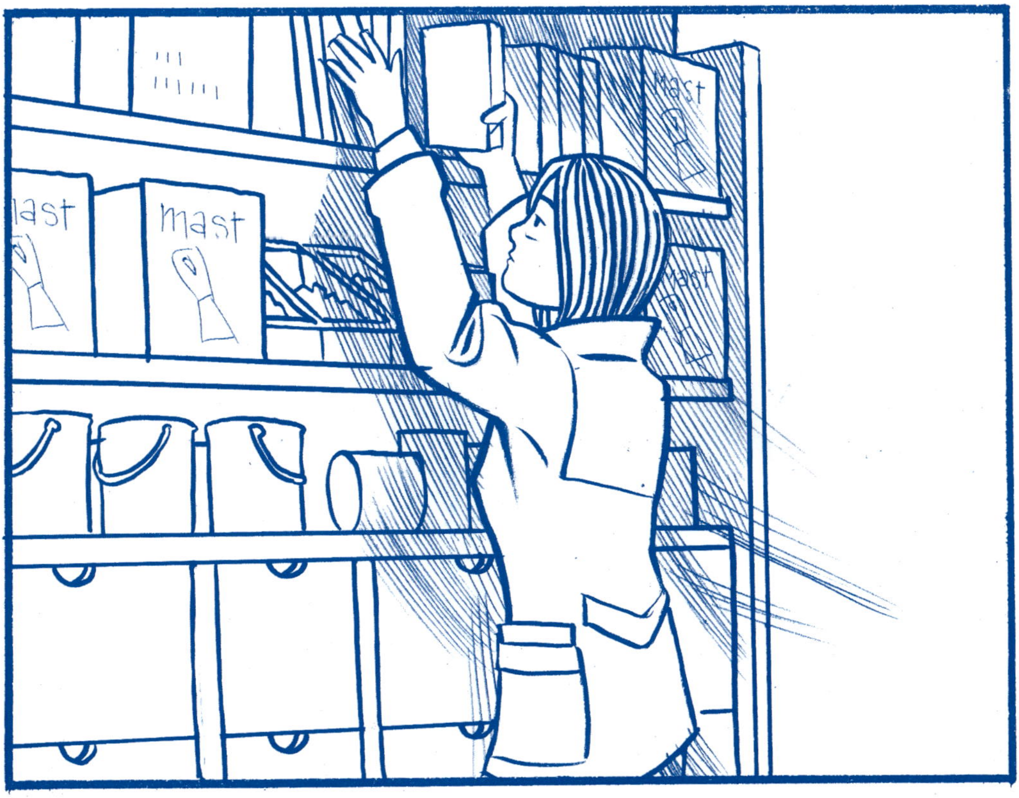
mast
mast

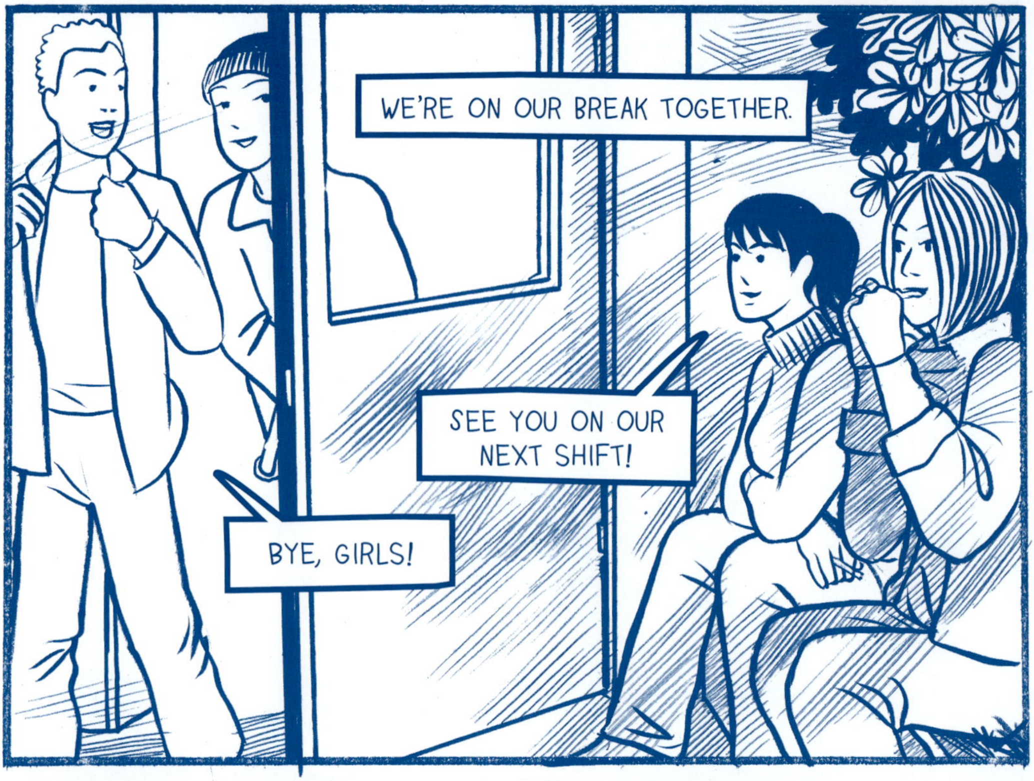
WE'RE ON OUR BREAK TOGETHER.
SEE YOU ON OUR NEXT SHIFT!
BYE, GIRLS!

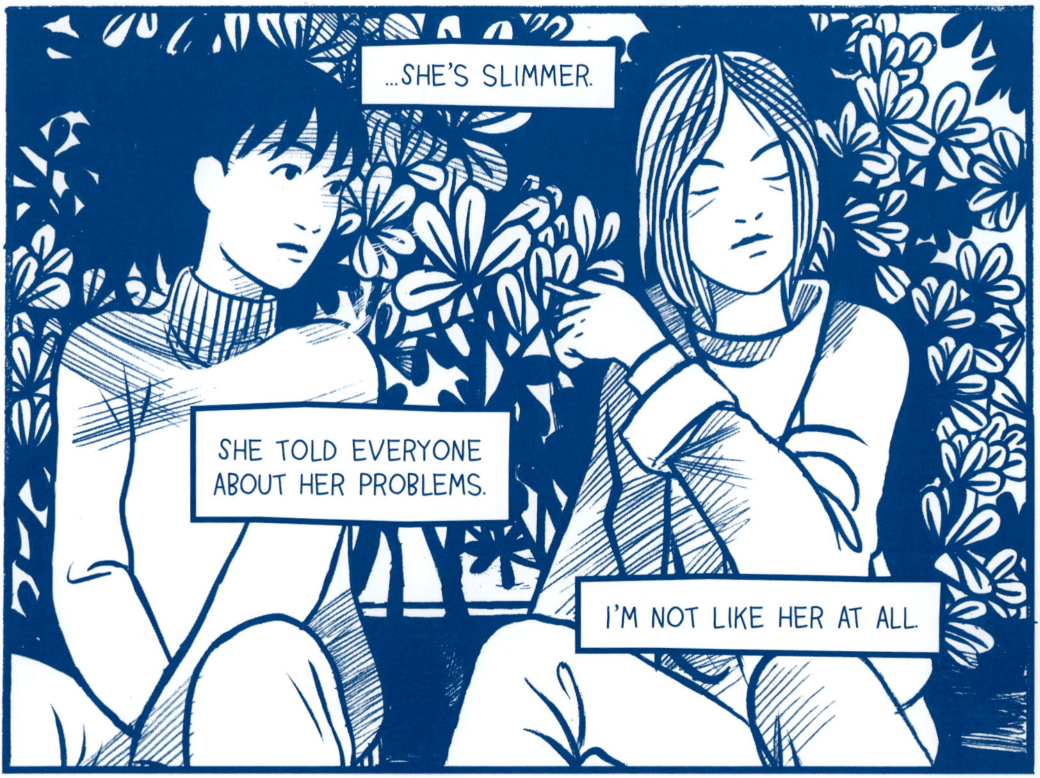
...SHE'S SLIMMER.
SHE TOLD EVERYONE ABOUT HER PROBLEMS.
I'M NOT LIKE HER AT ALL.

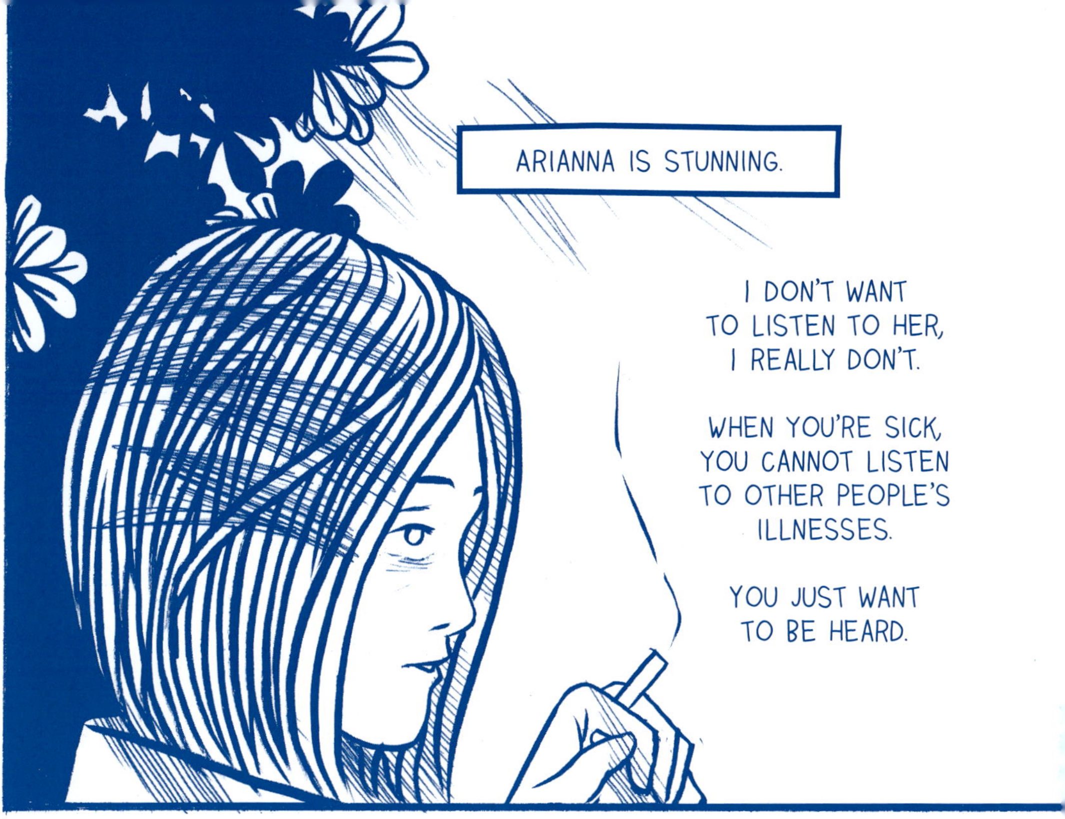
ARIANNA IS STUNNING.
I DON'T WANT TO LISTEN TO HER, I REALLY DON'T.
WHEN YOU'RE SICK, YOU CANNOT LISTEN TO OTHER PEOPLE'S ILLNESSES.
YOU JUST WANT TO BE HEARD.

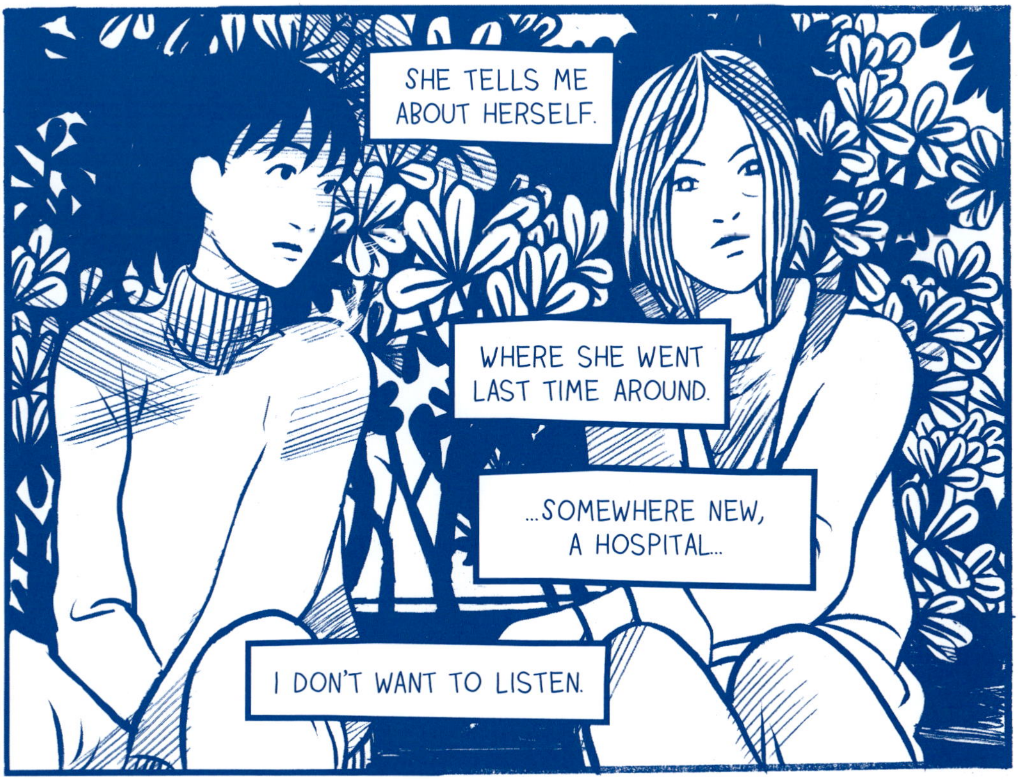
SHE TELLS ME ABOUT HERSELF.
WHERE SHE WENT LAST TIME AROUND.
...SOMEWHERE NEW, A HOSPITAL...
I DON'T WANT TO LISTEN.

IT'S... IT'S AS THOUGH SHE LIKES BEING SICK.

YOU'RE CONSTANTLY THE CENTER OF ATTENTION, I SUPPOSE.
MY THOUGHTS TURN TO MARCO.
MARCO KNEW HE WAS ILL... HE KNEW... YET HE WAS ALWAYS ON THE GO.

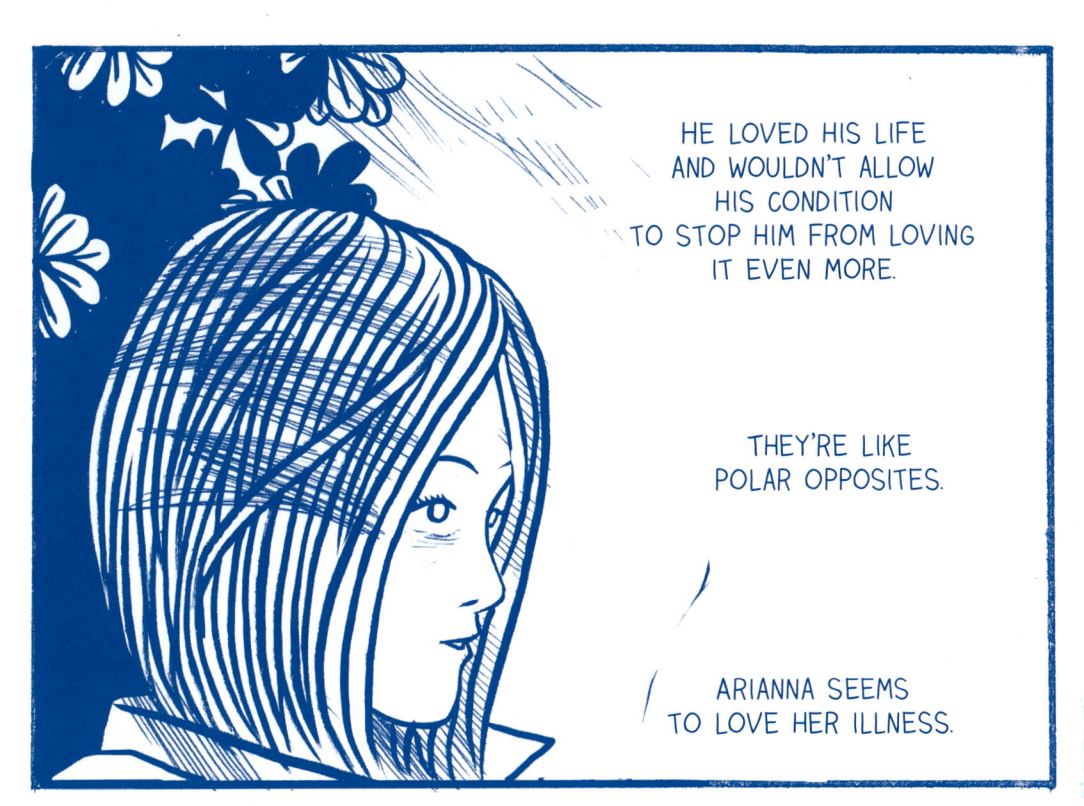

HE LOVED HIS LIFE AND WOULDN'T ALLOW HIS CONDITION TO STOP HIM FROM LOVING IT EVEN MORE.

THEY'RE LIKE POLAR OPPOSITES.

ARIANNA SEEMS TO LOVE HER ILLNESS.

BEING AROUND HER MAKES ME FEEL SICK TOO.

WHAT'S A HEADACHE?

WHERE DOES IT COME FROM?

GOOD QUESTION:
A TUMMY ACHE COMES
FROM YOUR STOMACH AND
IS CAUSED BY SOMETHING YOU ATE...
WHAT ABOUT A HEADACHE?

WHAT DID IT EAT?

IT'S LATE AND I CANNOT SLEEP.
I THINK OF WHAT ARIANNA SAID...
I THINK ABOUT MARCO.
IT'S ONLY BEEN TWO WEEKS.
IT'S WORSE AT THE START, YOU TELL YOURSELF.
HEADACHES...
THIS FEELING OF SPIDERS DROWNING IN DEEP WATER.

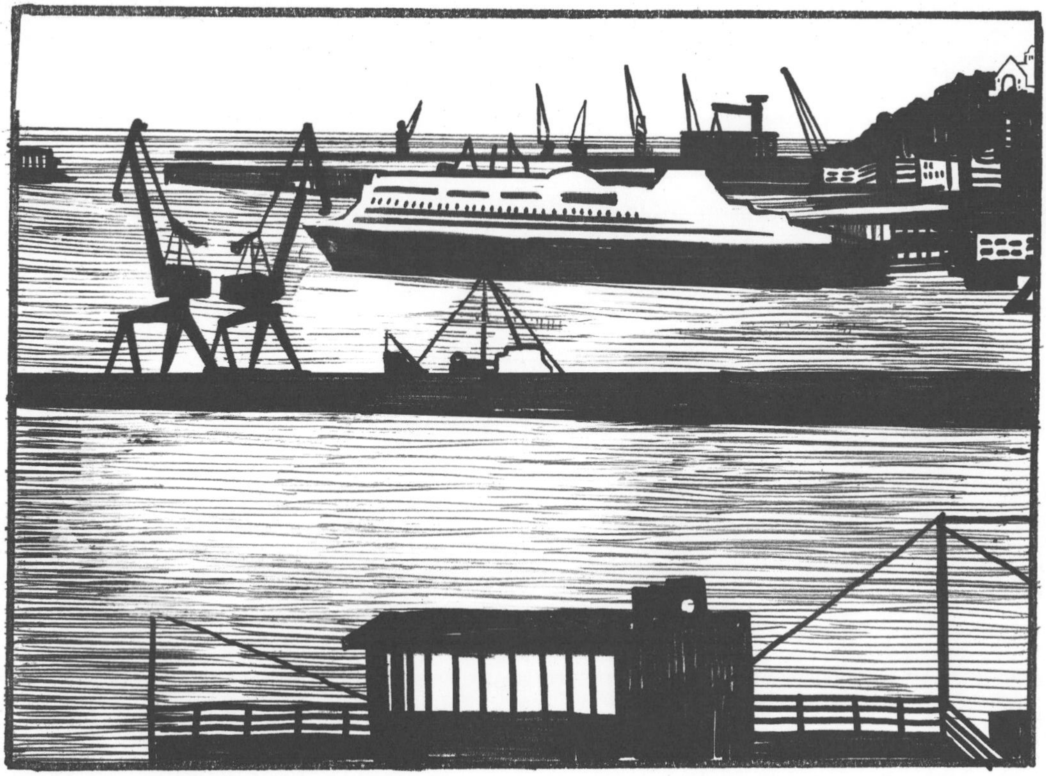

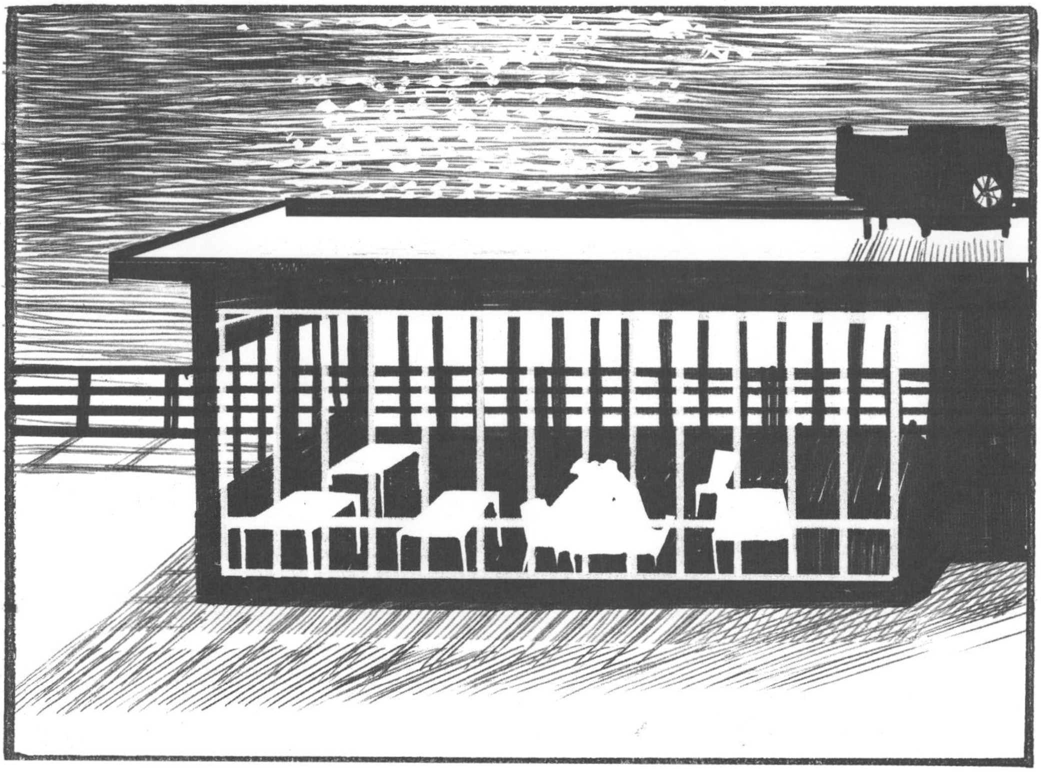

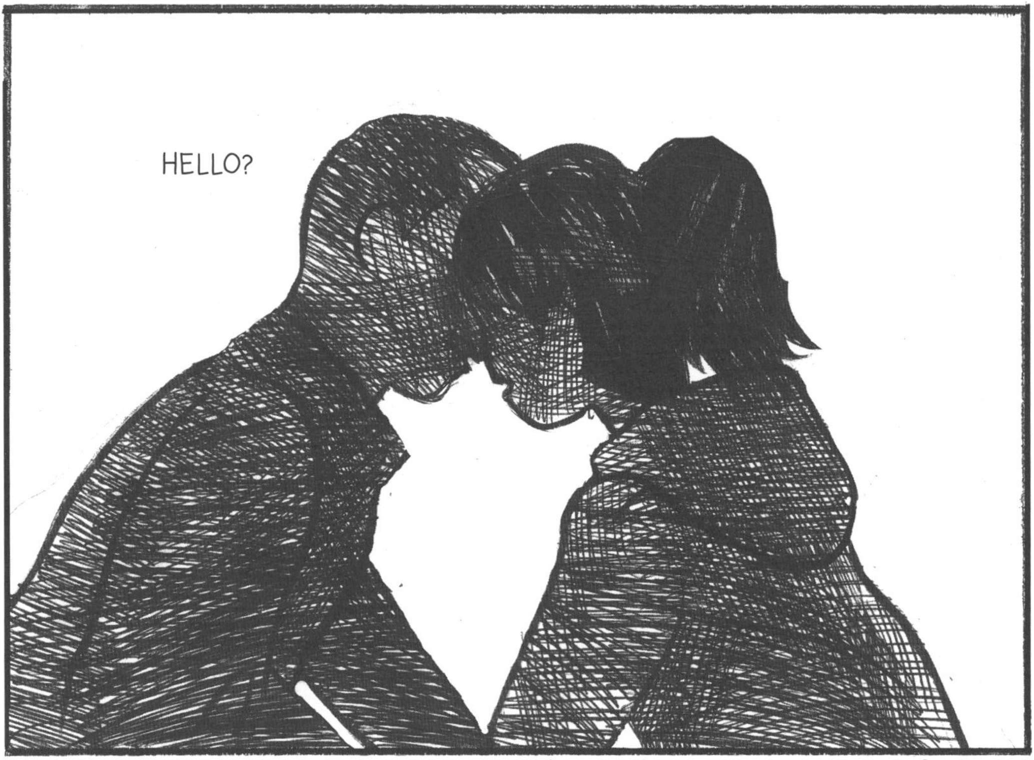
HELLO?

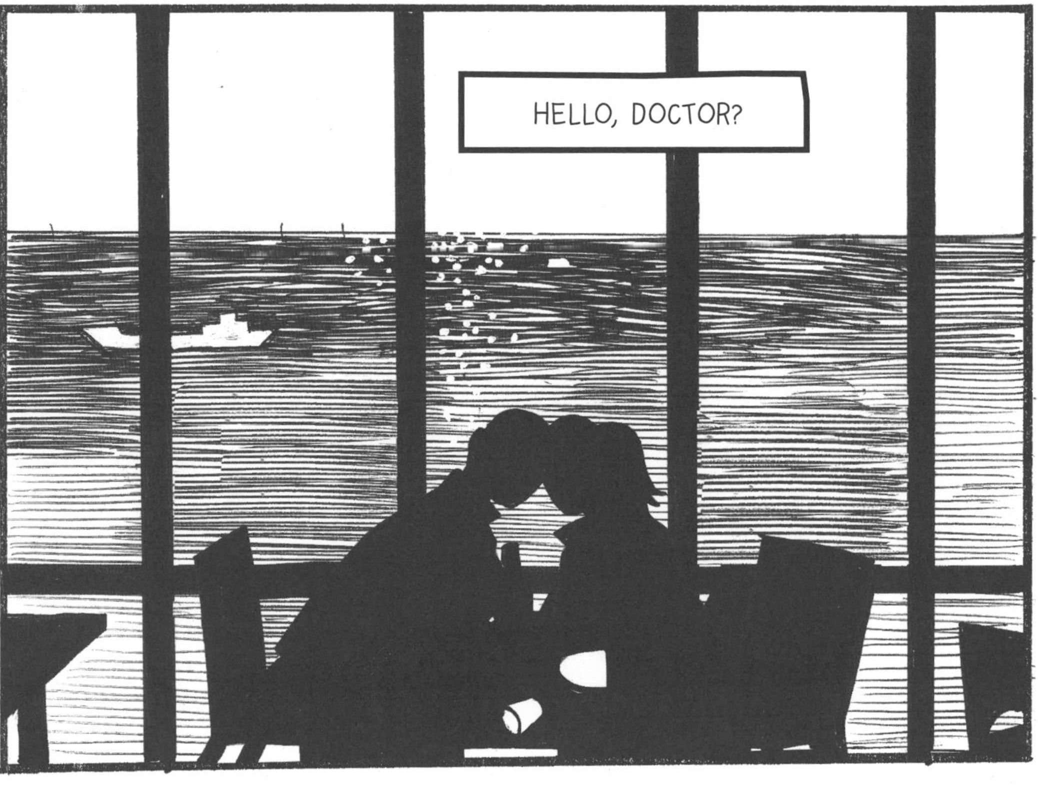
HELLO, DOCTOR?

HELLO?
DOCTOR?

THERE'S BLOOD...

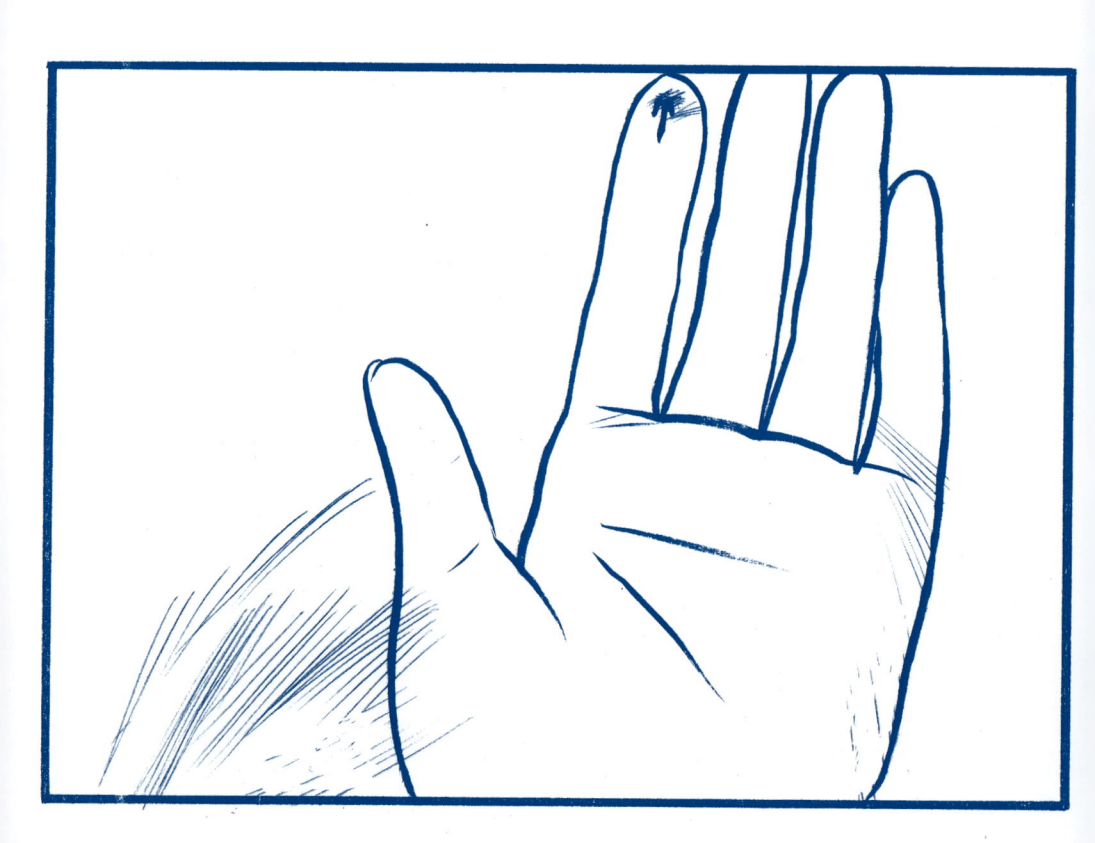

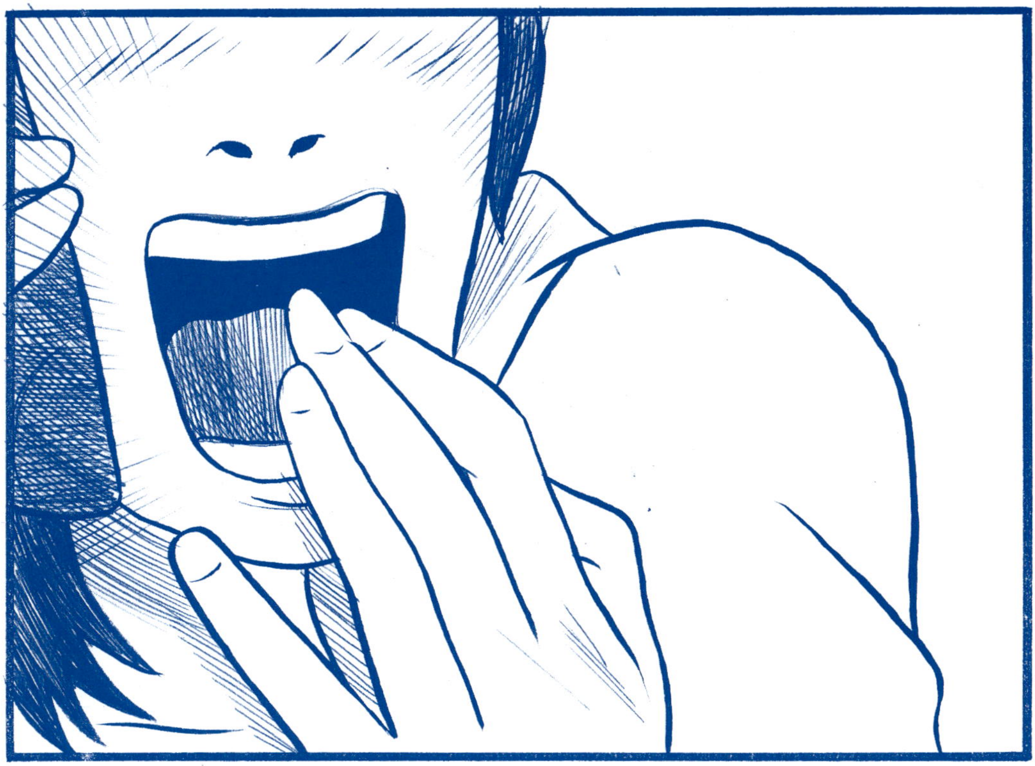

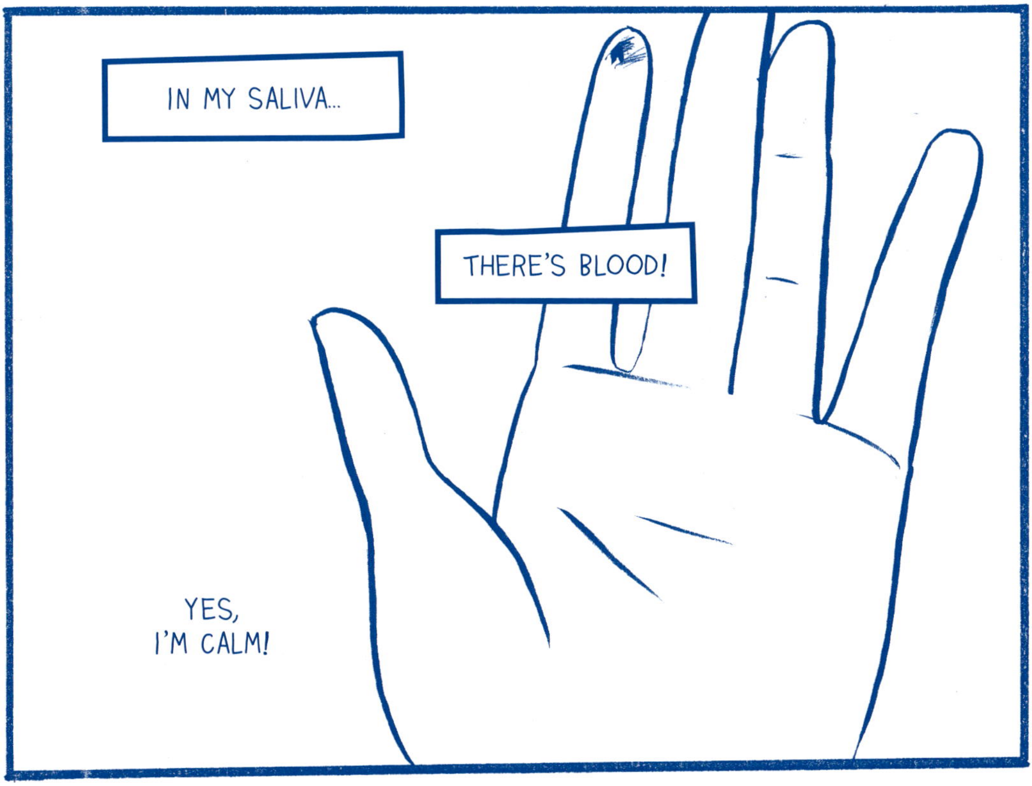
IN MY SALIVA...
THERE'S BLOOD!
YES,
I'M CALM!

SAYS ON THE BOX...

...SAYS ON THE BOX THAT... THAT THERE COULD BE BLEEDING.
YES, I'M CALM!
OK, I'LL SIT DOWN...

YES, I'M SITTING...
...BUT IN THE CONTRAINDICATION WARNINGS, IT SAYS...
WHY?
I HAVE BEEN CAREFUL!
WHY SHOULDN'T I WORRY?

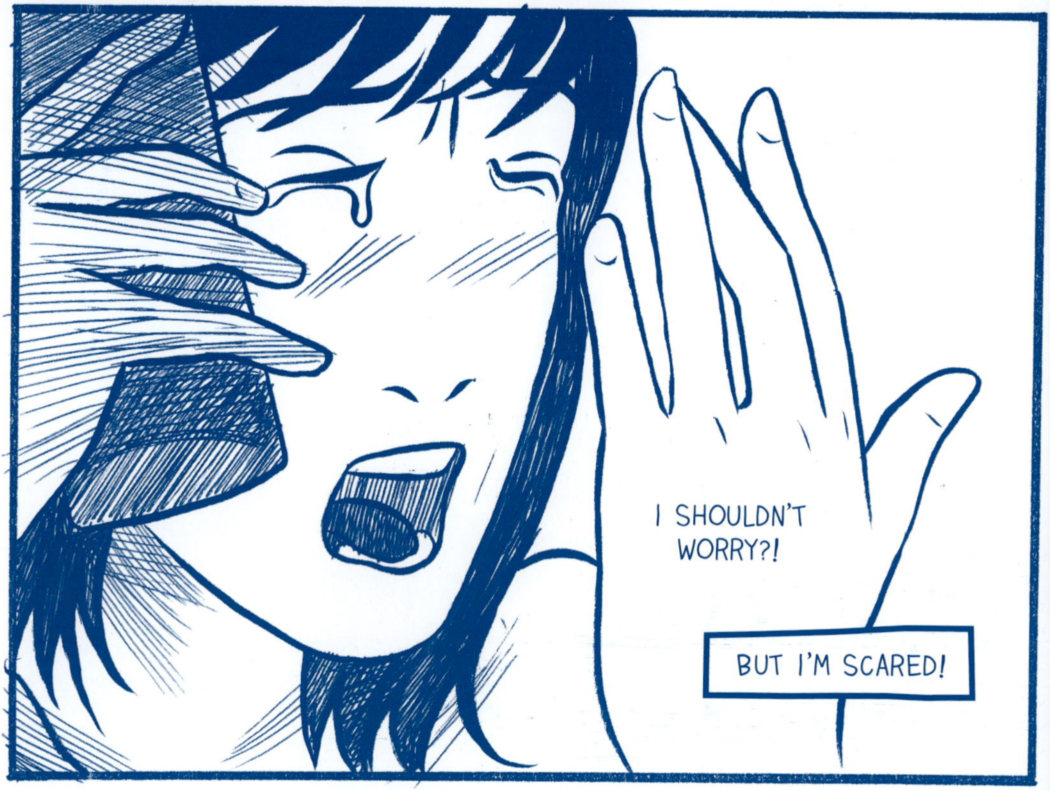
I SHOULDN'T WORRY?!
BUT I'M SCARED!

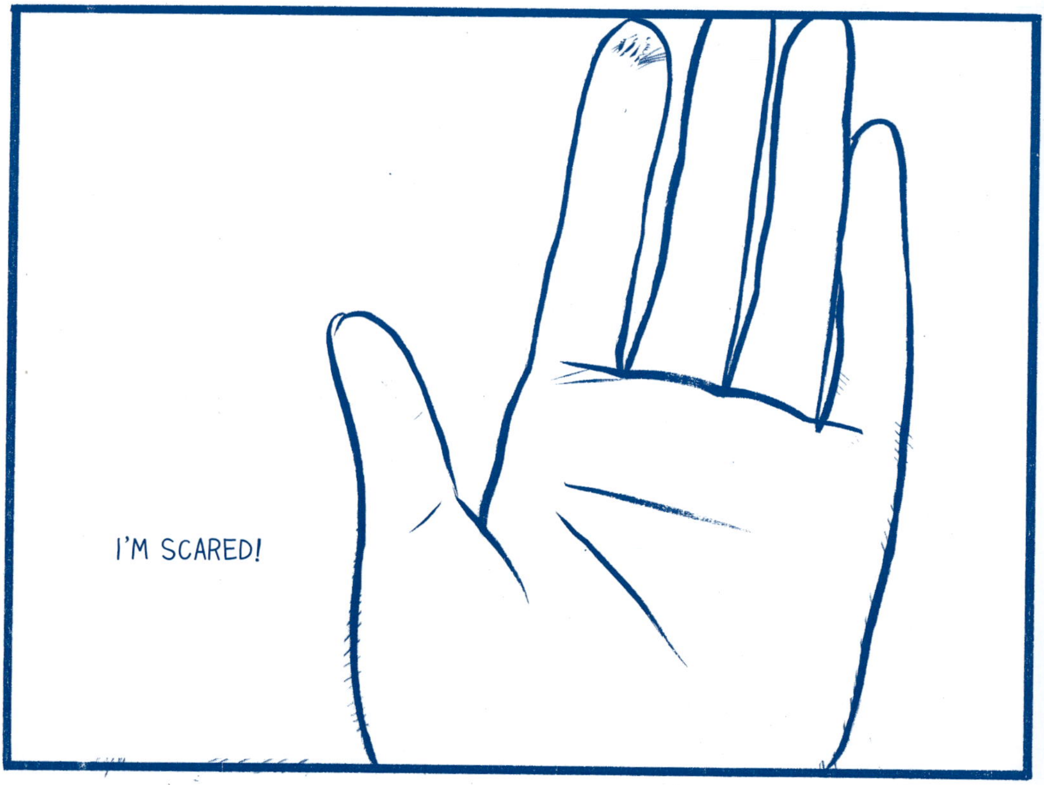
I'M SCARED!

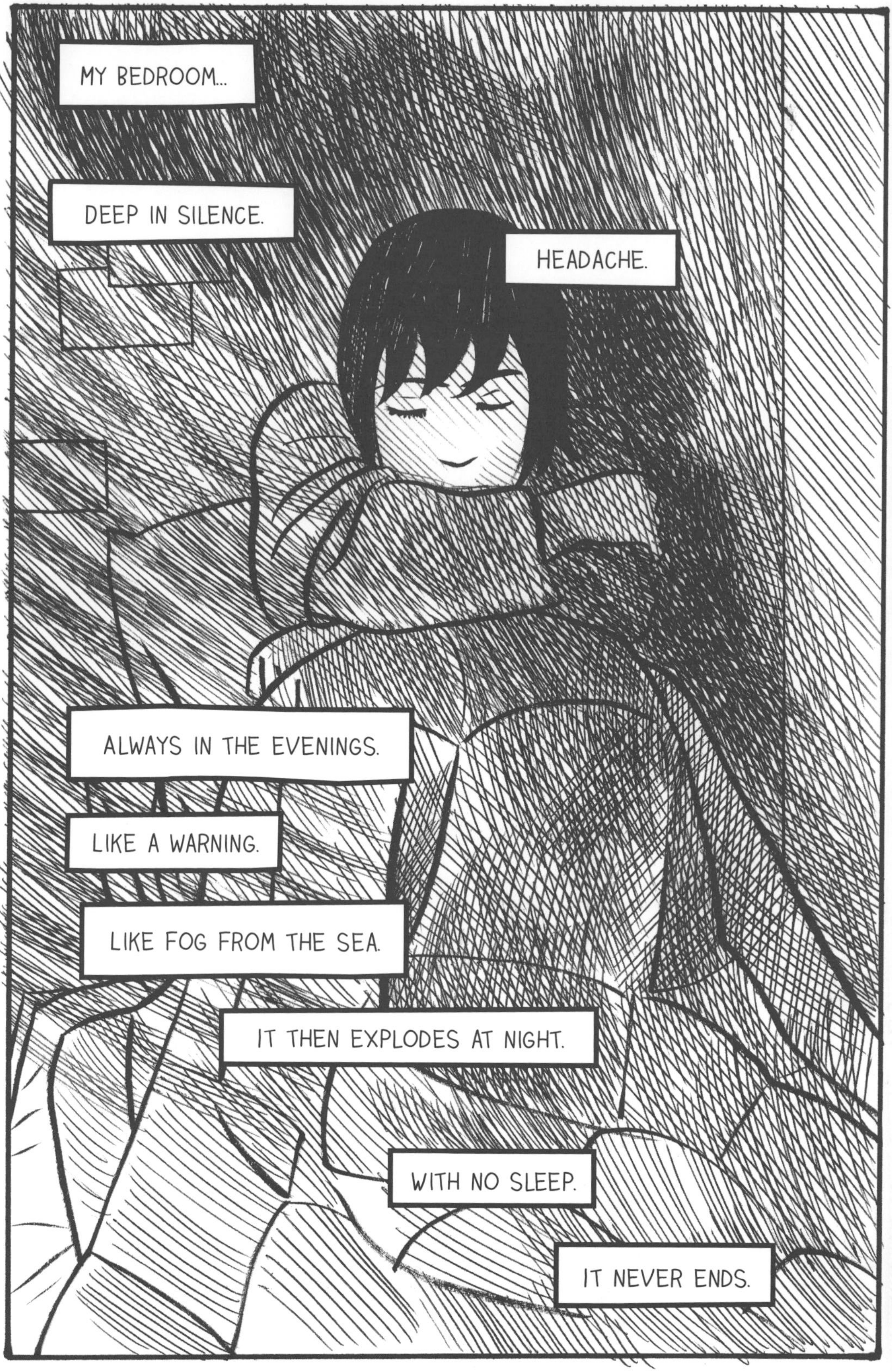
MY BEDROOM...
DEEP IN SILENCE.
HEADACHE.
ALWAYS IN THE EVENINGS.
LIKE A WARNING.
LIKE FOG FROM THE SEA.
IT THEN EXPLODES AT NIGHT.
WITH NO SLEEP.
IT NEVER ENDS.

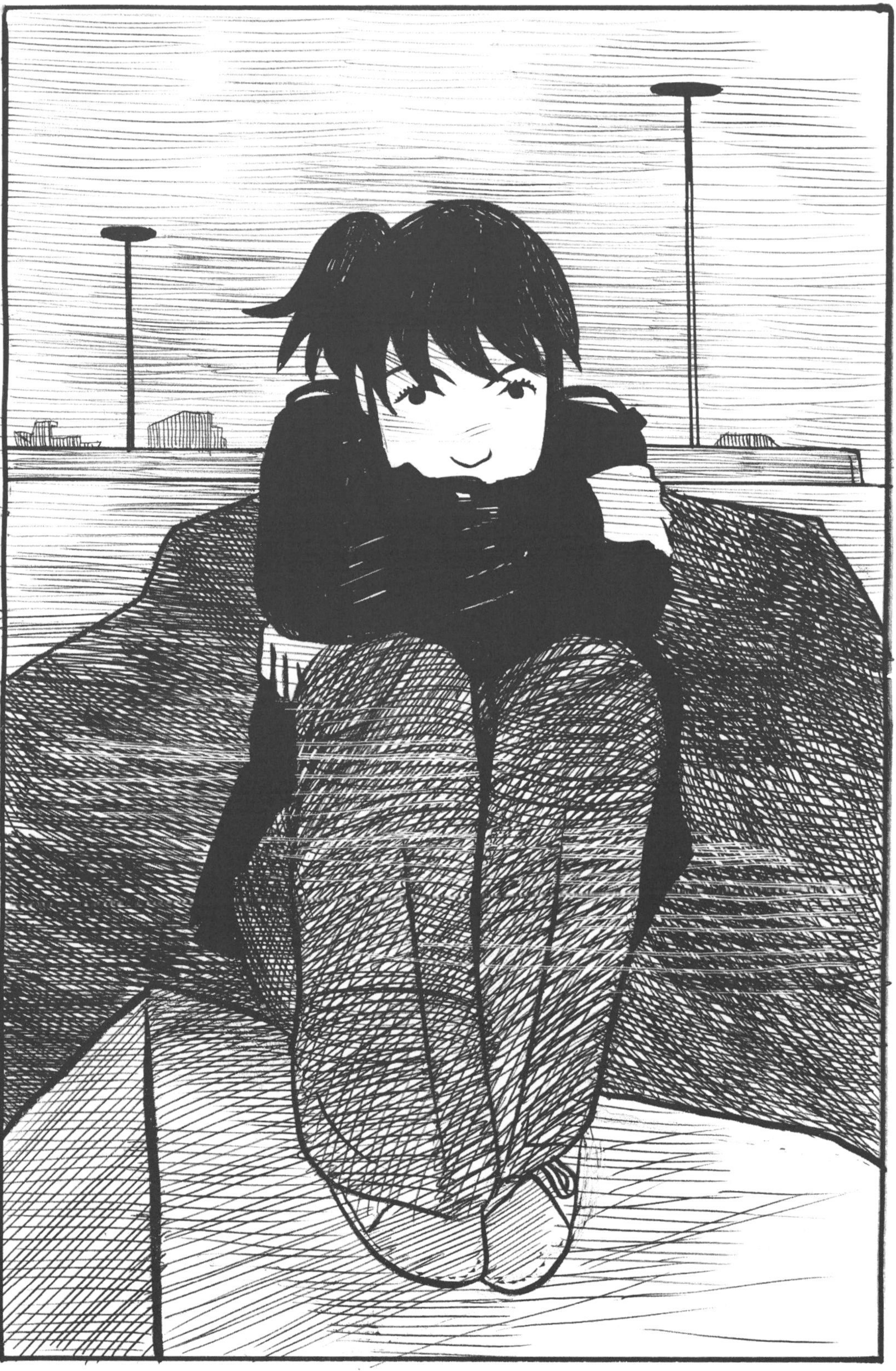

IS THIS IT THEN? WE'RE THROUGH?!
I'VE HAD IT!
DON'T BE LIKE THAT, PLEASE!
WHAT DO YOU THINK I SHOULD DO?
HOW SHOULD I REACT?

WHAT HURTS ME THE MOST IS THAT YOU CAN'T EVEN SEE WHO'S RIGHT BY YOUR SIDE.

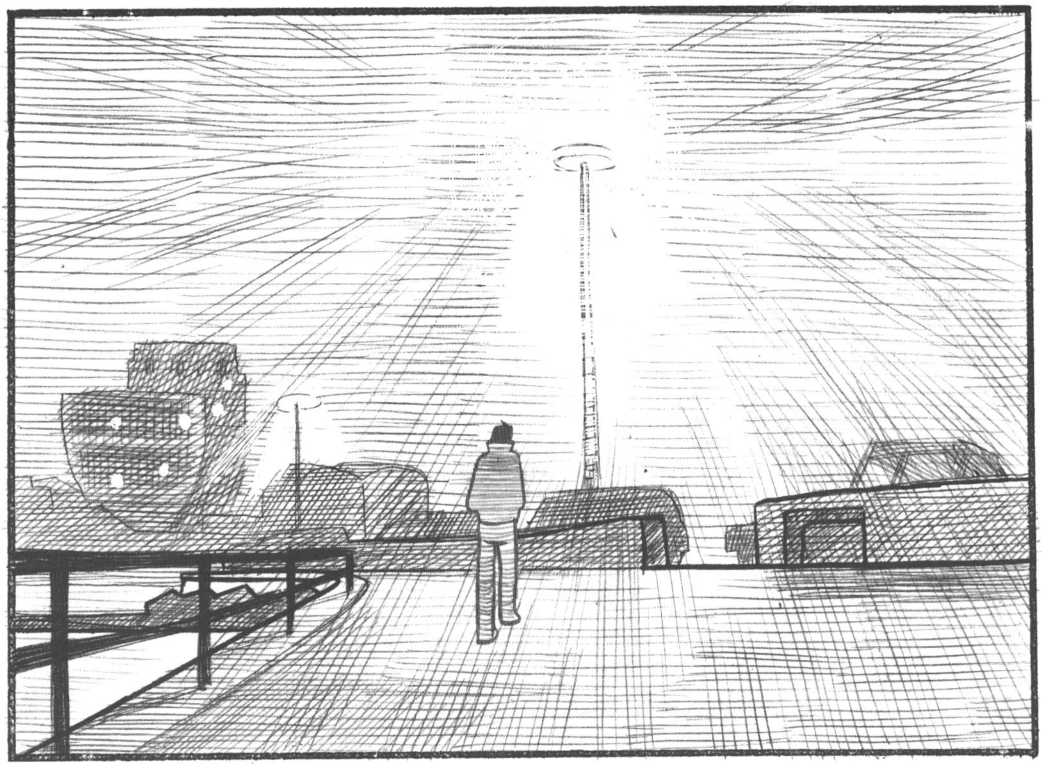

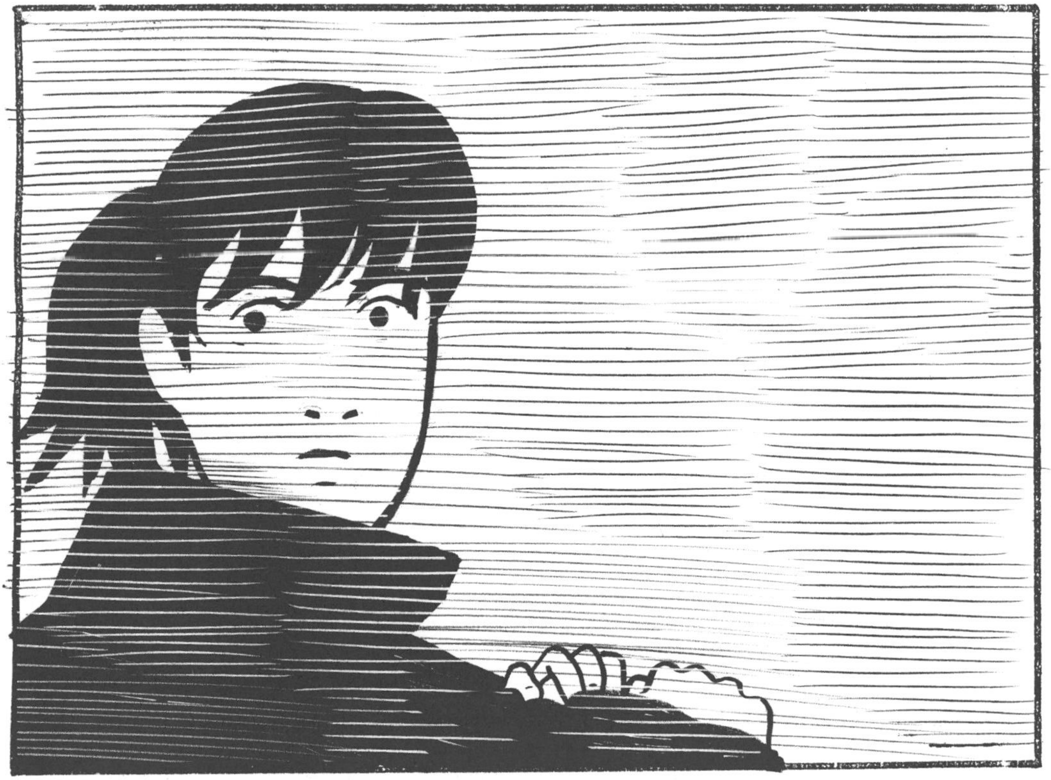

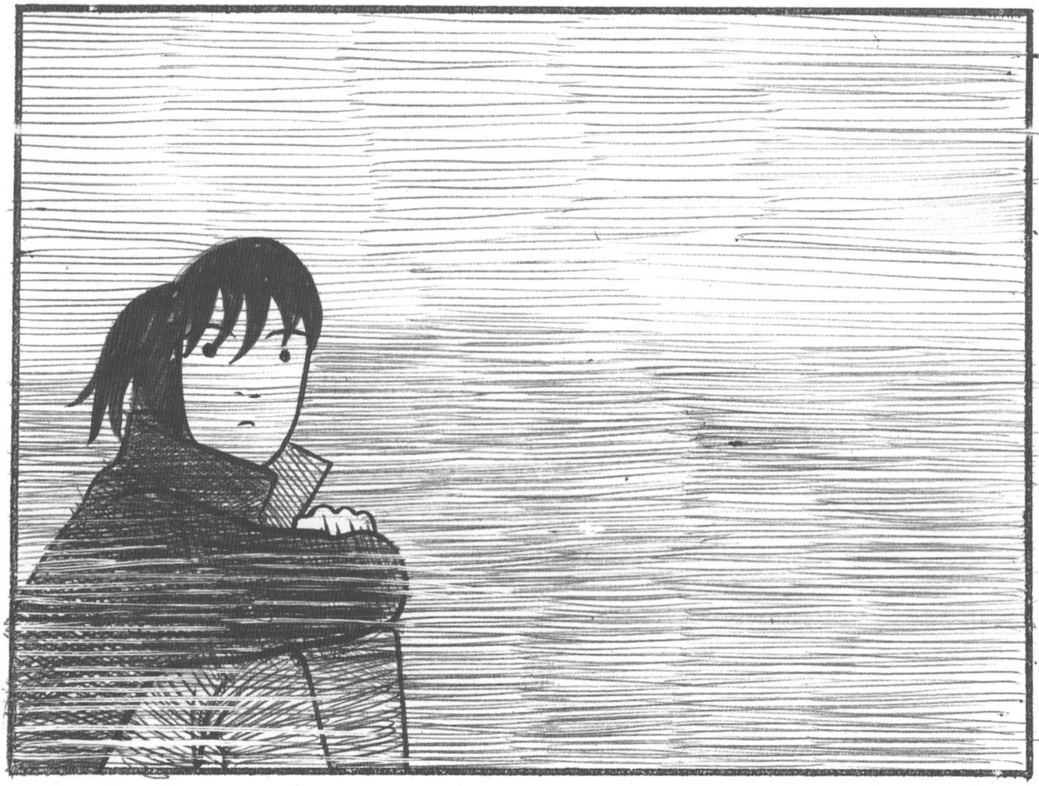
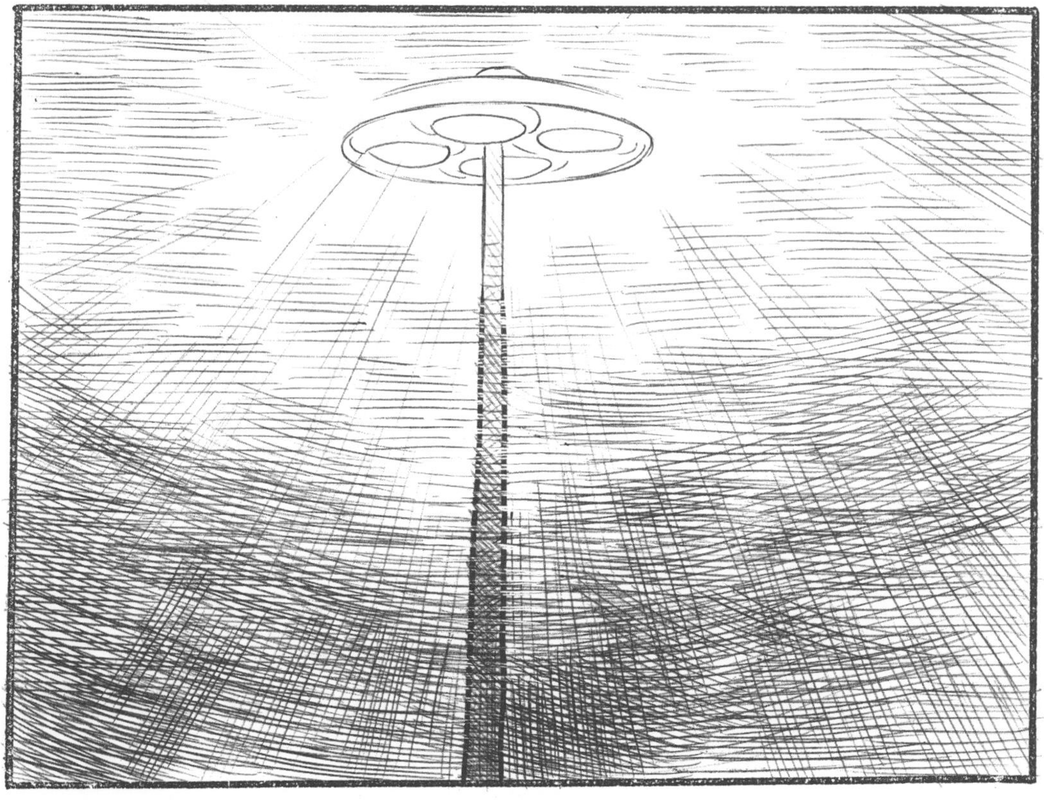

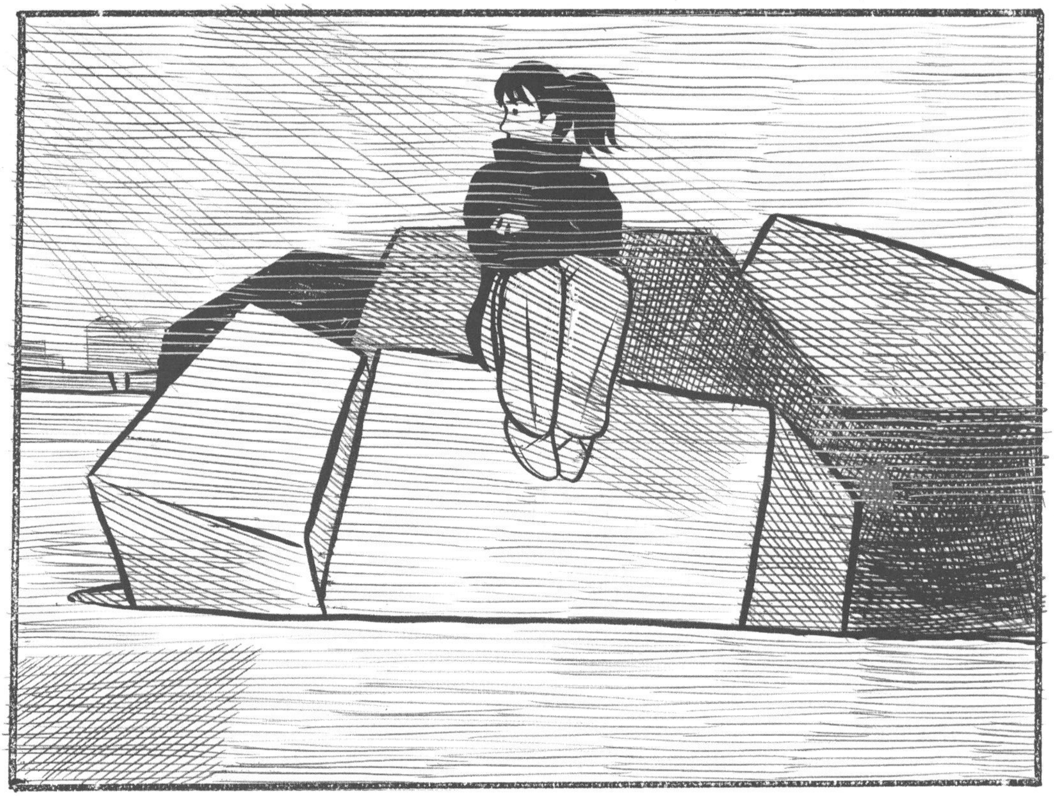

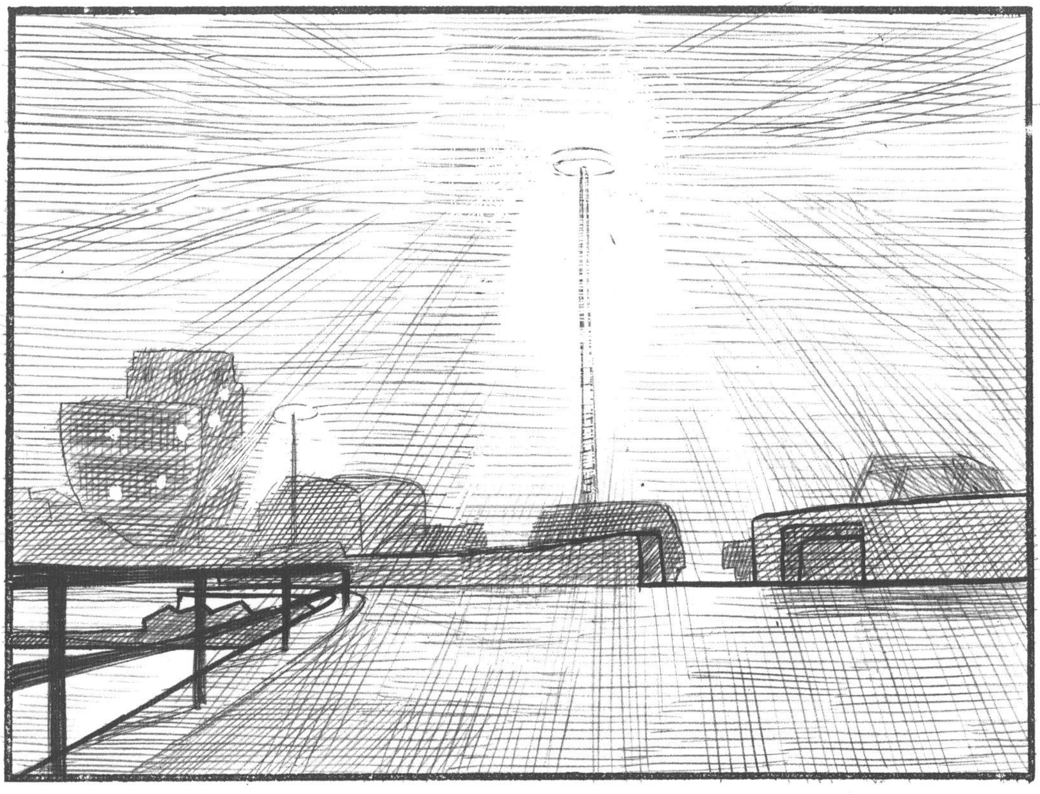

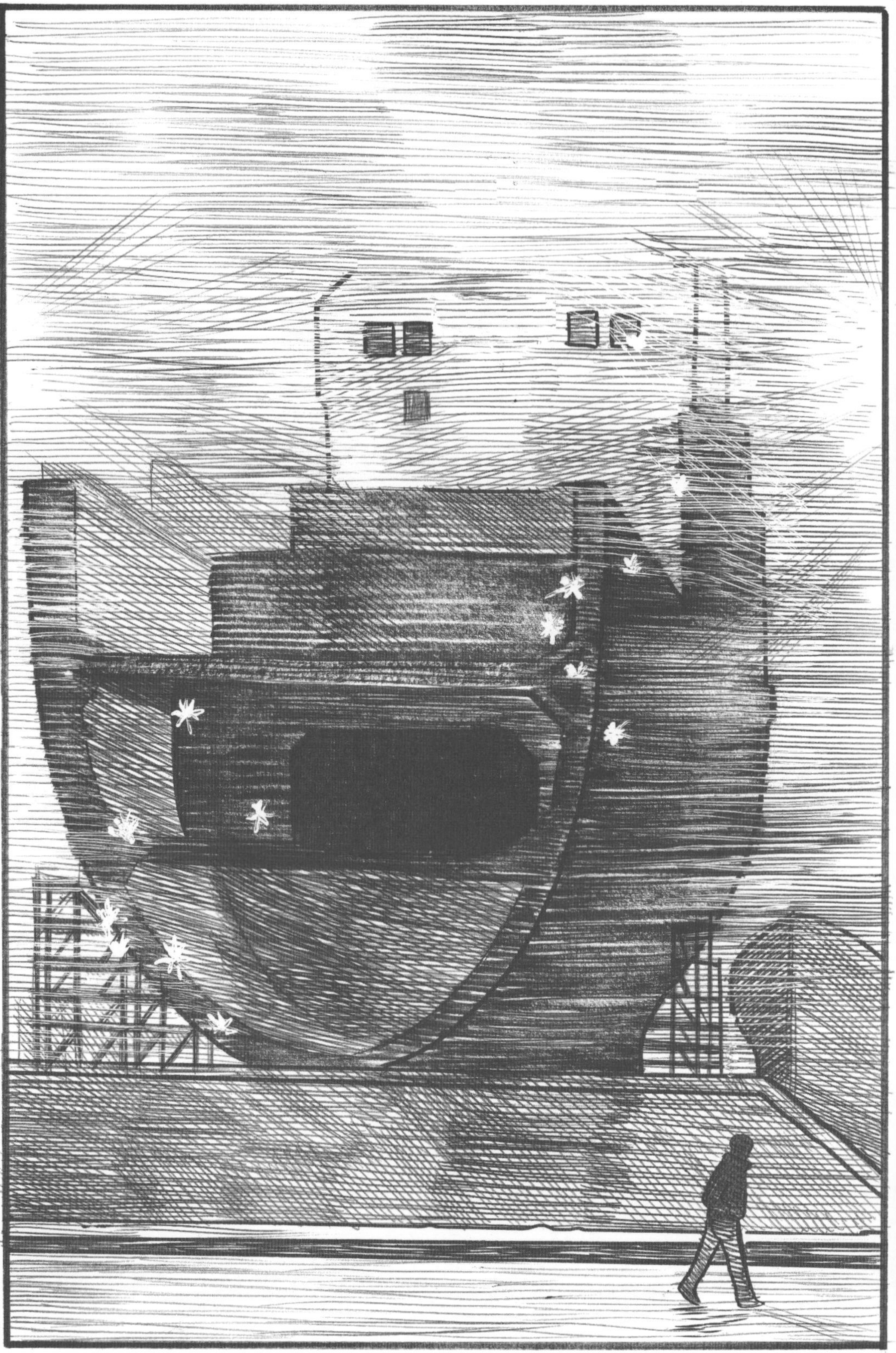

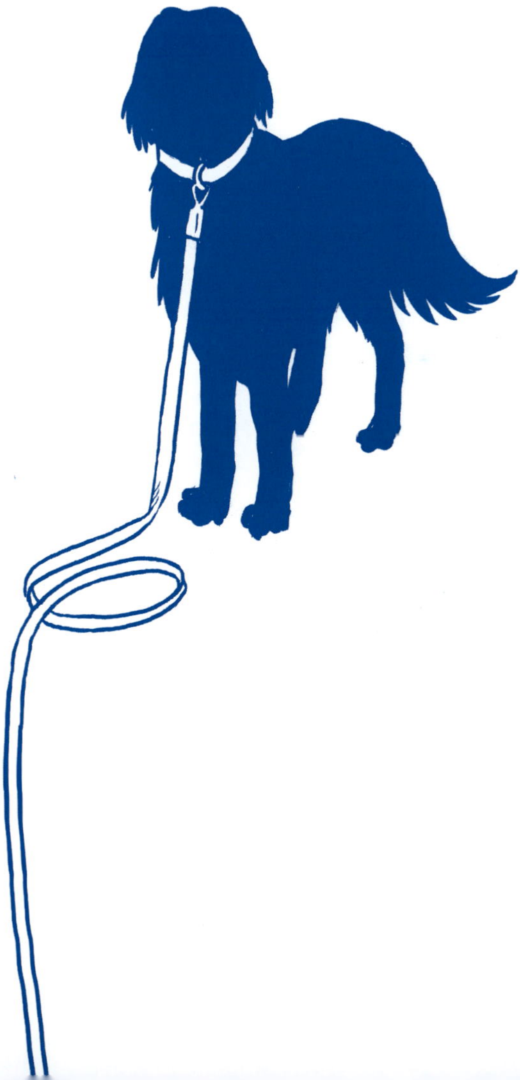

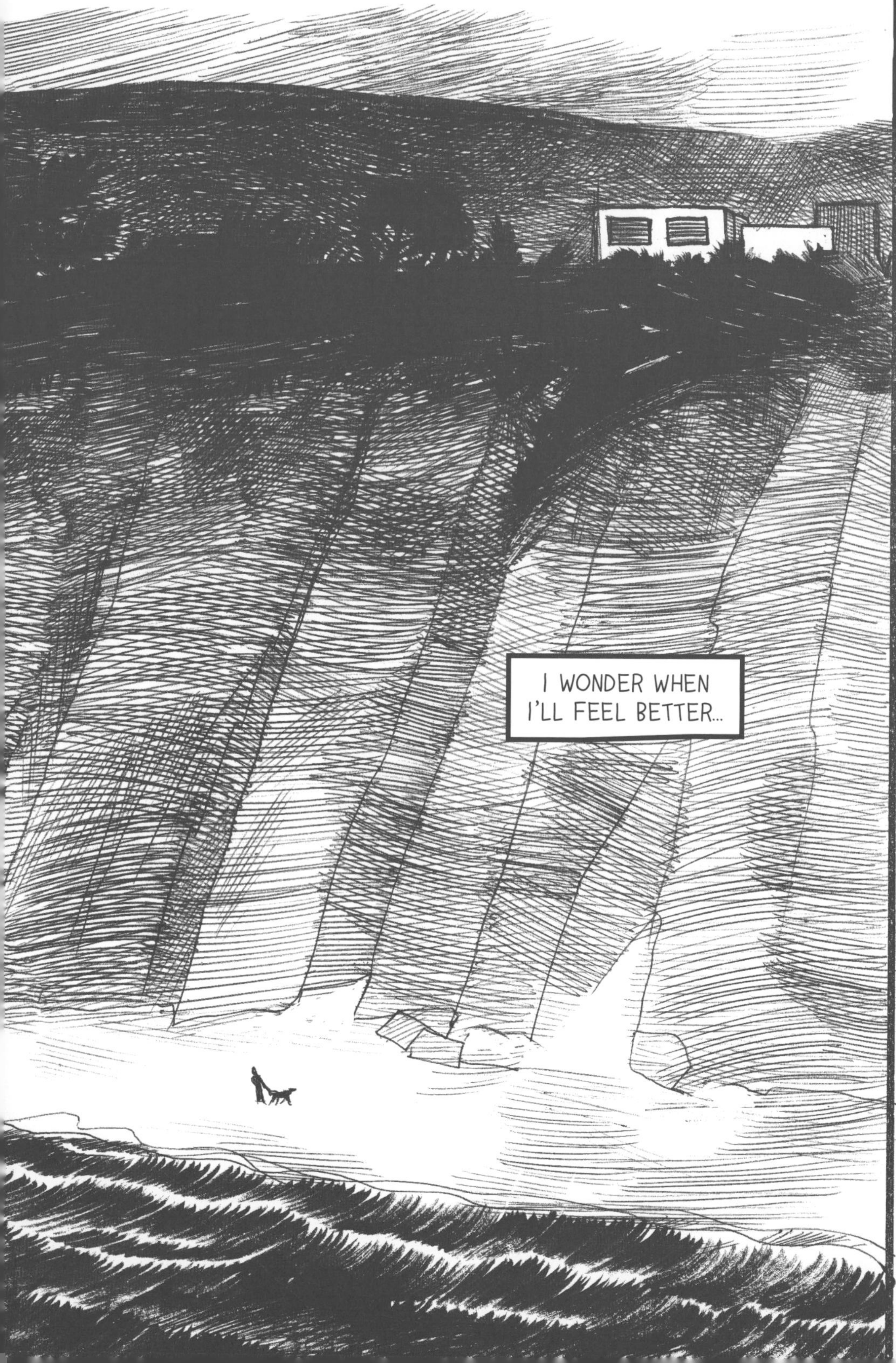
I WONDER WHEN I'LL FEEL BETTER...

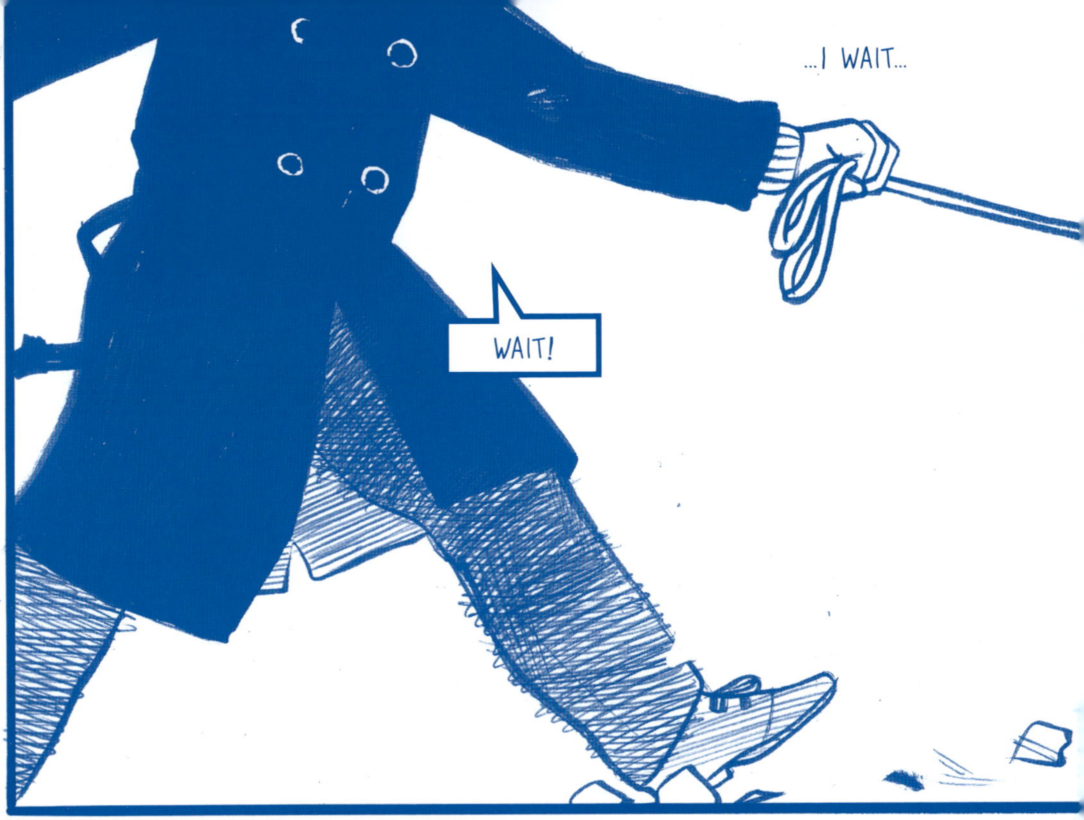
...I WAIT...
WAIT!

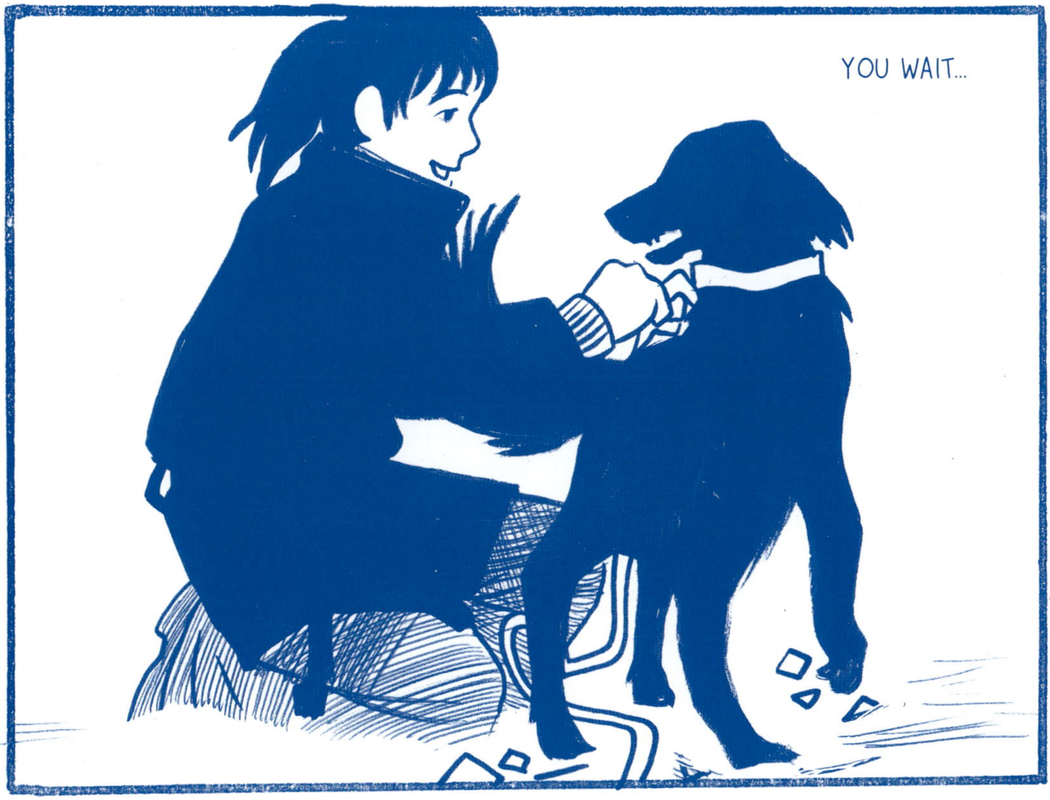
YOU WAIT...

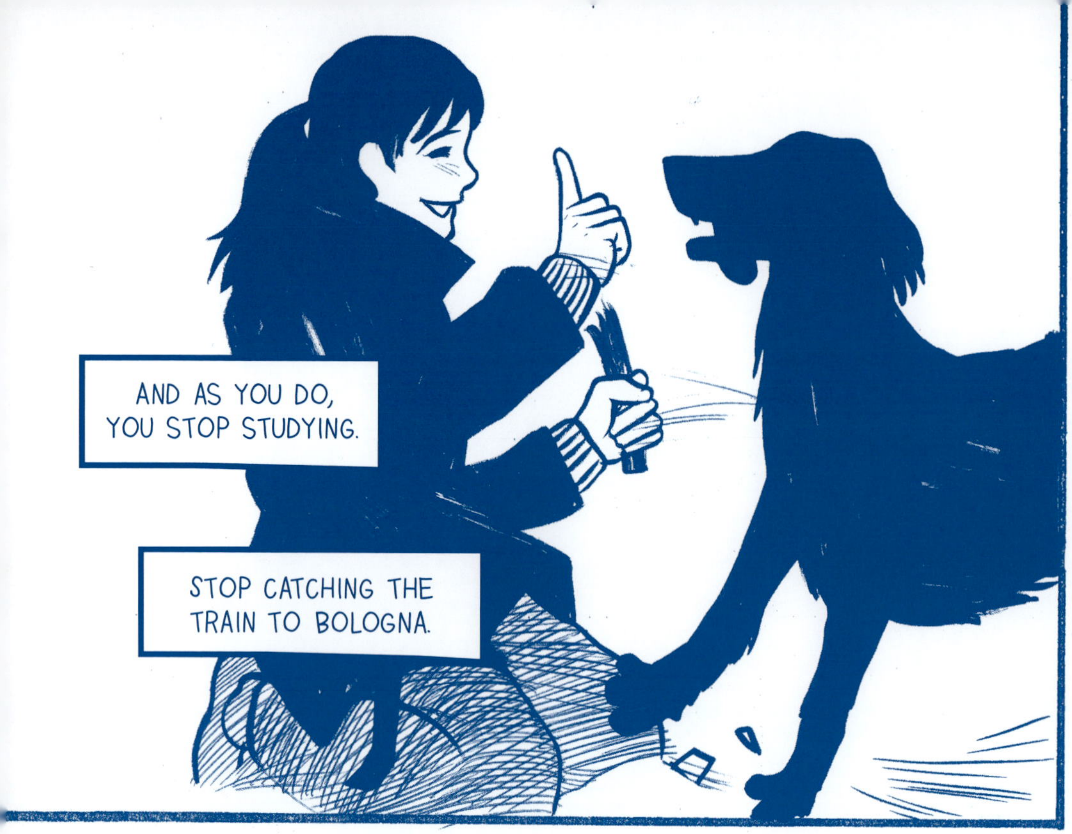
AND AS YOU DO, YOU STOP STUDYING.
STOP CATCHING THE TRAIN TO BOLOGNA.

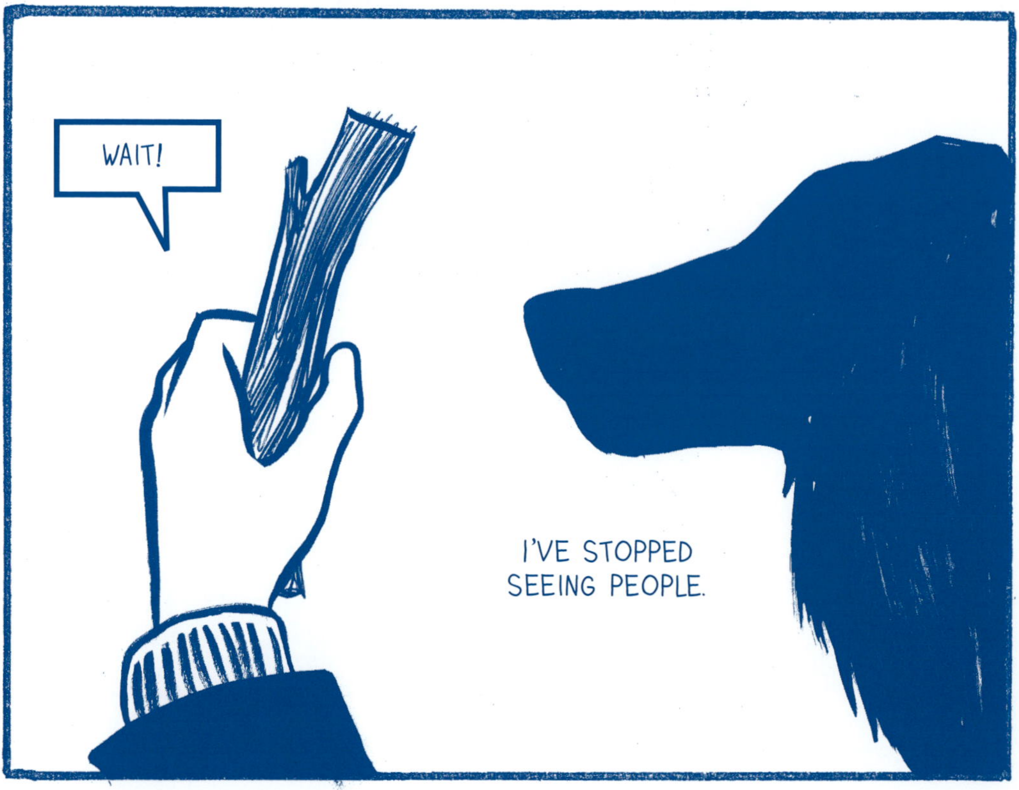
WAIT!
I'VE STOPPED SEEING PEOPLE.

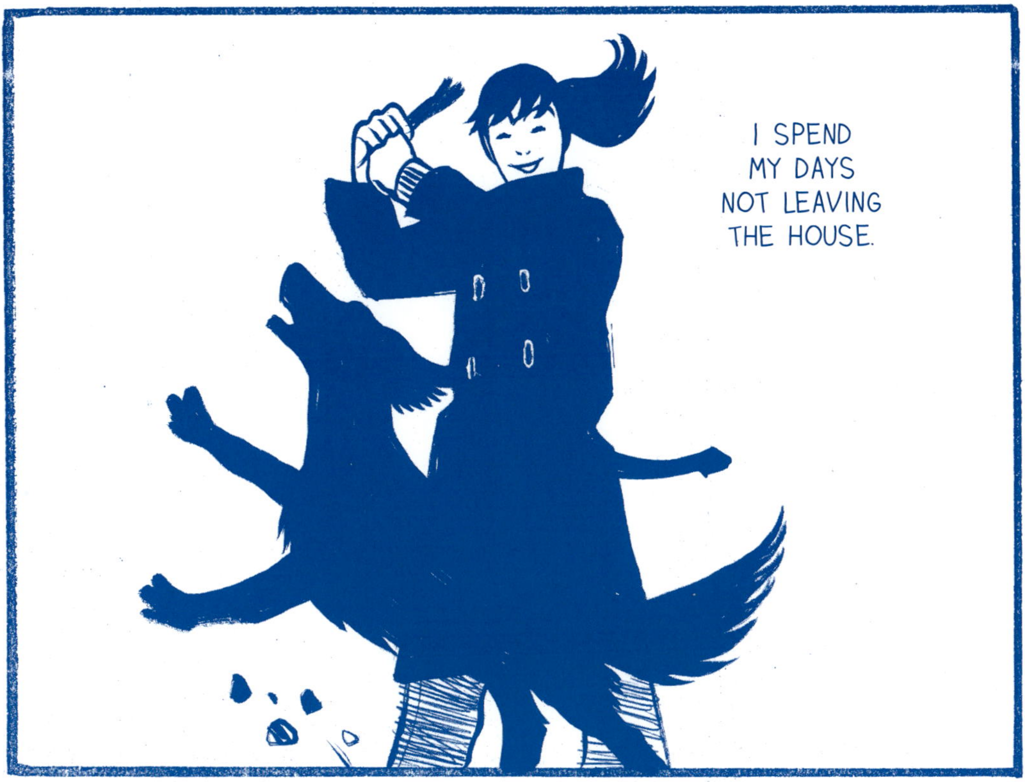
I SPEND MY DAYS NOT LEAVING THE HOUSE.

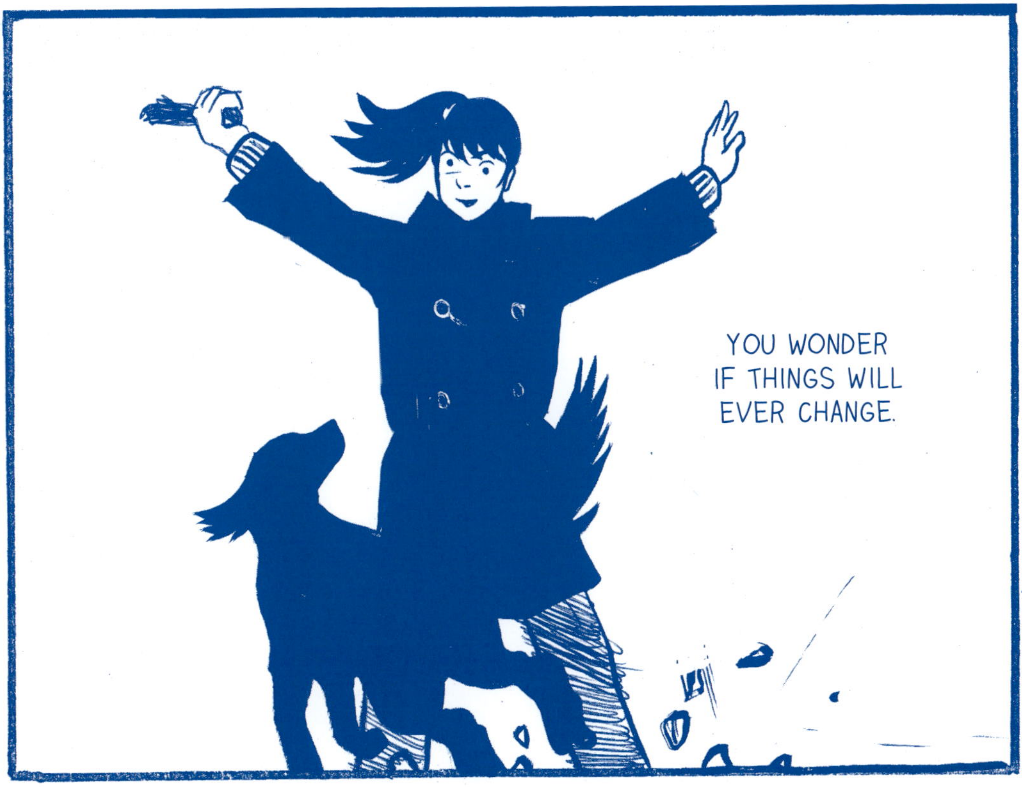
YOU WONDER IF THINGS WILL EVER CHANGE.

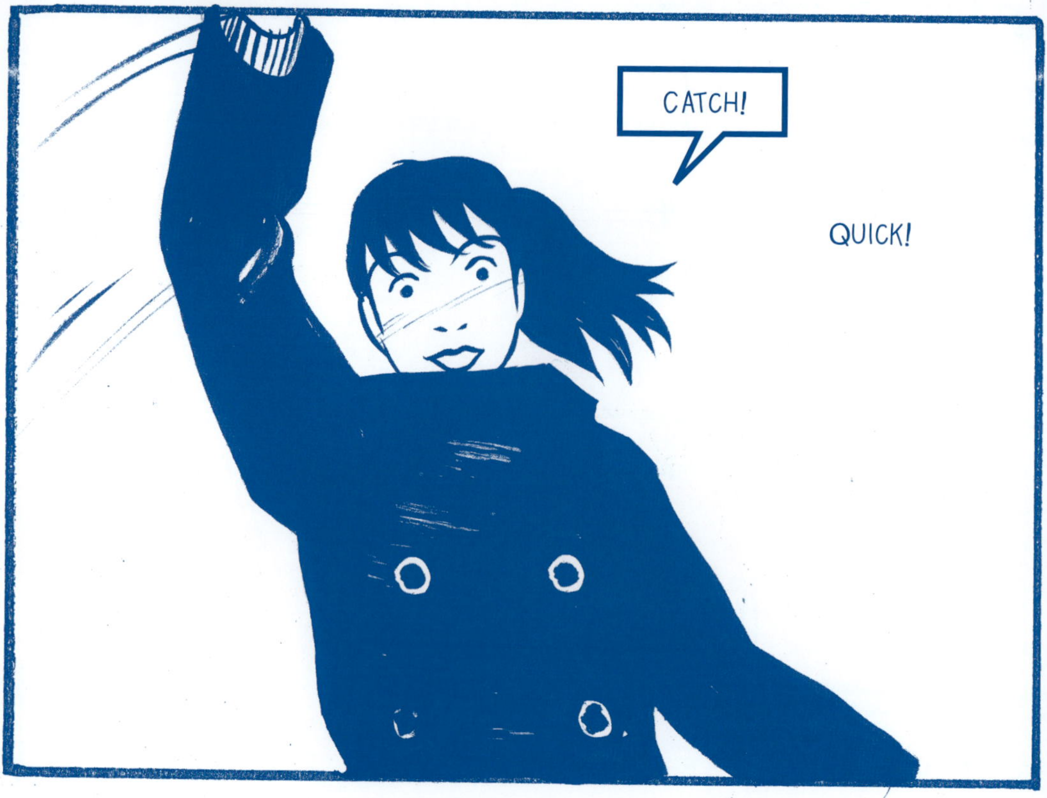
CATCH!
QUICK!

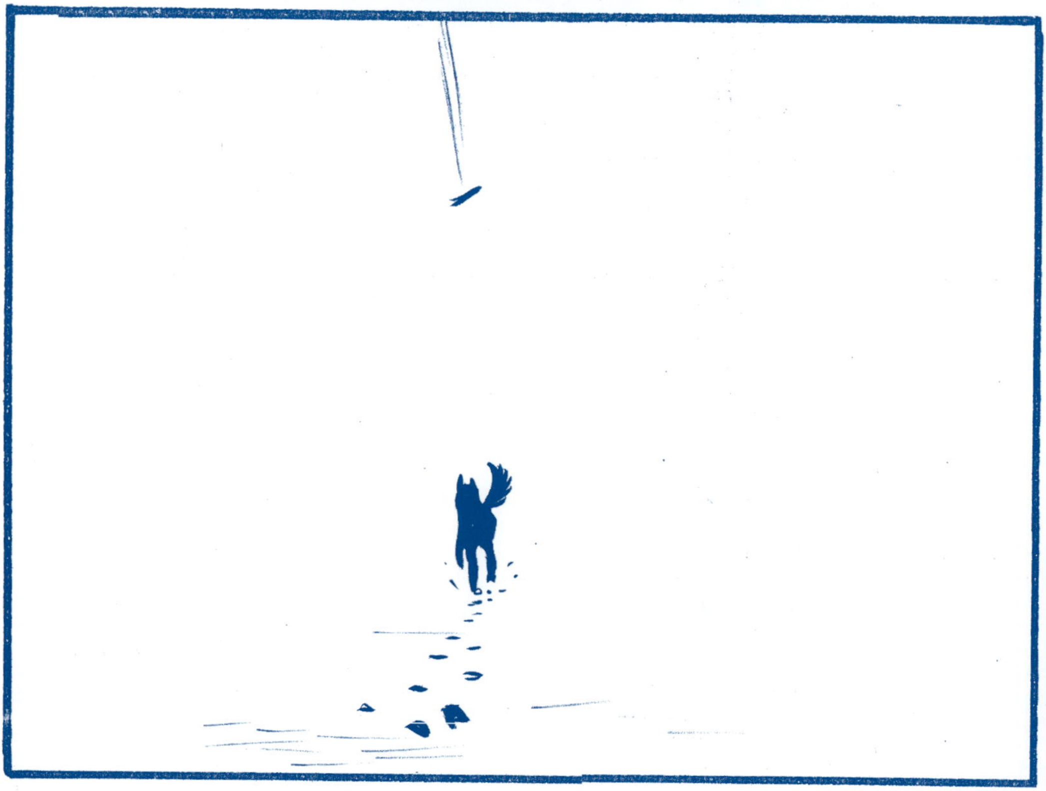

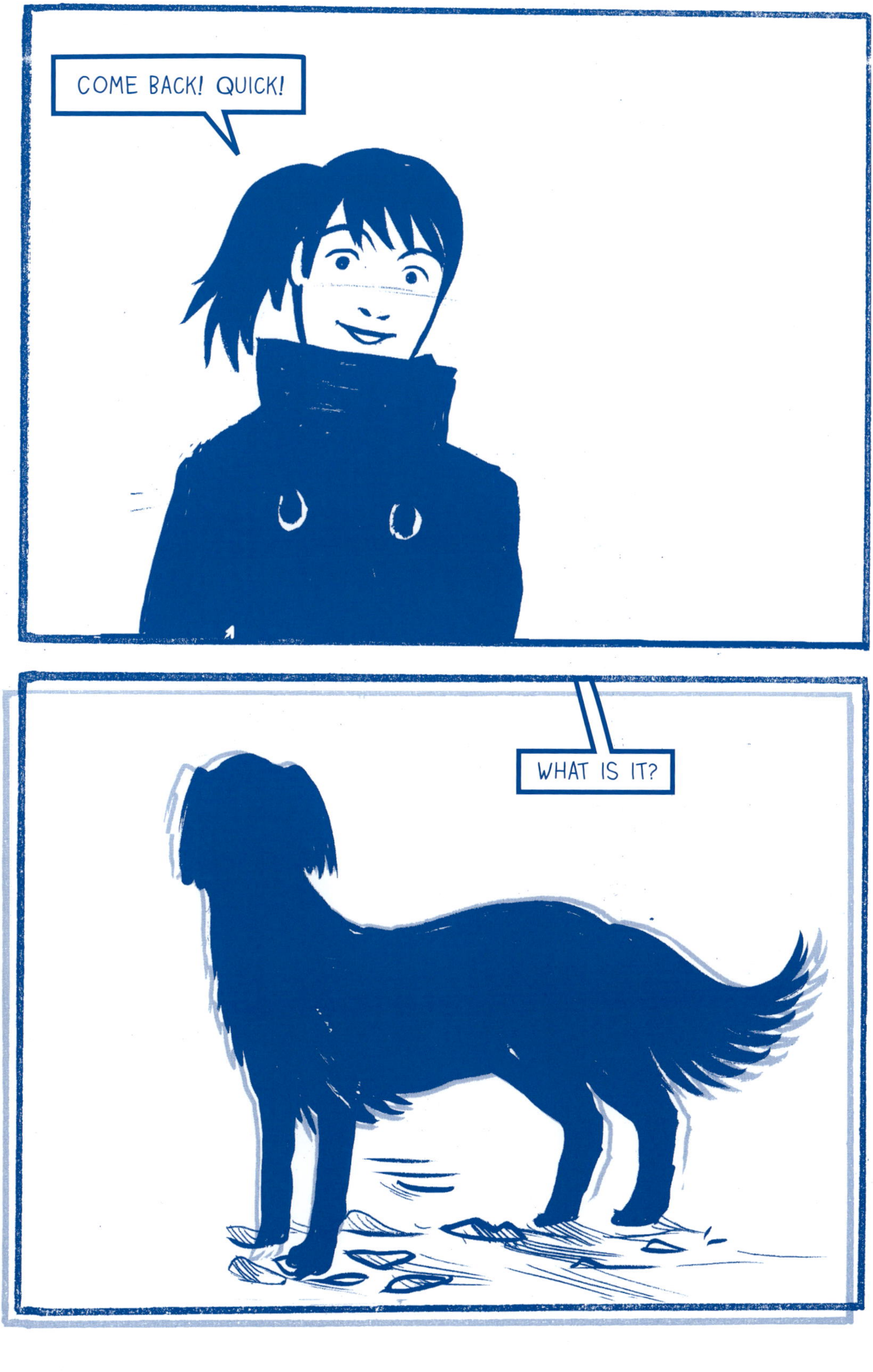
COME BACK! QUICK!
WHAT IS IT?

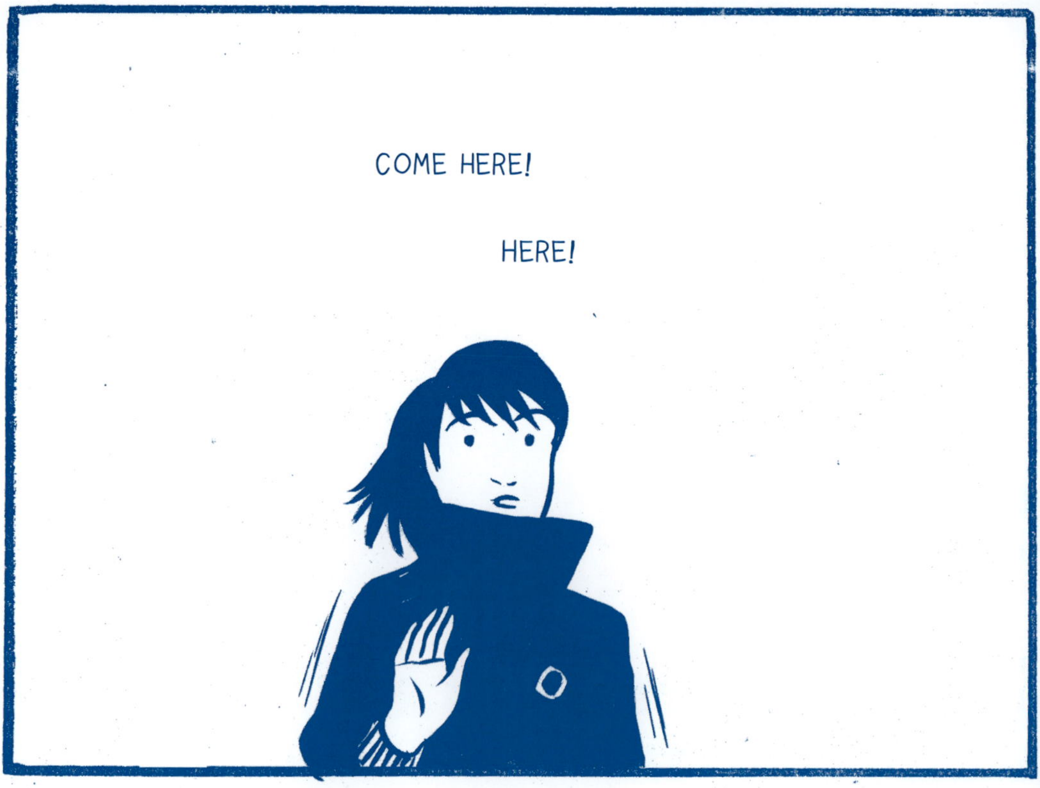
COME HERE!
HERE!

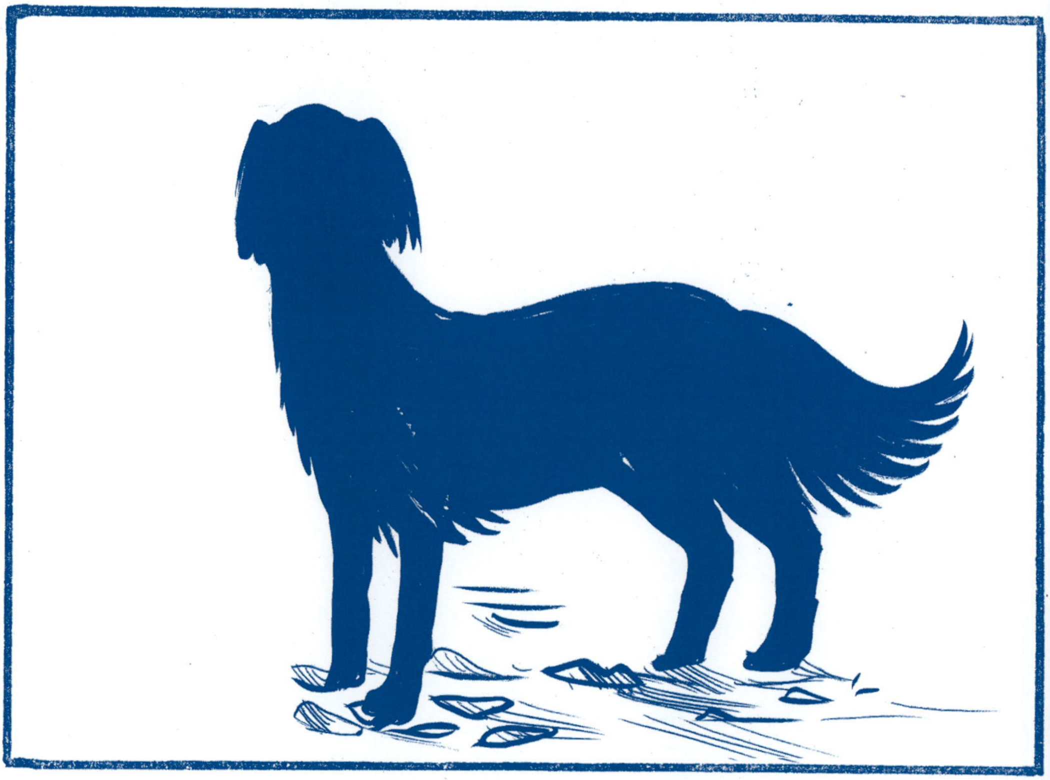

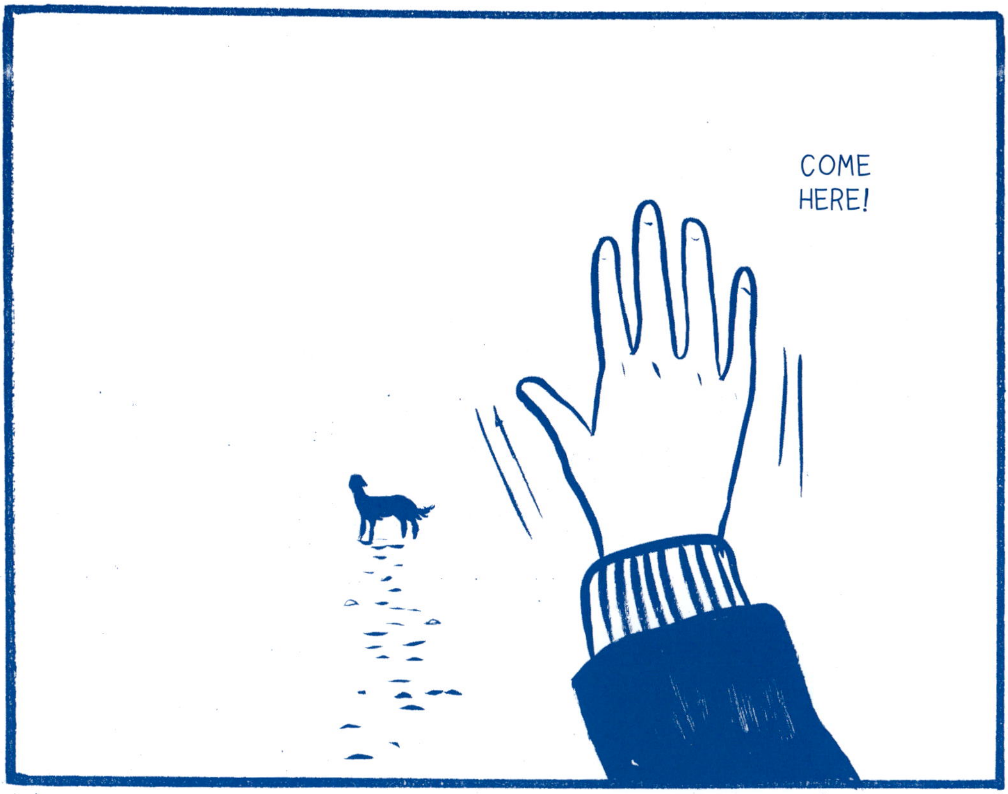
COME
HERE!

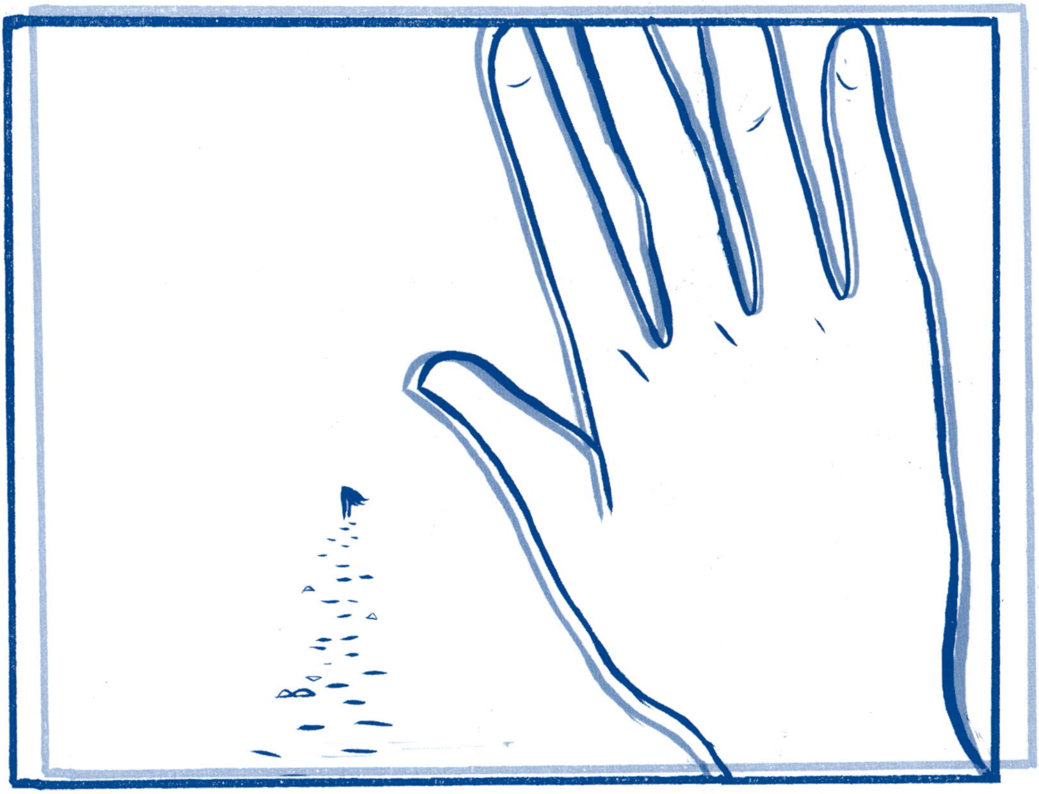

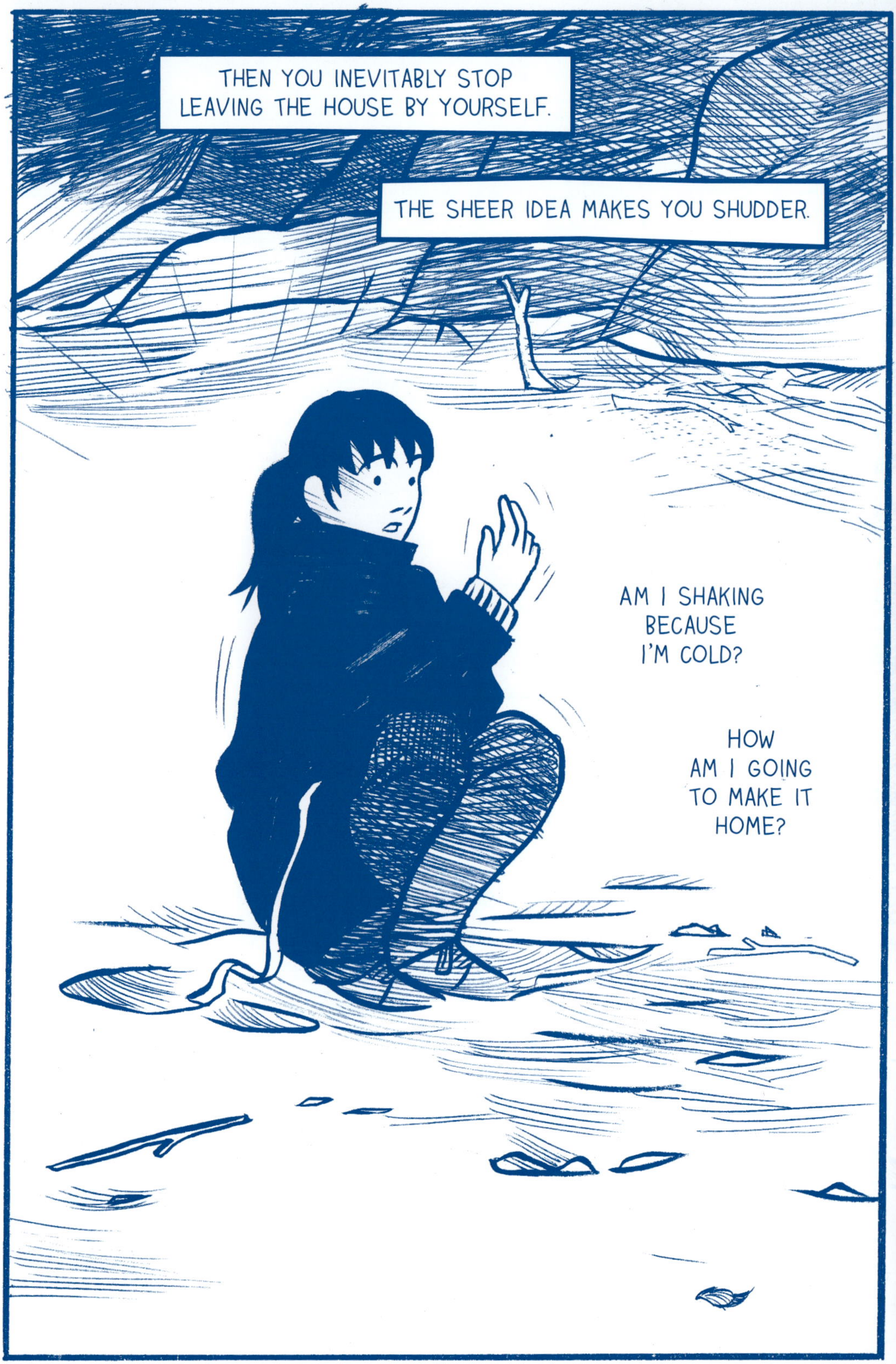
THEN YOU INEVITABLY STOP LEAVING THE HOUSE BY YOURSELF.
THE SHEER IDEA MAKES YOU SHUDDER.
AM I SHAKING BECAUSE I'M COLD?
HOW AM I GOING TO MAKE IT HOME?

I CAN'T GO HOME, NOW!
SO YOU JUST SIT AND WAIT.
YOU WAIT FOR IT ALL TO END, SOONER OR LATER.
BUT IT DOESN'T.
THE END IS FURTHER AWAY.

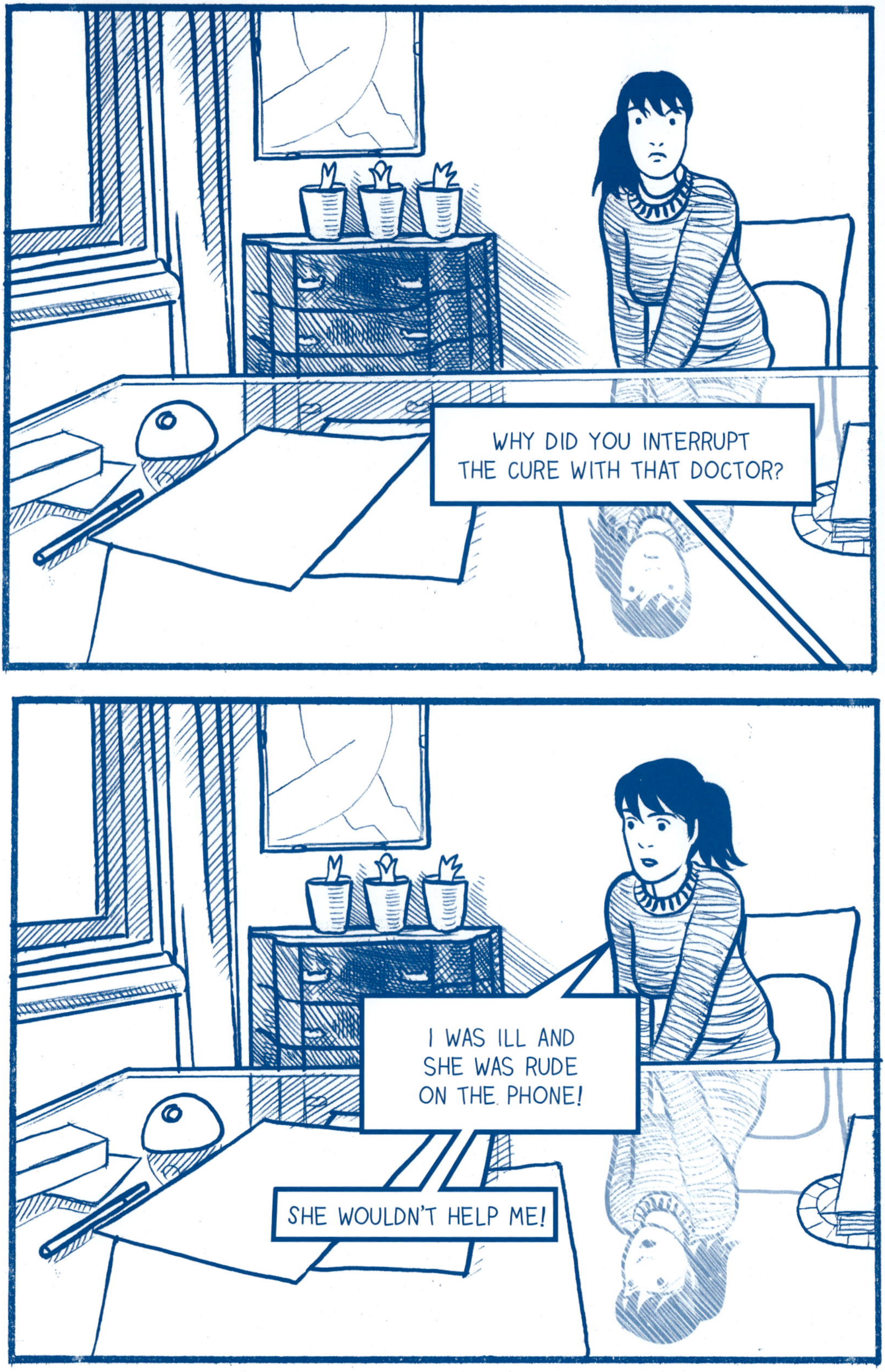
WHY DID YOU INTERRUPT THE CURE WITH THAT DOCTOR?
I WAS ILL AND SHE WAS RUDE ON THE PHONE!
SHE WOULDN'T HELP ME!

IT WAS ABOUT A MONTH AGO: I WAS SCARED. I FOUND BLOOD... IN MY SALIVA.
I WAS TAKING PILLS WHICH I STOPPED TAKING THERE AND THEN...
MMMH... AND THEN YOU CAME TO ME?

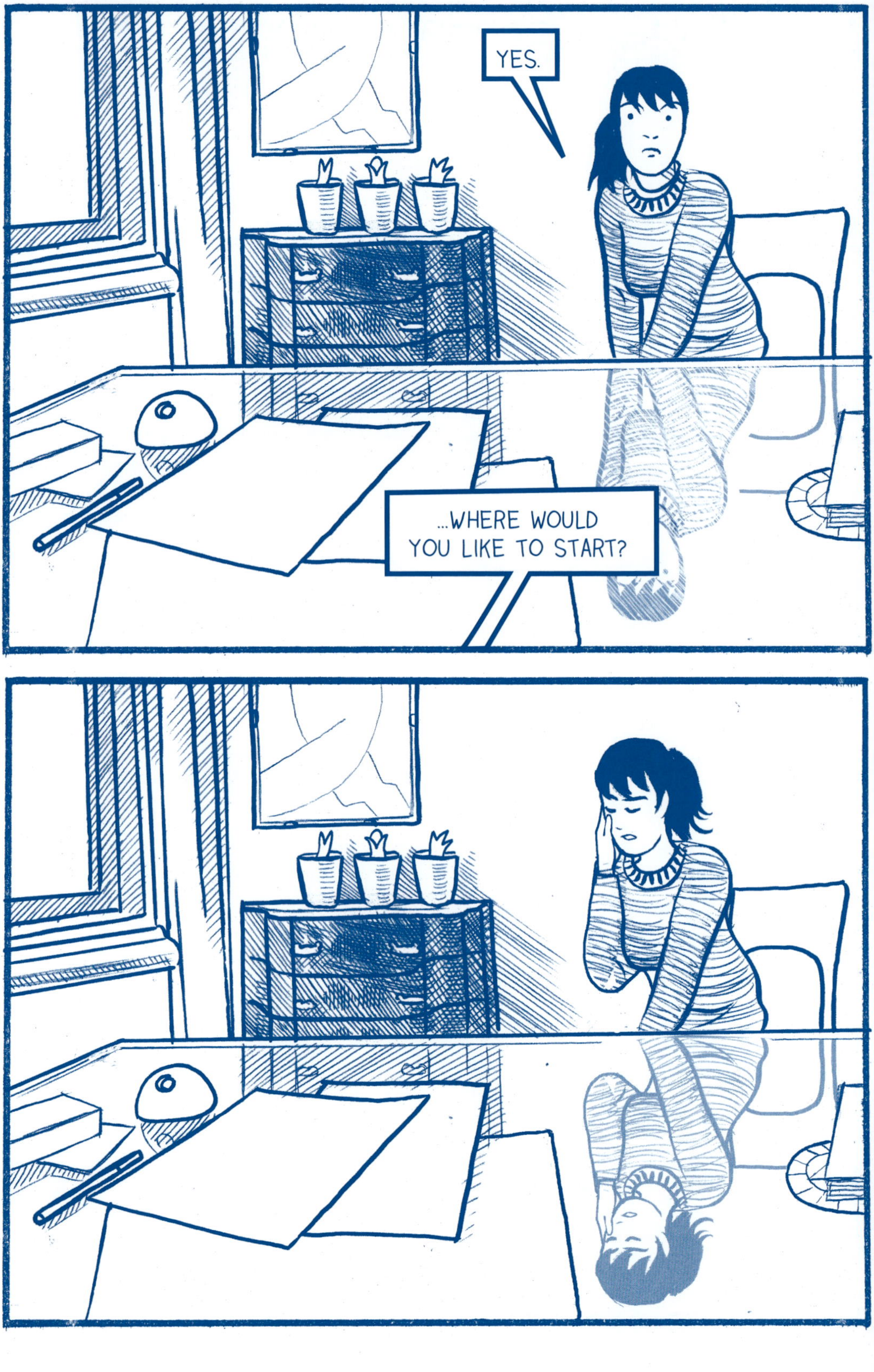
YES.
...WHERE WOULD YOU LIKE TO START?

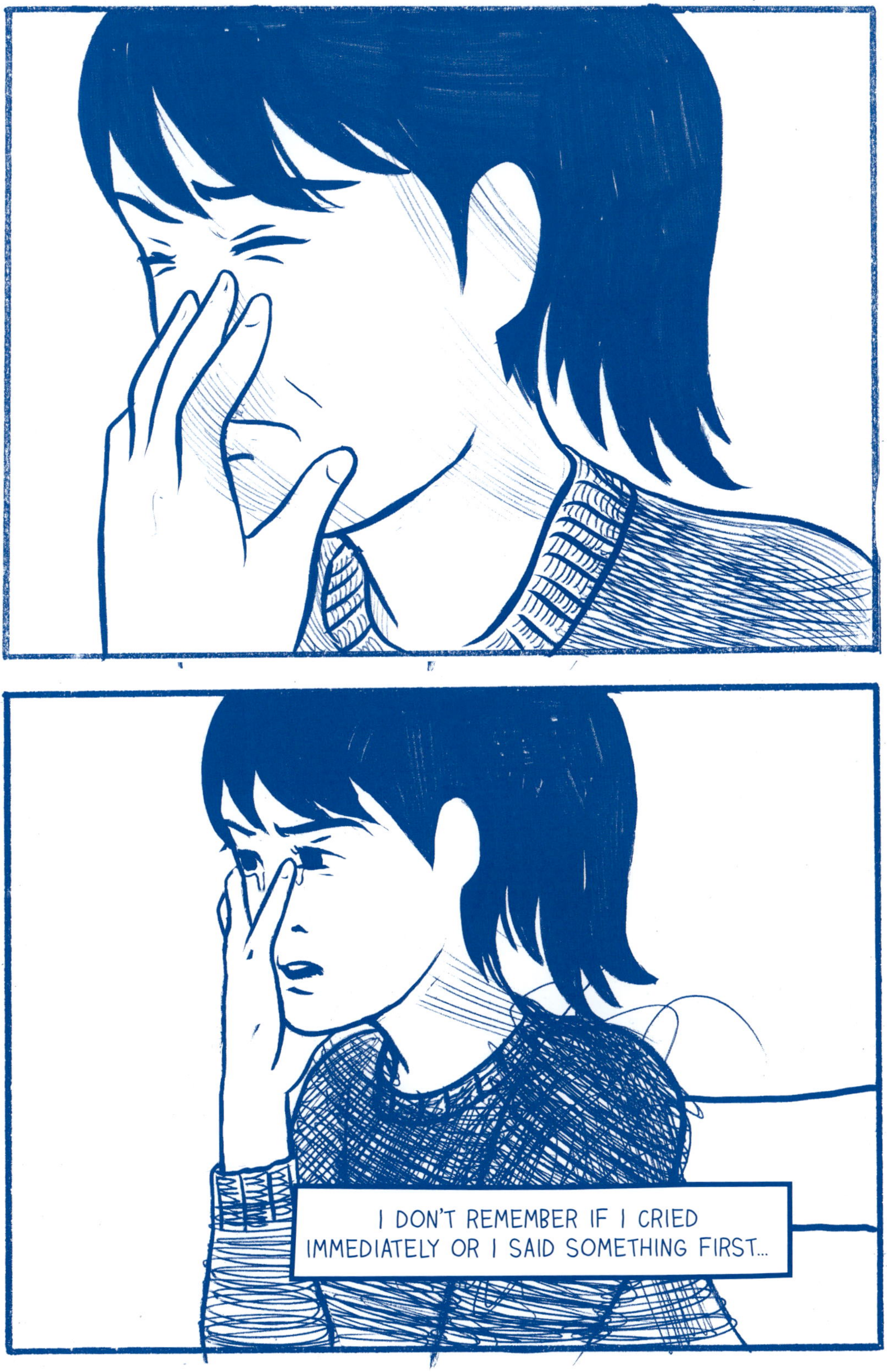
I DON'T REMEMBER IF I CRIED IMMEDIATELY OR I SAID SOMETHING FIRST...

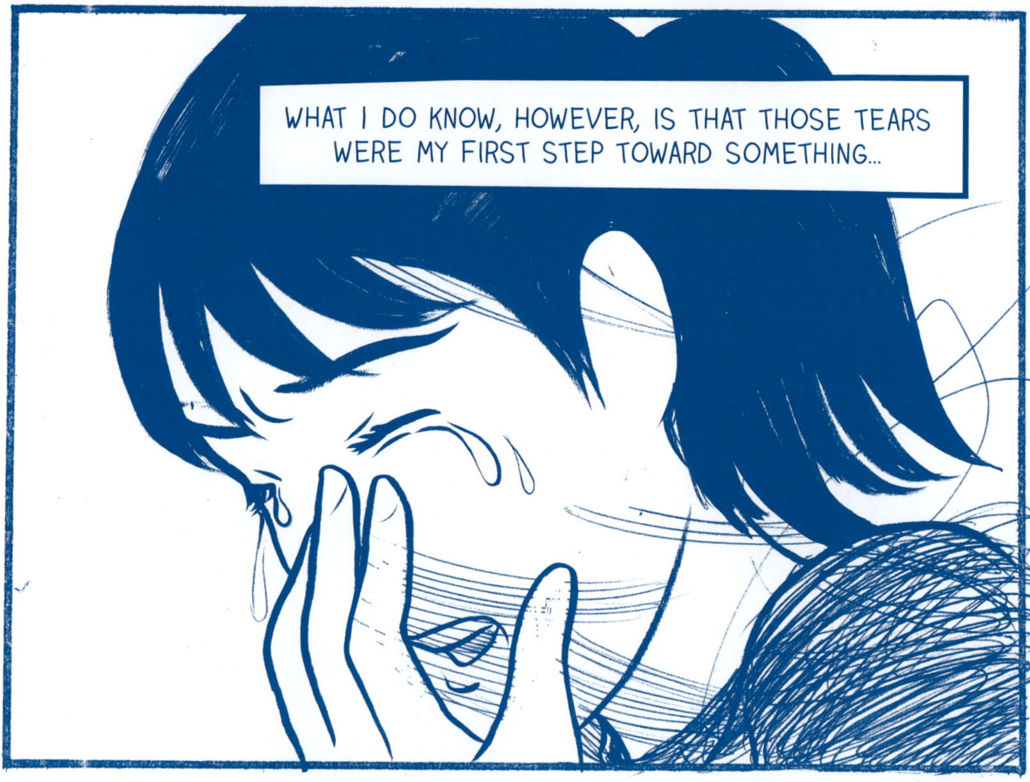
WHAT I DO KNOW, HOWEVER, IS THAT THOSE TEARS WERE MY FIRST STEP TOWARD SOMETHING...

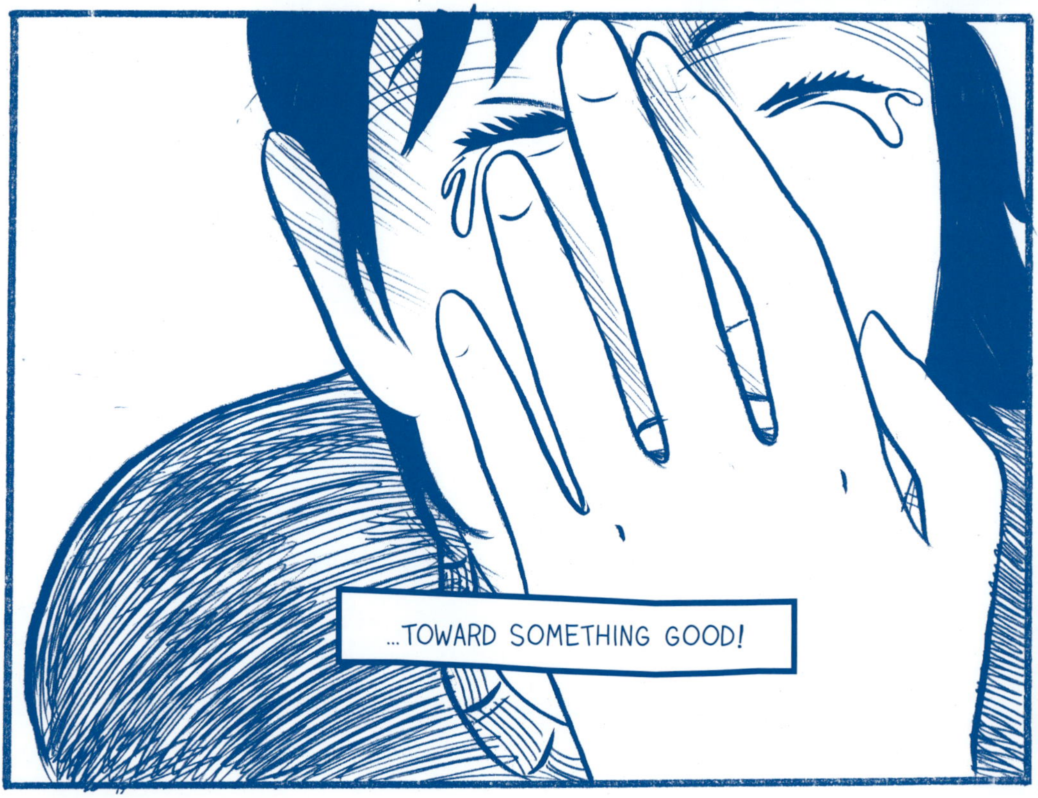
...TOWARD SOMETHING GOOD!

MY WHOLE LIFE
I'D BEEN GETTING ALONG
WITH MY BODY JUST FINE.
I RELIED ON IT.

BUT NOW
IT FEARED ME.

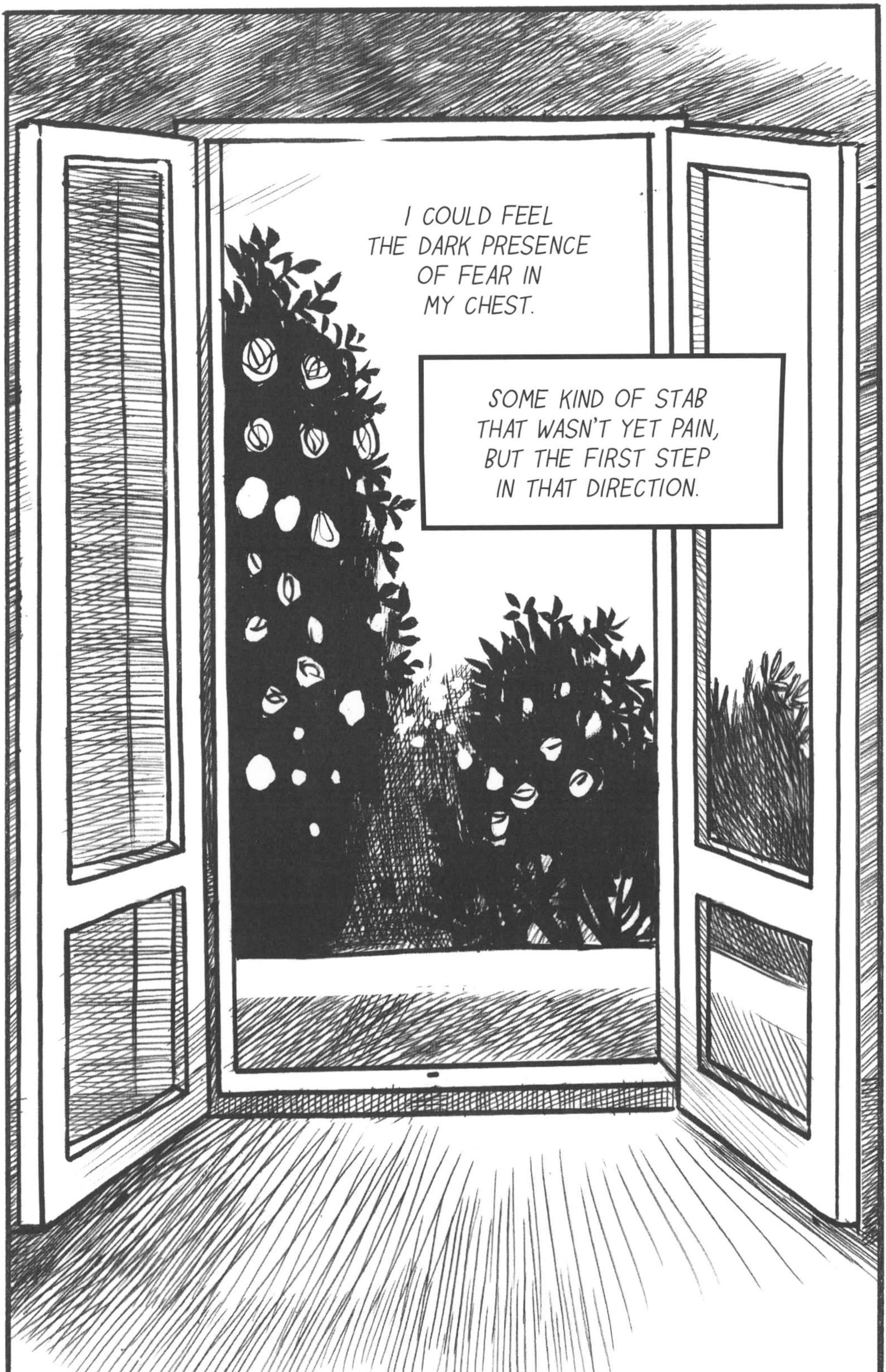
I COULD FEEL THE DARK PRESENCE OF FEAR IN MY CHEST.
SOME KIND OF STAB THAT WASN'T YET PAIN, BUT THE FIRST STEP IN THAT DIRECTION.

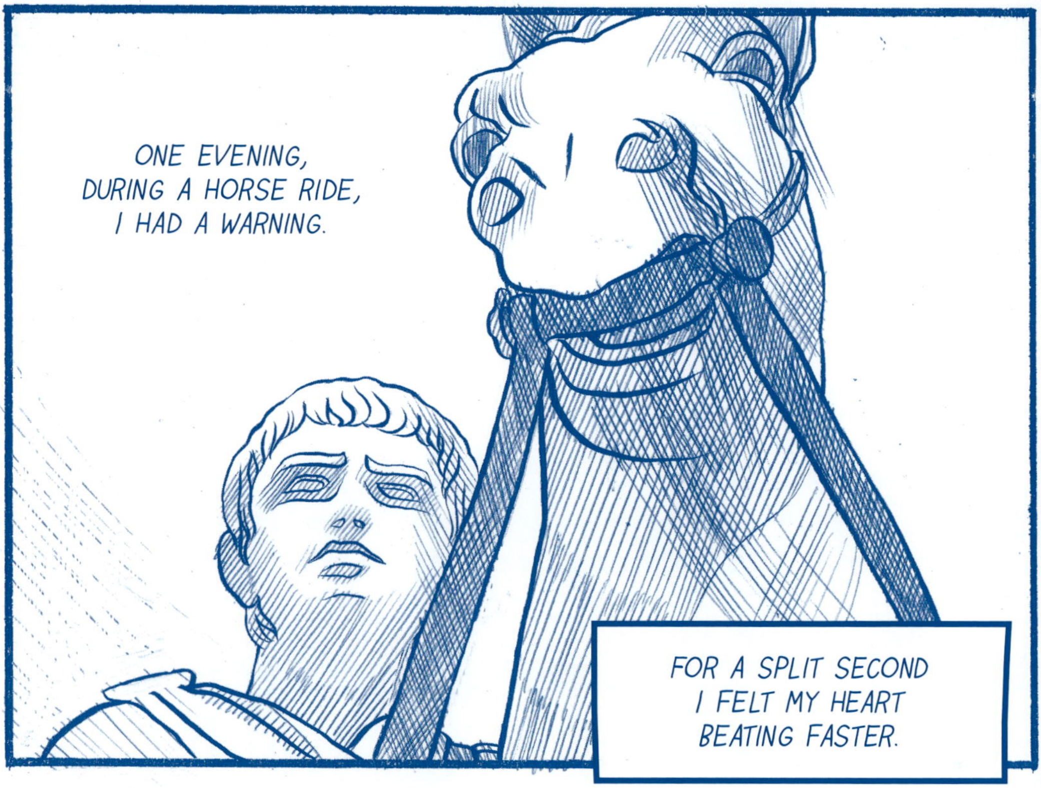
ONE EVENING,
DURING A HORSE RIDE,
I HAD A WARNING.
FOR A SPLIT SECOND
I FELT MY HEART
BEATING FASTER.

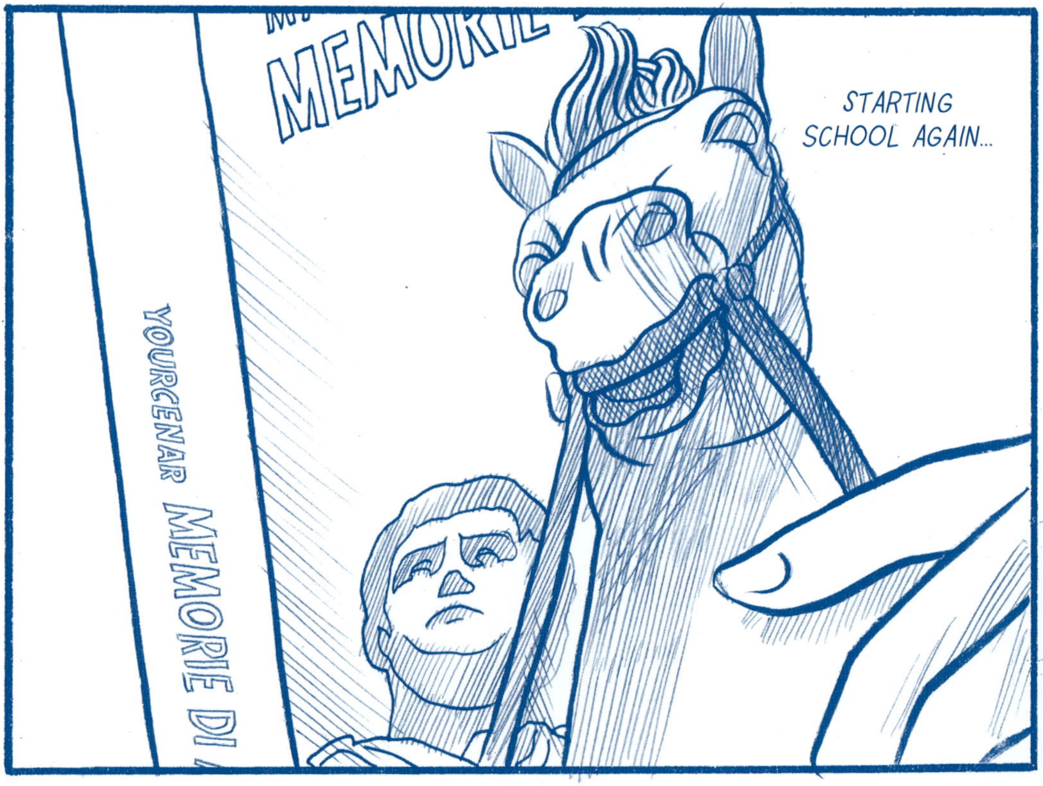
MEMORIE
STARTING
SCHOOL AGAIN...
YOURCENAR
MEMORIE DI

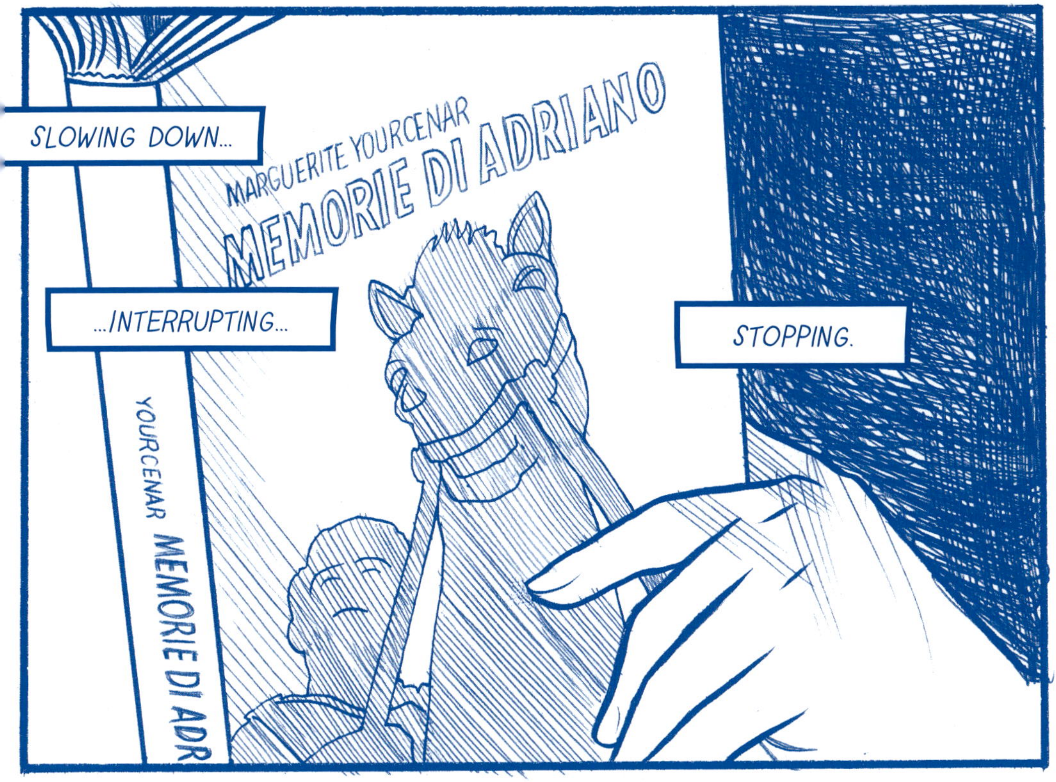
SLOWING DOWN...
MARGUERITE YOURCENAR
MEMORIE DI ADRIANO
...INTERRUPTING...
STOPPING.
YOURCENAR MEMORIE DI ADR

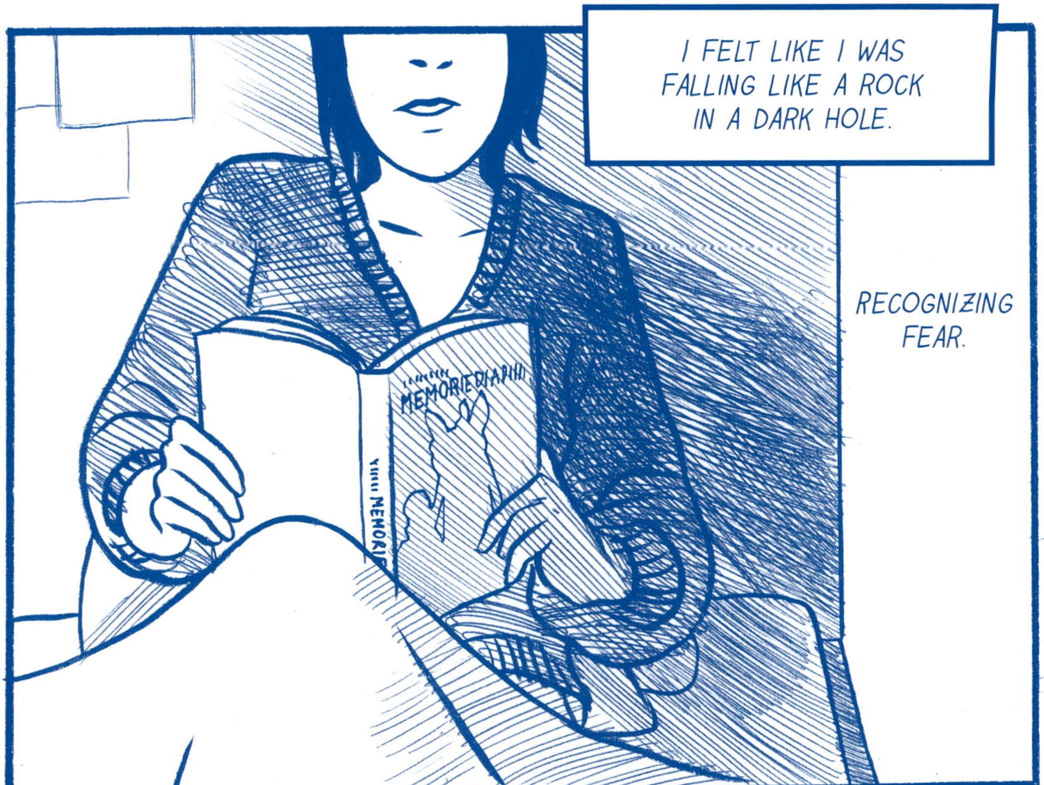
I FELT LIKE I WAS FALLING LIKE A ROCK IN A DARK HOLE.
RECOGNIZING FEAR.
MEMORIE DI ADRI
MEMORI

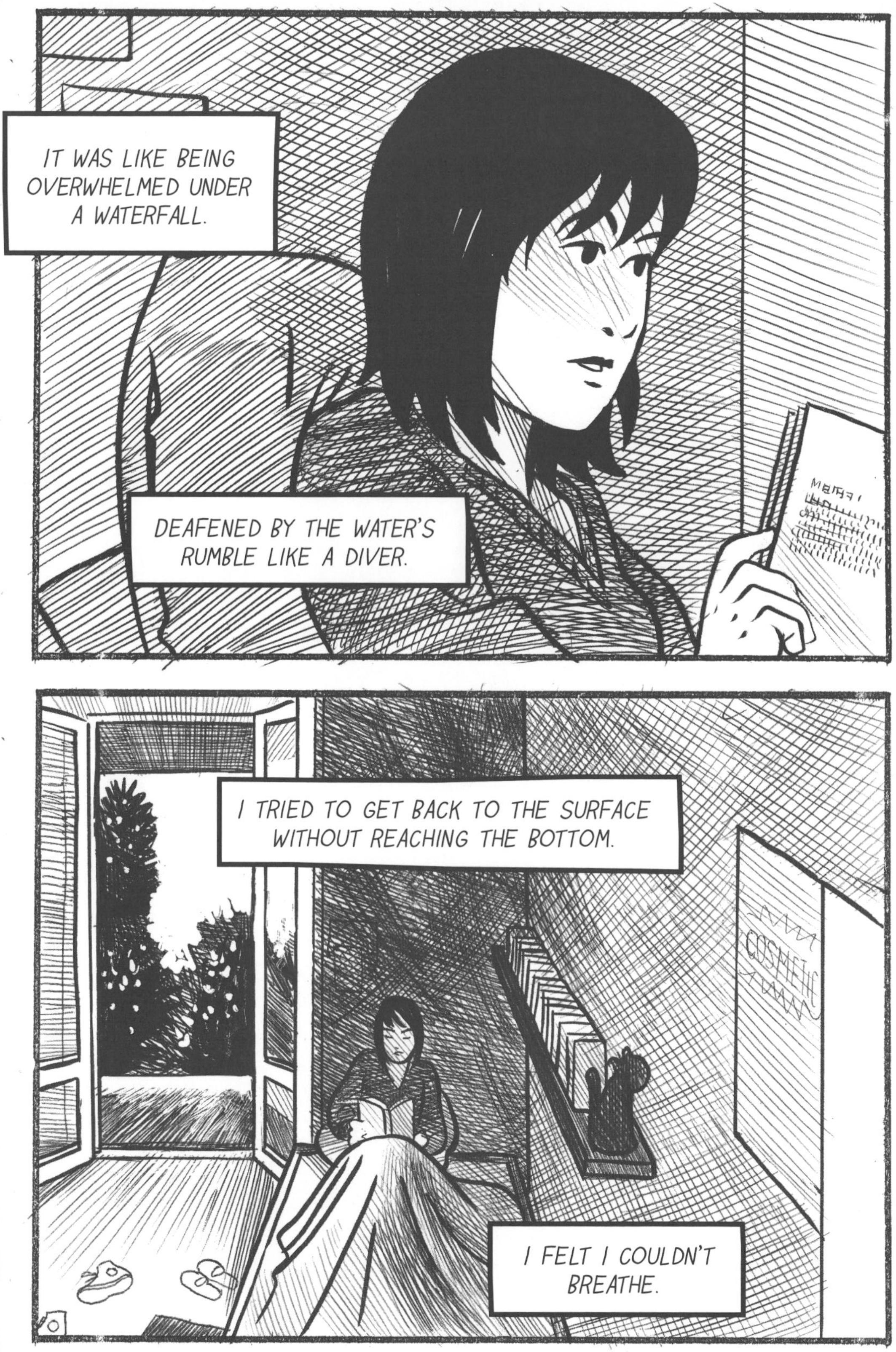
IT WAS LIKE BEING OVERWHELMED UNDER A WATERFALL.
DEAFENED BY THE WATER'S RUMBLE LIKE A DIVER.
I TRIED TO GET BACK TO THE SURFACE WITHOUT REACHING THE BOTTOM.
COSMETIC
I FELT I COULDN'T BREATHE.

ACKNOWLEDGING
PANIC ATTACKS AS AN ILLNESS
IS VERY IMPORTANT.

AT LEAST YOU STOP
ALL THOSE POINTLESS
CHECKUPS...

AND YOU REALIZE
YOU'RE NOT ALONE, AT LAST...
OTHERS LIKE YOU DON'T
KNOW THIS...
DIDN'T KNOW IT.

YOU MAY FEEL STUPID,
BUT AT LEAST YOU'RE NOT
ALONE ANYMORE.

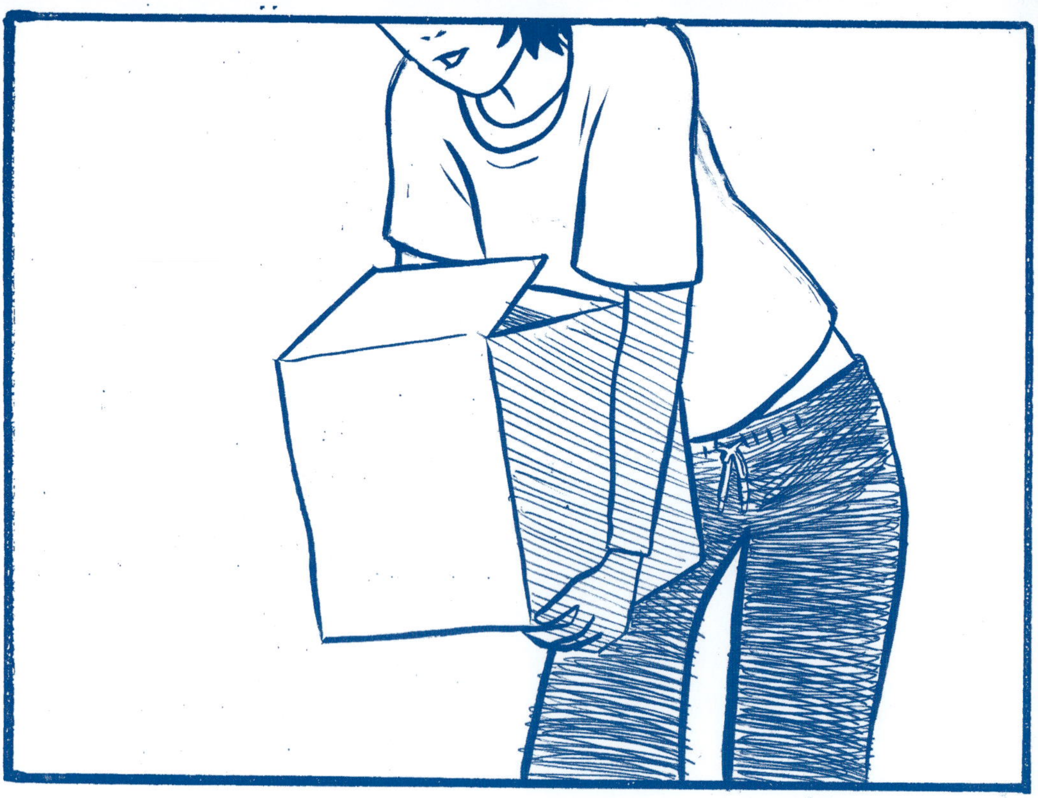

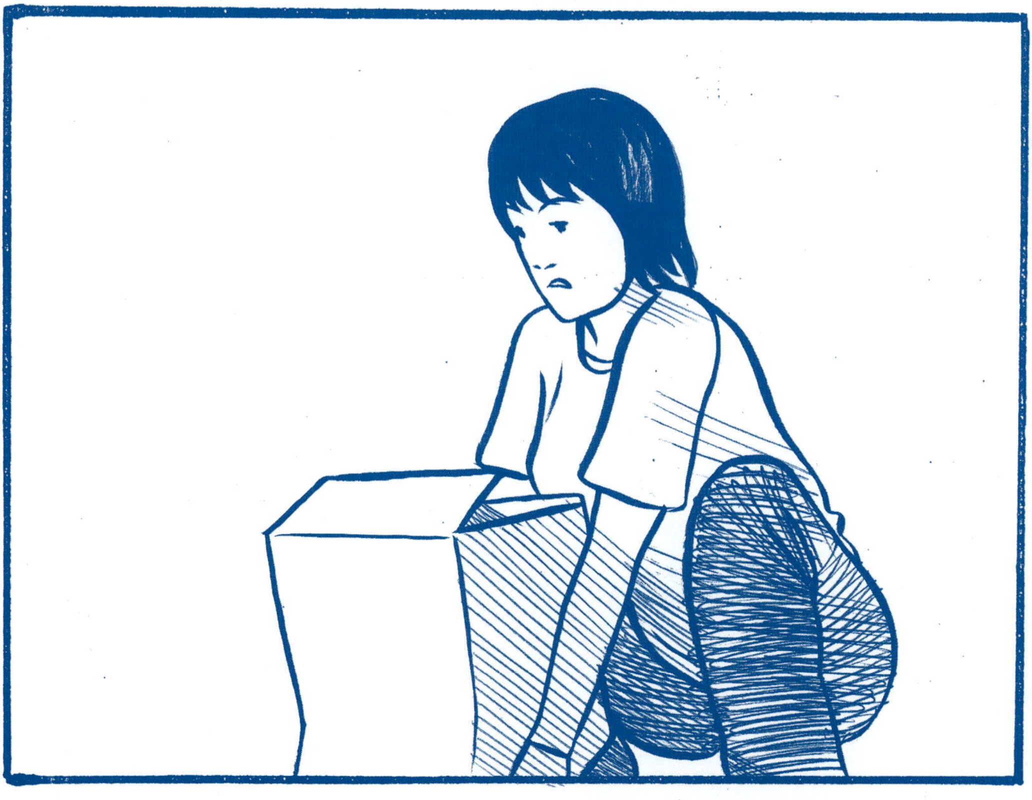

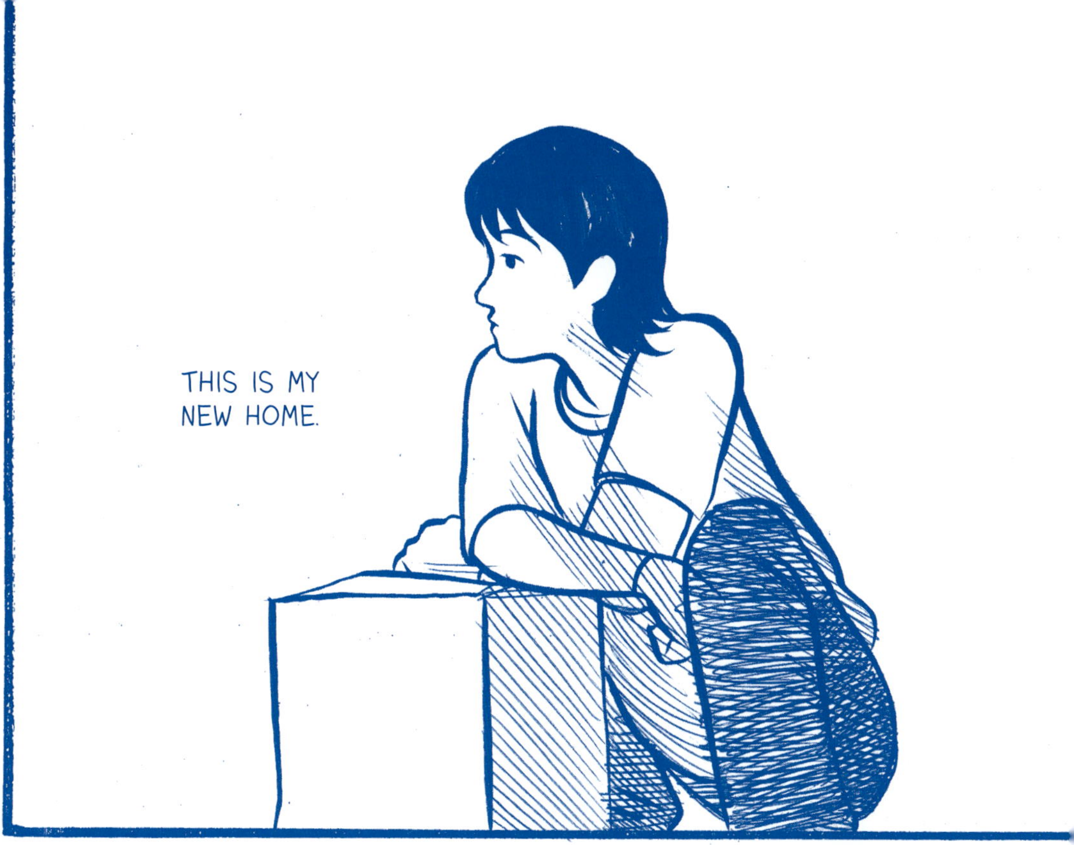
THIS IS MY
NEW HOME.

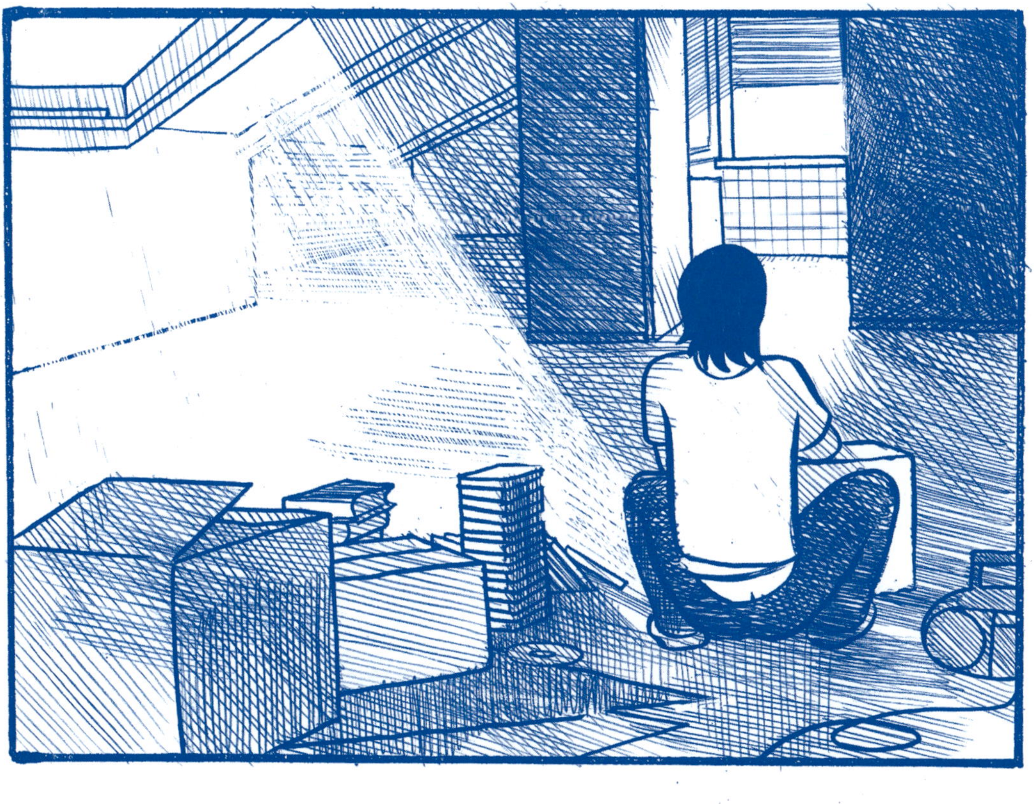

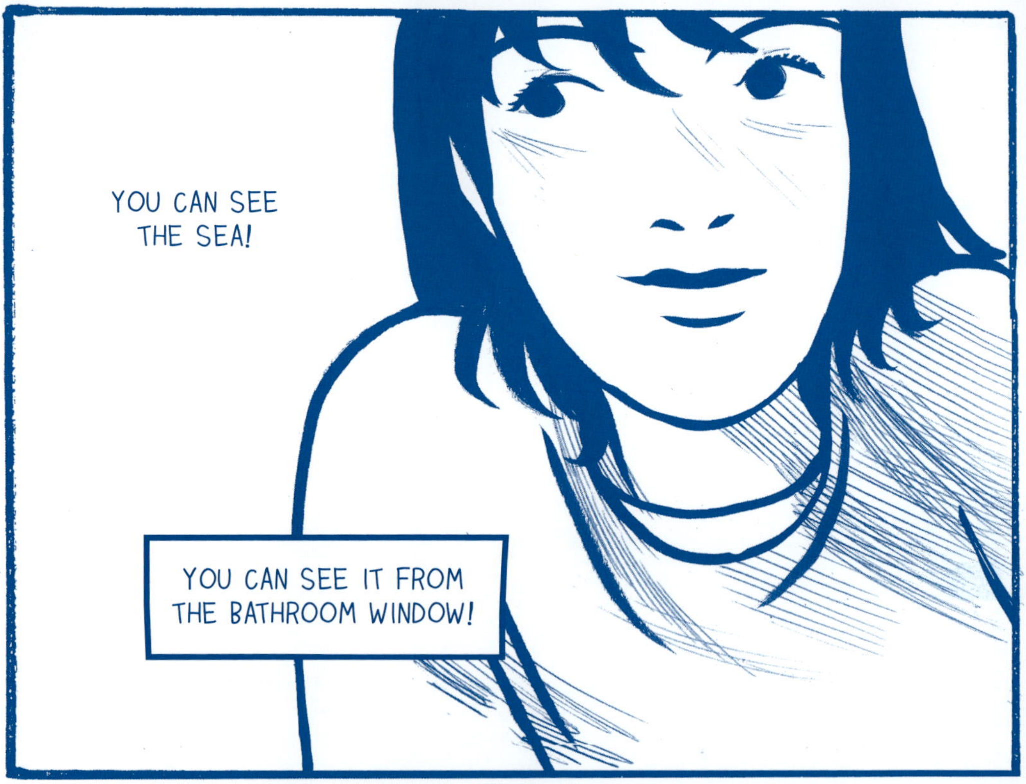
YOU CAN SEE THE SEA!
YOU CAN SEE IT FROM THE BATHROOM WINDOW!

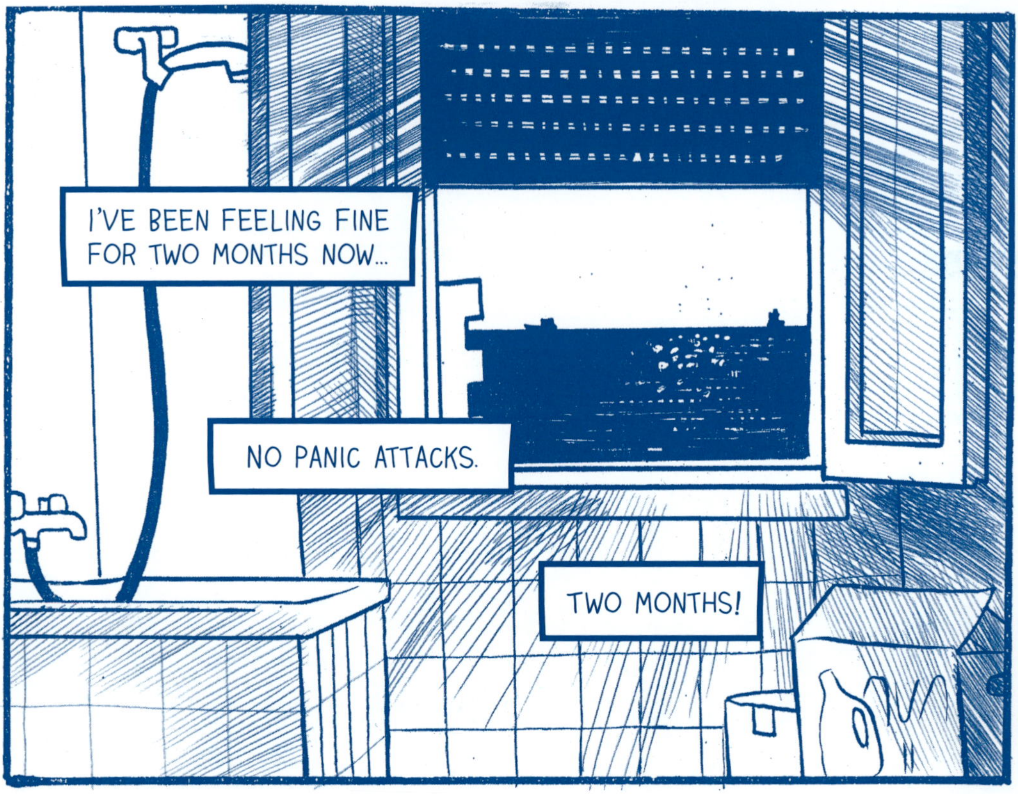
I'VE BEEN FEELING FINE FOR TWO MONTHS NOW...
NO PANIC ATTACKS.
TWO MONTHS!

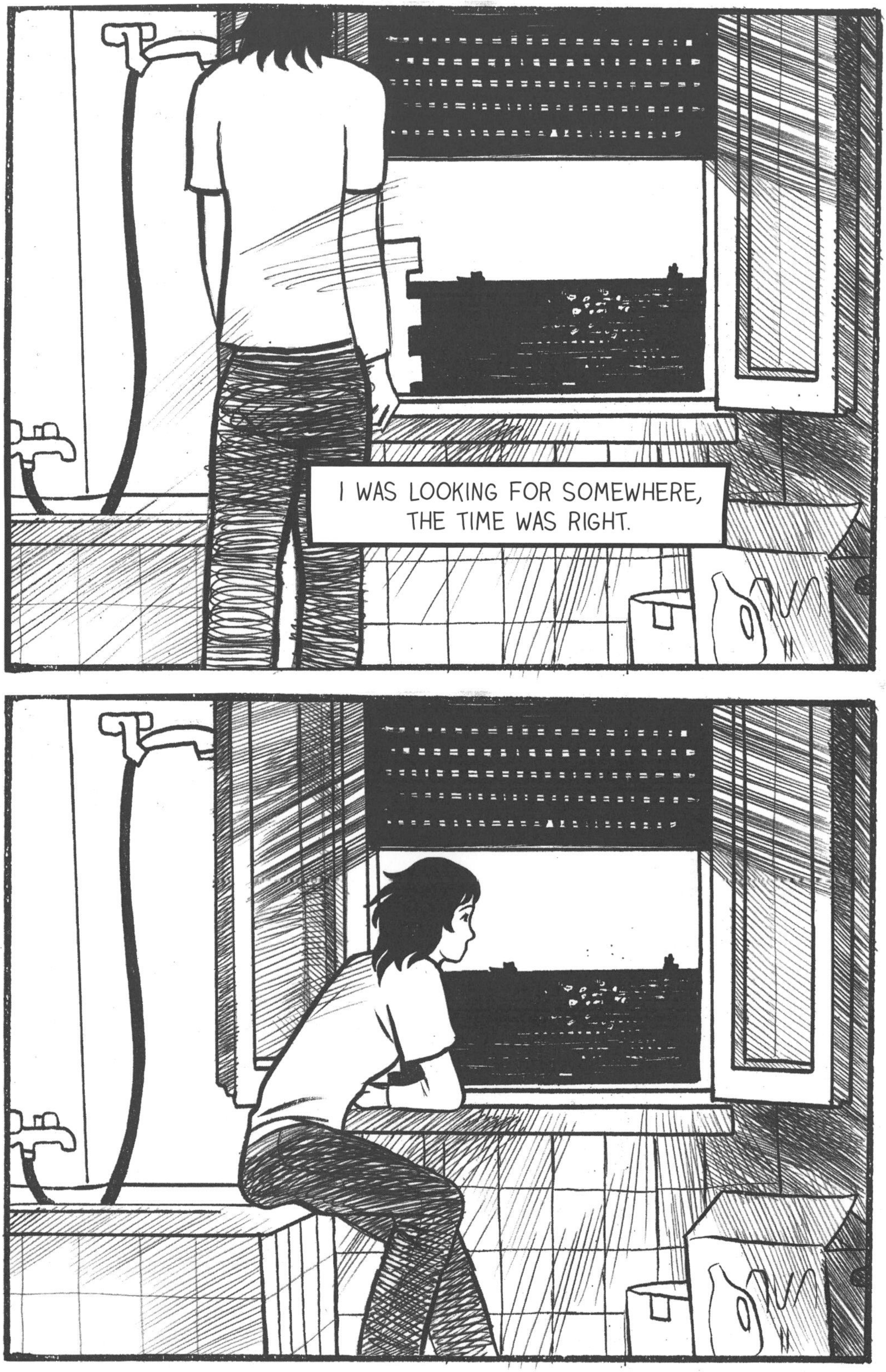
I WAS LOOKING FOR SOMEWHERE,
THE TIME WAS RIGHT.

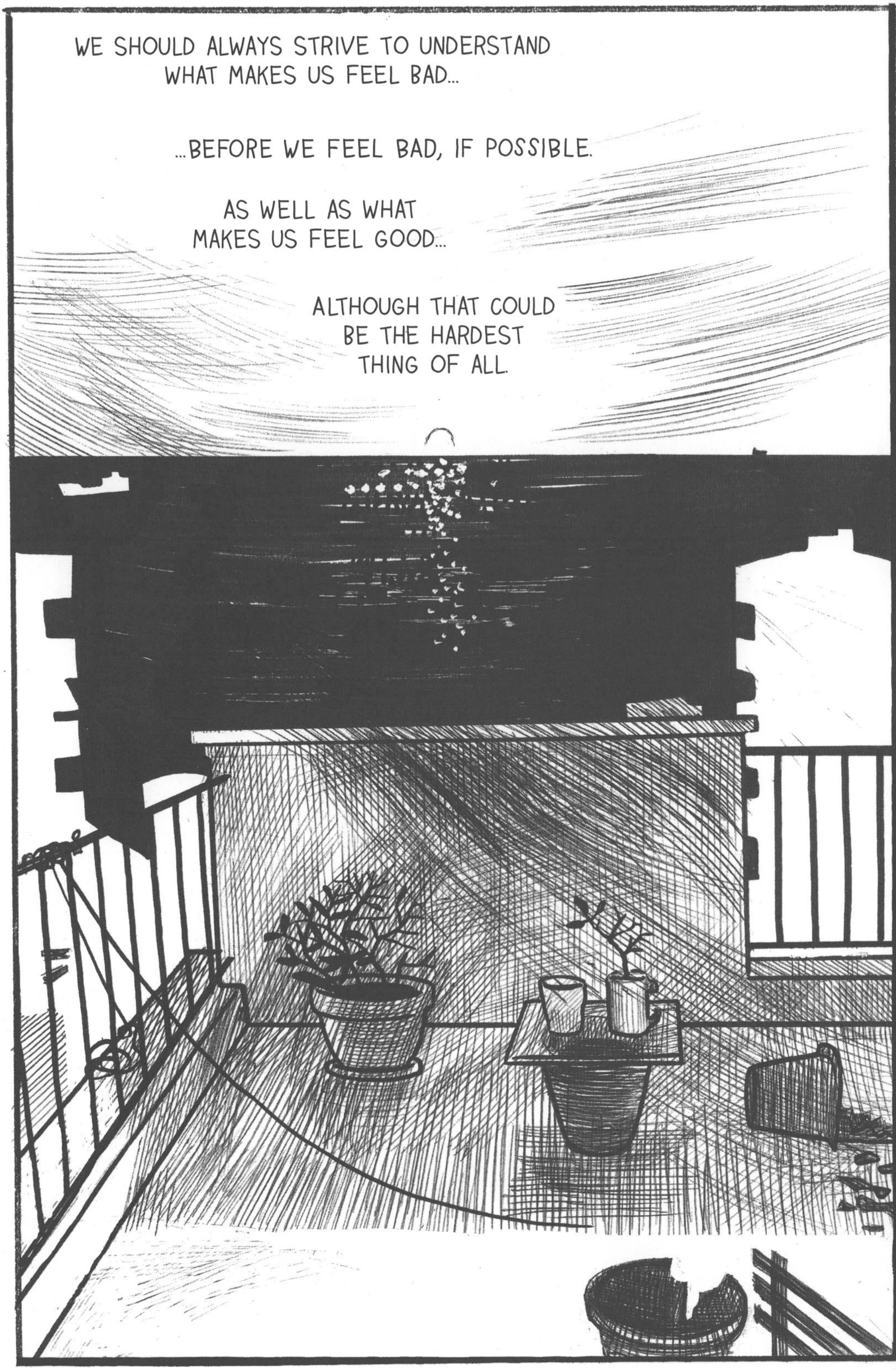
WE SHOULD ALWAYS STRIVE TO UNDERSTAND WHAT MAKES US FEEL BAD...
...BEFORE WE FEEL BAD, IF POSSIBLE.
AS WELL AS WHAT MAKES US FEEL GOOD...
ALTHOUGH THAT COULD BE THE HARDEST THING OF ALL.

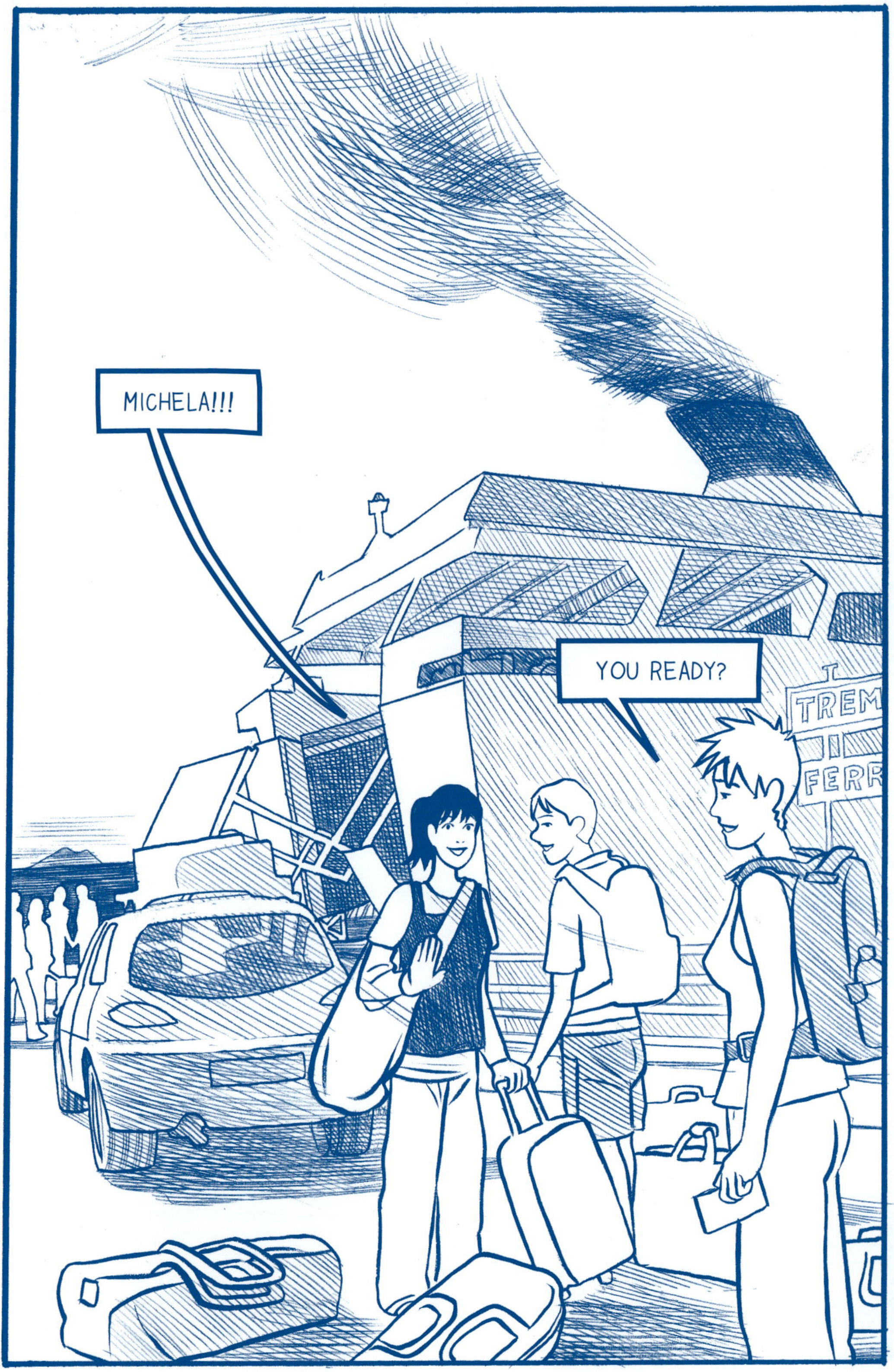
MICHELA!!!
YOU READY?
TREM
FERR

I'M SHAKING!
I'M EXCITED!
THRILLED!
THEY'RE WAITING FOR US ON THE BOAT. THE EQUIPMENT'S ALREADY THERE.

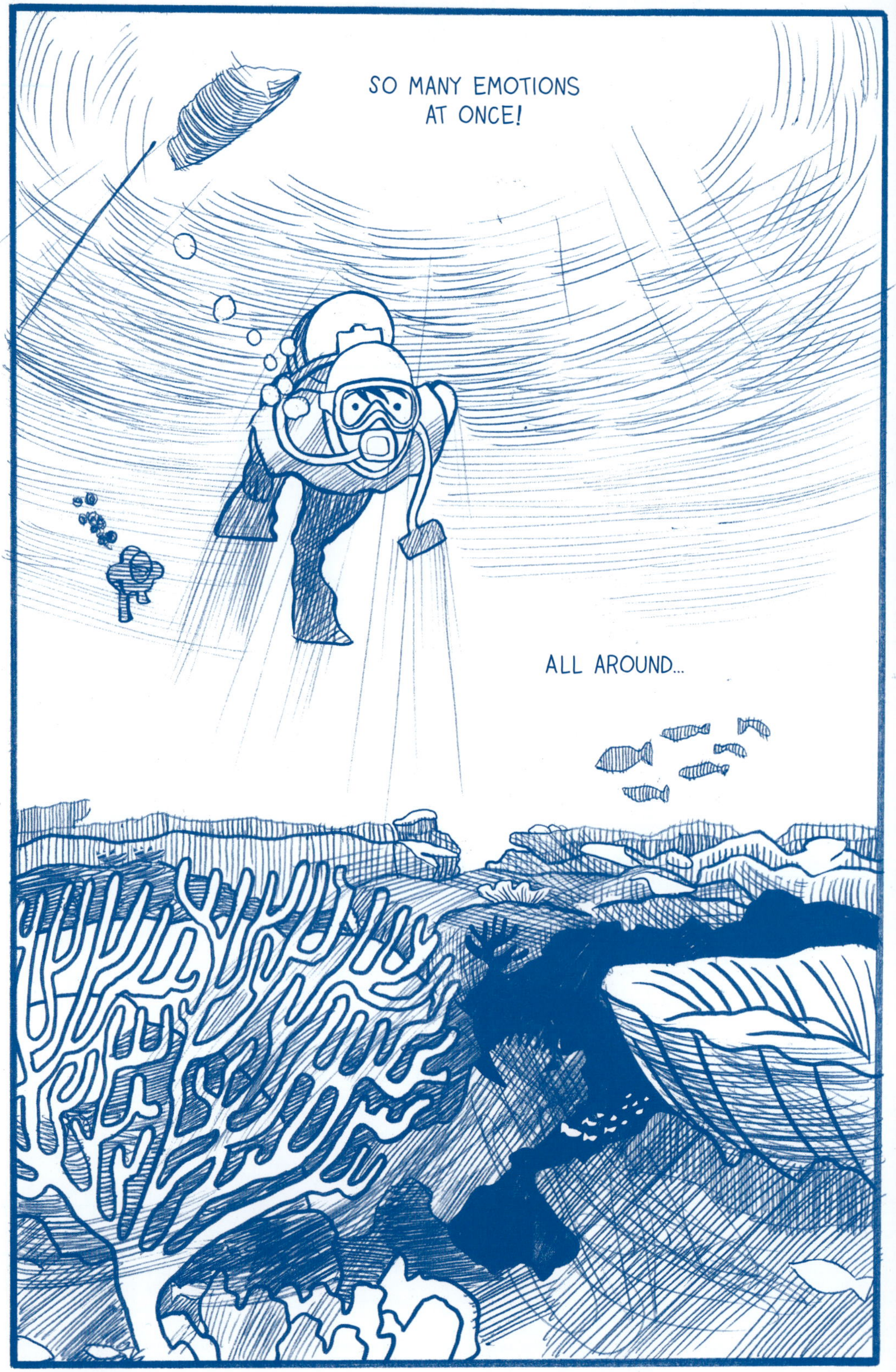
SO MANY EMOTIONS AT ONCE!
ALL AROUND...

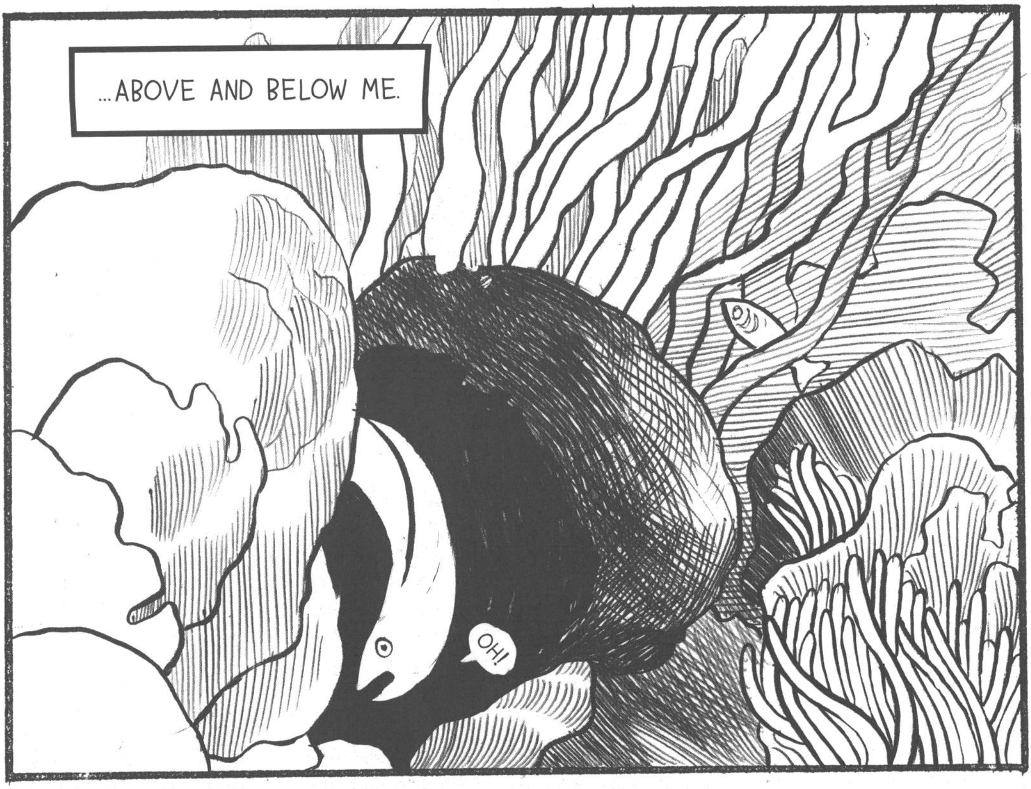
...ABOVE AND BELOW ME.
OH!

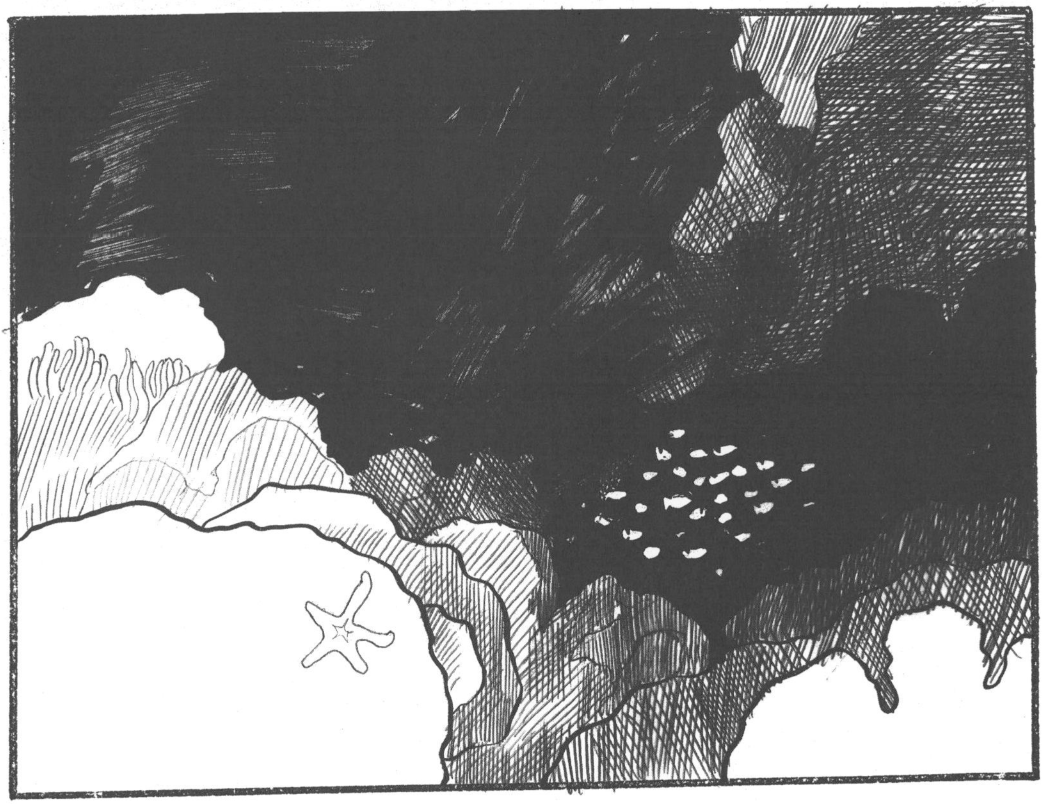

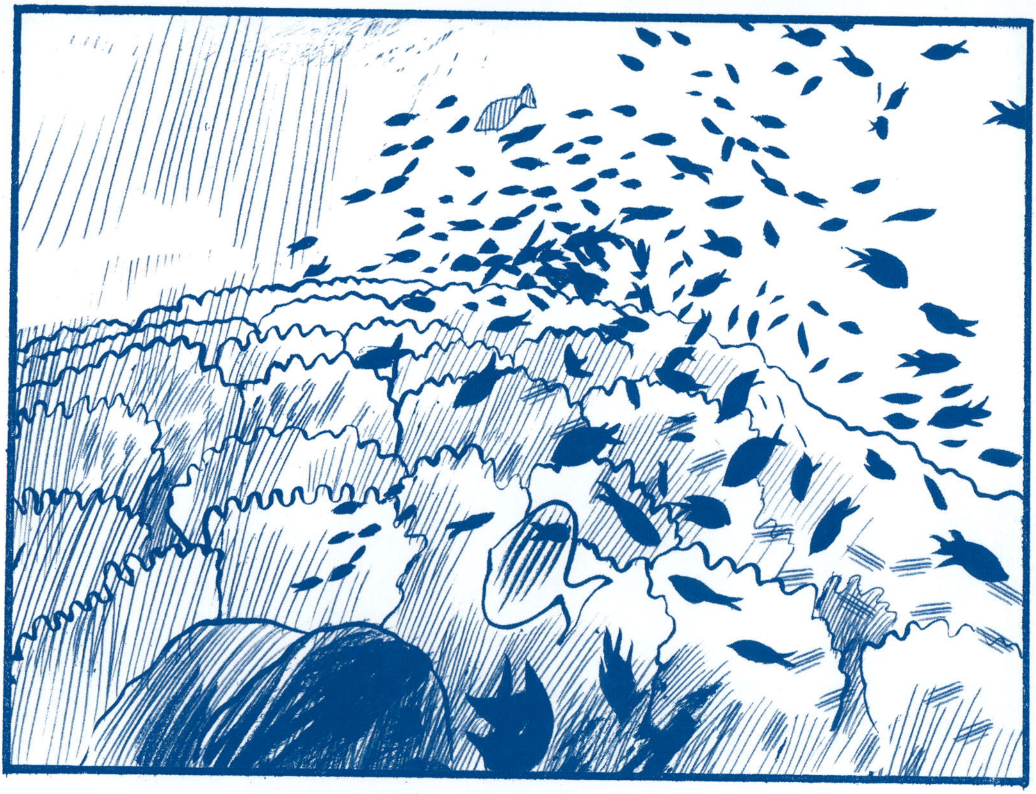

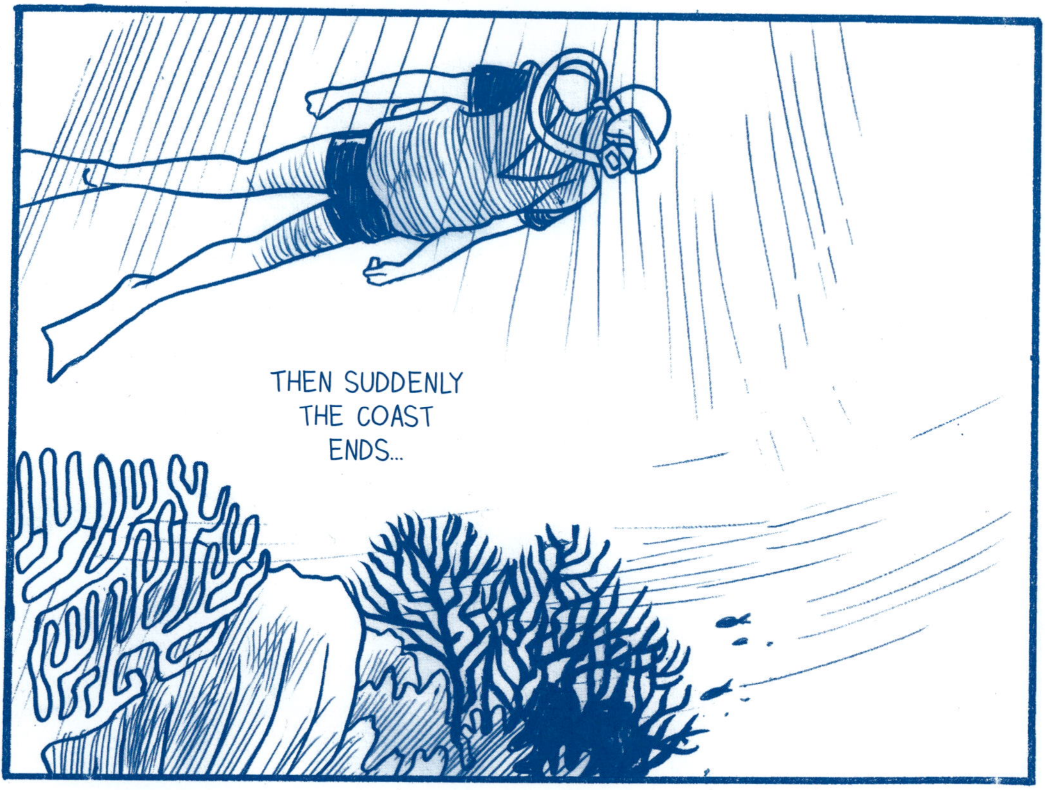
THEN SUDDENLY
THE COAST
ENDS...

WHAT A STRANGE FEELING...
EVERYTHING TURNS BLUE!
BELOW ME IS NOTHING, BOTTOMLESS, BUT I'M NOT FALLING.

THE WATER KEEPS ME UP...

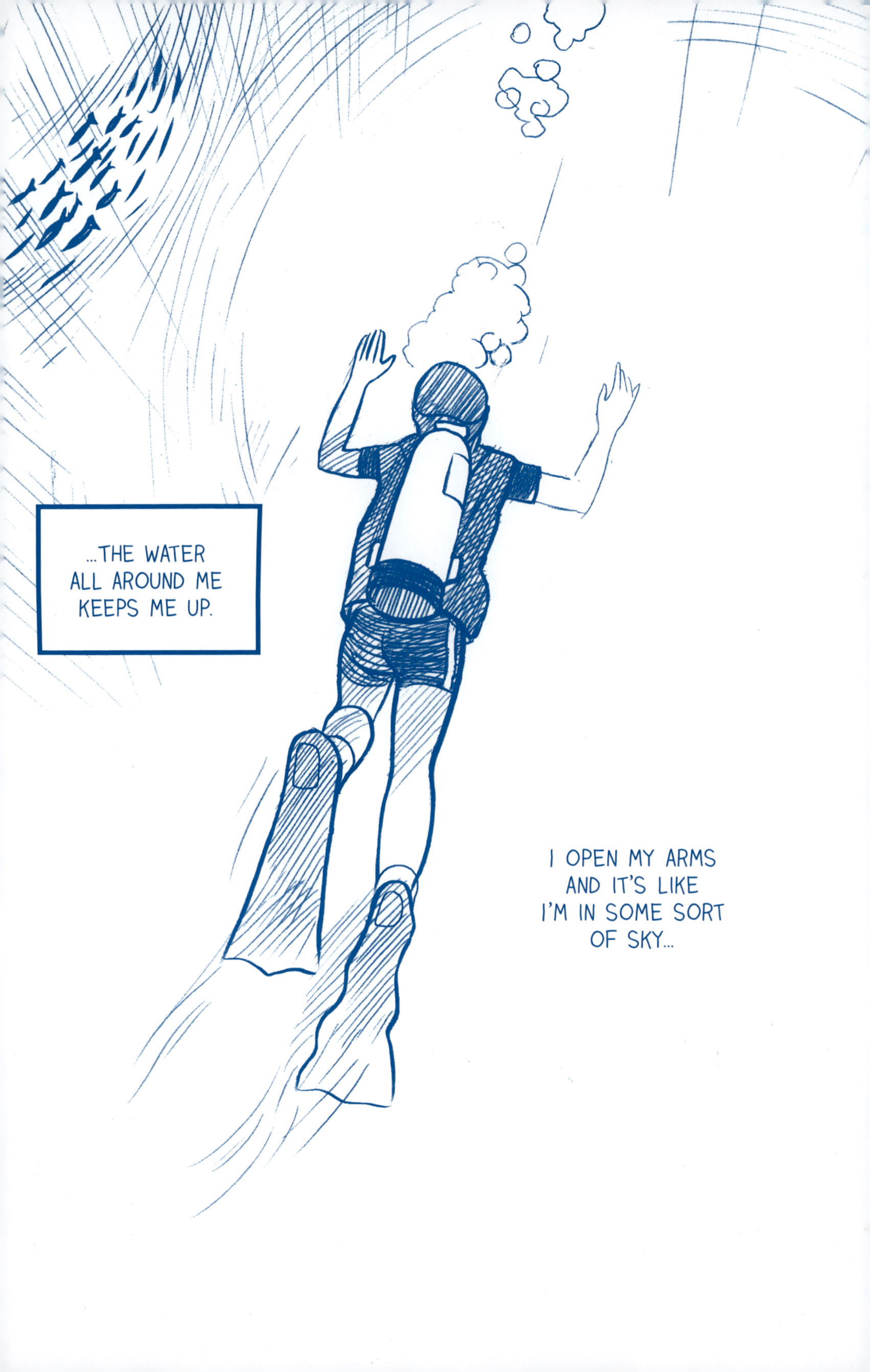
...THE WATER ALL AROUND ME KEEPS ME UP.
I OPEN MY ARMS AND IT'S LIKE I'M IN SOME SORT OF SKY...

A SKY AS BLUE AS THE SEA...

BLUE AS THE SEA LIKE
THE NIGHT SKY...

AND I FEEL LIKE
I'M FLYING.

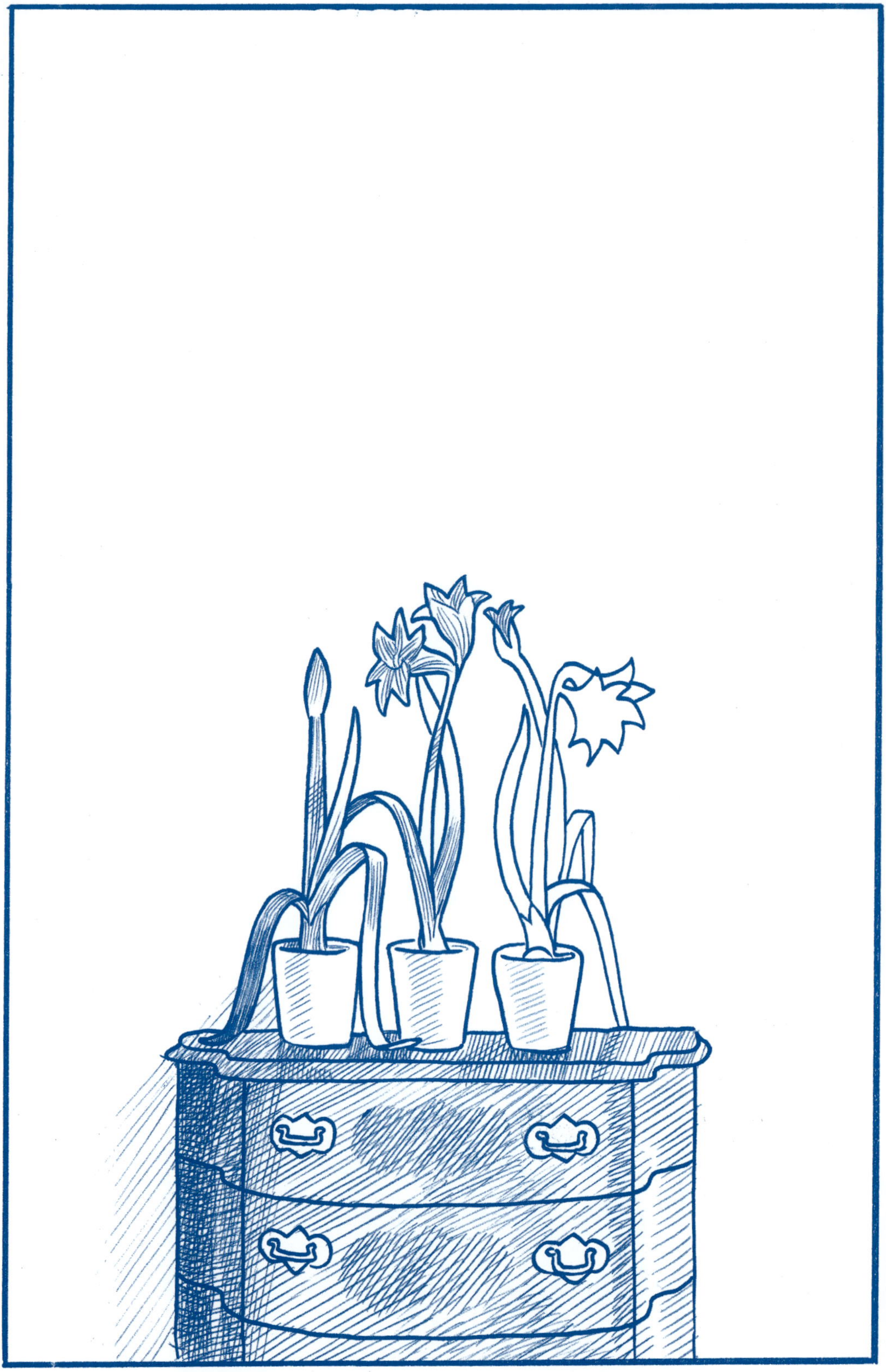

THE END

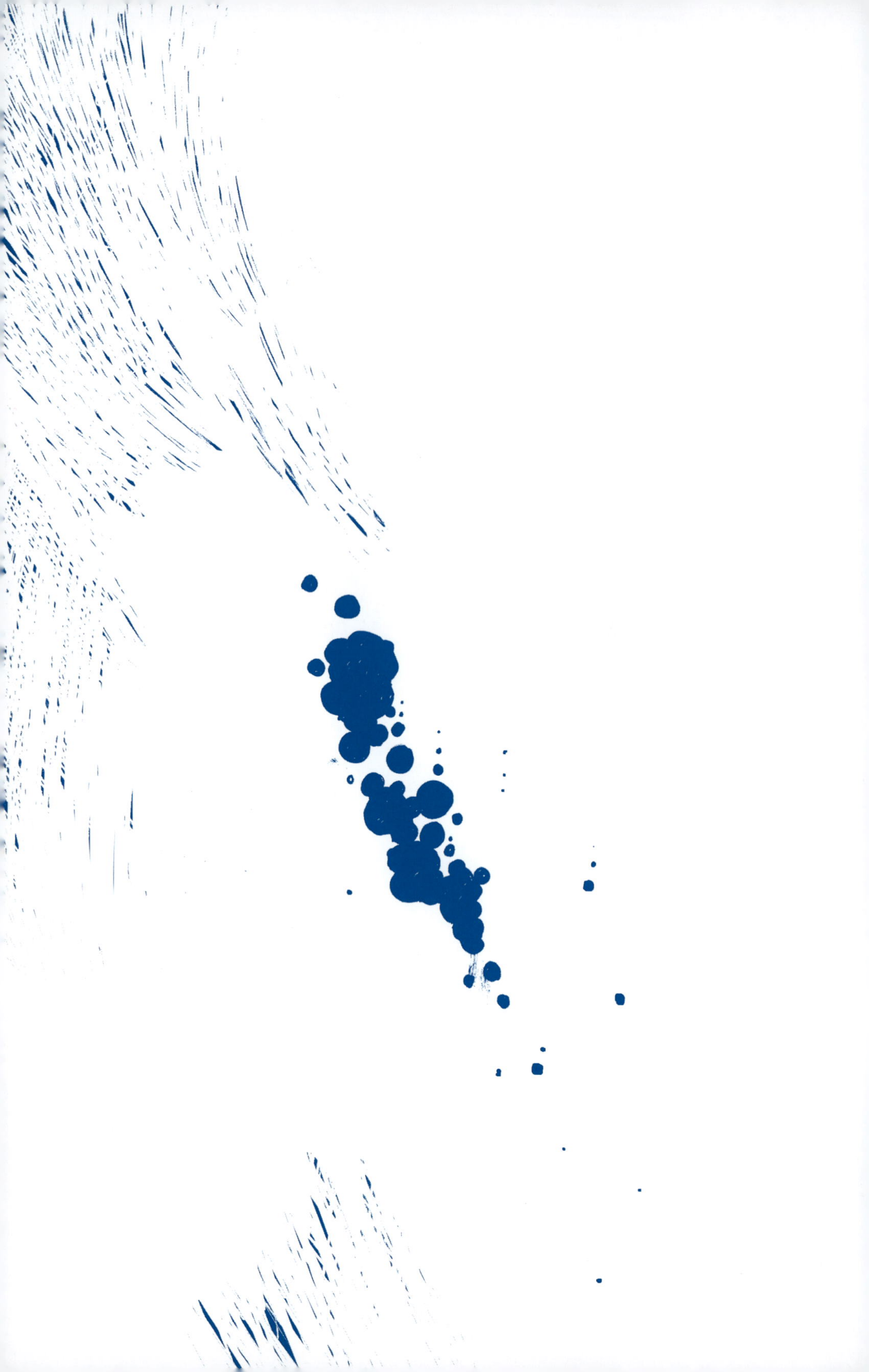

ALESSANDRO BARONCIANI IS A CARTOONIST, ILLUSTRATOR, ART DIRECTOR, GRAPHIC DESIGNER, AND MUSICIAN. BORN IN PESARO, ITALY, HE QUICKLY BECAME AN HONORARY MILANESE.

WITH BLACK VELVET HE PUBLISHED **UNA STORIA A FUMETTI**, A COLLECTION OF HIS SELF-PUBLISHED WORK, WRITTEN AND THEN DISTRIBUTED BY MAIL. STILL WITH BLACK VELVET, HE PUBLISHED **WHEN EVERYTHING TURNED BLUE (QUANDO TUTTO DIVENTÒ BLU)** AND **LE RAGAZZE DELLO STUDIO DI MUNARI**. THE REMASTERED EDITIONS OF THESE WERE PRINTED BY BAO PUBLISHING IN 2017 AND 2020. HIS COLLABORATION WITH BAO ACTUALLY DATES BACK TO 2015, WITH THE PUBLICATION OF **RACCOLTA - 1992/2012**, ONLY TO CONTINUE, STILL IN 2015, WITH **LA DISTANZA**, A GRAPHIC NOVEL OF GREAT SUCCESS AMONG BOTH READERS AND CRITICS, WRITTEN IN JOINT COLLABORATION WITH THE MUSICIAN COLAPESCE. IN 2016 HE PUBLISHED THE COMIC **COME SVANIRE COMPLETAMENTE**, AN EXPERIMENTAL WORK COUNTING MORE THAN FORTY ILLUSTRATED STORIES, BORN OUT OF AN ONLINE FUNDRAISER.

IN 2018 HE PUBLISHED **NEGATIVA**, STILL WITH BAO PUBLISHING.

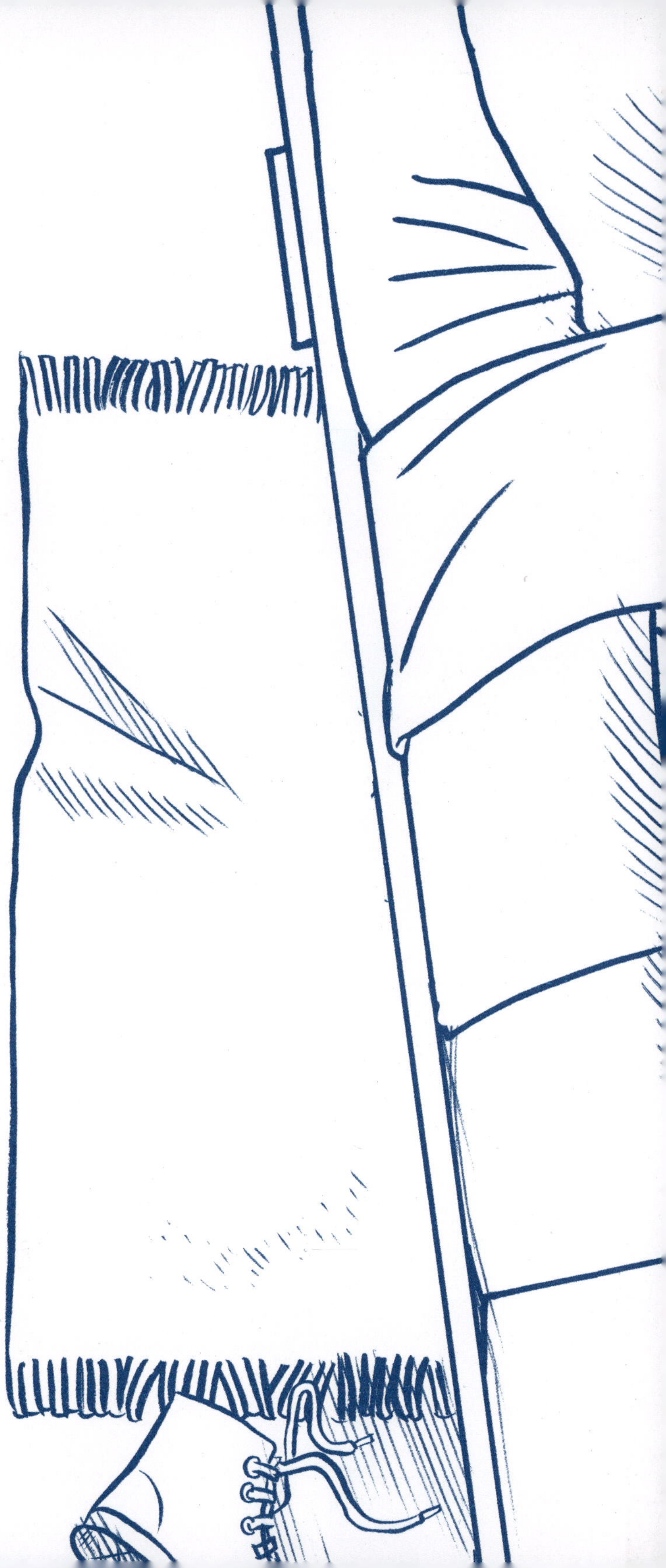